"Tell me what's going on! You're pale as a ghost."

David tried to take her hand, but she waved him off. "I was just remembering…" She clamped her mouth shut. Instinctively. She'd been about to tell him she remembered who he was. But something inside made her stop. Something told her it was a matter of life or death.

Oh, God, why?

"I…I think I just need to rest. You were right, David. It's the sun. I shouldn't have been out. I'll be fine. Really."

And something cold sank in her stomach as he carried her to her room. Because she knew she couldn't tell him what she knew about him. Because her life and the lives of others depended on it.

She just didn't understand why….

Dear Reader,

Get ready for this month's romantic adrenaline rush from Silhouette Intimate Moments. First up, we have RITA® Award-winning author Kathleen Creighton's next STARRS OF THE WEST book, *Secret Agent Sam* (#1363), a high-speed, action-packed romance with a tough-as-nails heroine you'll never forget. RaeAnne Thayne delivers the next book in her emotional miniseries THE SEARCHERS, *Never Too Late* (#1364), which details a heroine's search for the truth about her mysterious past…and an unexpected detour in love.

As part of Karen Whiddon's intriguing series THE PACK—about humans who shape-shift into wolves—*One Eye Closed* (#1365) tells the story of a wife who is in danger and turns to the only man who can help: her enigmatic husband. Kylie Brant heats up our imagination in *The Business of Strangers* (#1366), where a beautiful amnesiac falls for the last man on earth she should love—a reputed enemy!

Linda Randall Wisdom enthralls us with *After the Midnight Hour* (#1367), a story of a heart-stopping detective's fierce attraction to a tormented woman…who was murdered by her husband a century ago! Can this impossible love overcome the bonds of time? And don't miss Loreth Anne White's *The Sheik Who Loved Me* (#1368), in which a dazzling spy falls for the sexy sheik she's supposed to be investigating. So, what will win out—duty or true love?

Live and love the excitement in Silhouette Intimate Moments, where emotion meets high-stakes romance. And be sure to join us next month for another stellar lineup.

Happy reading!

Patience Smith
Associate Senior Editor

Please address questions and book requests to:
Silhouette Reader Service
U.S.: 3010 Walden Ave., P.O. Box 1325, Buffalo, NY 14269
Canadian: P.O. Box 609, Fort Erie, Ont. L2A 5X3

The Sheik Who Loved Me

LORETH ANNE WHITE

Silhouette®

INTIMATE MOMENTS™

Published by Silhouette Books

America's Publisher of Contemporary Romance

SILHOUETTE BOOKS

ISBN 0-373-27438-6

THE SHEIK WHO LOVED ME

Copyright © 2005 by Loreth Beswetherick

This edition published by arrangement with Harlequin Books S.A.

® and TM are trademarks of Harlequin Books S.A., used under license.
Trademarks indicated with ® are registered in the United States Patent
and Trademark Office, the Canadian Trade Marks Office and in other
countries.

Visit Silhouette Books at www.eHarlequin.com

Printed in U.S.A.

Books by Loreth Anne White

Silhouette Intimate Moments

Melting the Ice #1254
Safe Passage #1326
The Sheik Who Loved Me #1368

LORETH ANNE WHITE

As a child in Africa, when asked what she wanted to be when she grew up, Loreth said a spy...or a psychologist, or maybe marine biologist, archaeologist or lawyer. Instead she fell in love, traveled the world and had a baby. When she looked up again she was back in Africa, writing and editing news and features for a large chain of community newspapers. But those childhood dreams never died. It took another decade, another baby and a move across continents before the lightbulb finally went on. She didn't *have* to grow up. She could be them all— the spy, the psychologist and all the rest—through her characters. She sat down to pen her first novel...and fell in love.

She currently lives with her husband, two daughters and their cats in a ski resort in the rugged Coast Mountains of British Columbia, where there is no shortage of inspiration for larger-than-life characters and adventure.

Prologue

Monstrous clouds of hot desert sand mushroomed in the fierce wind, blotting out a sun that boiled blood-orange over an angry black sea. Panic squeezed Kamilah's heart. She scrambled up the dune as fast her little six-year-old legs would carry her. She shouldn't be out in this storm. Her father would be furious.

But it didn't matter now. Nothing mattered. She had to get help or the mermaid might die. After all this time, all this waiting, she had finally come.

But she was broken.

Tears stung Kamilah's face. Her lungs burned. The wind clawed at the very roots of her hair. The ocean behind her boomed as she ran, heaving foaming water onto the outlying coral reefs, pounding it into the bay, making the ordinarily placid waters swell and surge with turbid life.

Daddy please help. Before the sea takes it away again.

The words screamed inside her brain, drowning out the gusts of wind. Words that wanted to be spoken out loud for the first time in a very, very long time.

Lightning cracked the sky. Kamilah flattened instantly to the ground, scrunched her eyes tight and waited for the crash of thunder. It resounded through her little body making her limbs tremble and her heart drum so fast she thought it might burst right through her chest.

But she had to move. She had to get Daddy. She scrambled up the sand bank, lurched over an exposed root, skidded back down. She grasped desperately for purchase as pain seared her hands, her knees. The sand stung her eyes.

But she could not give up. She would *not* let the sea take it back. Because Mummy had sent this mermaid. She just knew it!

David Rashid pushed a yellow pin into the large map that covered the entire back wall of his office. The pin denoted the last of the Rashid International oilfields to be reclaimed from the rebels. It too was now in full production, drawing rich black gold up to the arid Saharan surface, oil that had for centuries been buried deep under the northern reaches of Azar. Oil his father had known was there.

The smaller red pins clustered into the map up near the Libyan and Egyptian borders flagged the final desert strongholds of the now-straggling rebel army. The two big blue pins to the southeast of Azar represented the biggest prize of all, the Rashid uranium mines. And it was no ordinary uranium that Rashid International was drawing out of the earth. It had a unique molecular structure that made it invaluable in cutting edge nuclear technology. David's mines were among only a handful in the world in a position to deliver this particular uranium. It had put Azar squarely back in the game.

David stepped back, folded his arms, and smiled. It was a coup he could be proud of. One his father had dreamed of. One that would rebuild his nation by bridging the old world with the new, that would fuel the economy and give pride and spirit back to a forgotten people, the Bedu of Azar, the warrior nomads of a country wedged between Chad and Sudan with Egypt and Libya to the north.

David's only wish was that his father had lived to see this. And to see how he'd managed to heal the bitter rift between himself and his half brother, Tariq.

He rubbed the stubble on his jaw as he studied the clusters of red pins on the map, vaguely aware of wind tearing at battened-down shutters, swirling and shrieking in the old castle's protected courtyards. The only question that still ate at his mind was, who was backing the rebels? But before he could chew on it, his office door flung open with a resounding crash.

David jolted, spun around. The storm winds blew fine desert sand up out of the courtyard and into his office. His daughter tumbled in with it. Her hair was a wild, dark tangle about her bloodless face, her chocolate-brown eyes wide with terror.

"Kamilah!" He lunged for the door, slammed it, shutting out the storm. He dropped to his knees and took her slight shoulders in his hands. She was trembling violently.

"Kamilah? What is it?"

Her eyes were impossibly huge, and they stared straight at him. *Into* him. David could barely breathe. She was trying to tell him something with those beautiful expressive eyes, eyes that hadn't gazed directly into his for almost two years.

Every muscle in his body tensed. The sound of the storm faded into far recesses of his mind. He was afraid to move, to breathe even, fearful any slight gesture might sever the tenuous connection between him and his child. It was like a thread, fine as gossamer. He didn't know whether to grab hold and yank it in to him, or to tread softly around for fear of breaking it. God, he never knew what to do with his beautiful baby girl. He swallowed, tentatively moved a tangled strand of hair from her pale cheek.

She didn't back away. It fed his courage, his hope. He breathed a little deeper. He took her tiny hands in his own, looked deep into her eyes and dropped his voice to a gentle, reassuring whisper. "What is it, Kamilah? Can you tell me?"

She drew in a shuddering breath. Her lips parted. David's heart stopped. He waited. Not a muscle moved in his body.

The struggle to form words showed painfully in Kamilah's dusky features. Then she suddenly closed her lips, compressing them into a tight line. David's heart dropped like lead. His pent-up breath came out in a whoosh. He closed his eyes and his chin sunk to his chest. He shouldn't have even dared to hope. Hope only bred despair.

"The…mermaid," she whispered.

His eyes flared open. *She spoke!* His heart stumbled and kicked into a light stutter.

"She…she needs help," Kamilah said hesitatingly, shrinking back from the sound of her own words. But to David it was pure music, her little voice sweet like rain on the sands of a drought-ridden desert. A ball of emotion expanded painfully in his throat. Kamilah hadn't uttered a single word in twenty-one long months. Not since the accident. Not since she'd watched in horror as the ocean had swallowed her injured, drowning mother. Not since she'd witnessed her own father fail to save his beloved wife from the choking grip of the sea.

David had begun to believe his baby daughter might never speak again. And now that she had, he was absolutely terrified he'd do the wrong thing, say the wrong words, make her stop again.

He couldn't even begin to find his own voice. All he could do was take her soft cheeks into his hands, stare into the depths of her dark eyes and let the emotion spill hot and wet over his face.

"Daddy?"

His heart clenched. Oh God, how could a word be so painfully sweet?

She tugged at his shirt, her eyes widening in dark intensity. "She…she's dying, Daddy."

Confusion clashed with the euphoria in his brain. He'd been so focused on the sound of her voice, on the fact she'd spoken, that he hadn't heard the meaning in her words. He blinked, registered. With cognizance came a hot thread of panic. Was his sensitive little girl losing her tenuous hold on reality? Was she reliving the accident? Imagining things?

"*Who* is dying, Kamilah?"

"The…the mermaid."

"Mermaid?"

She nodded.

He hesitated. Hell, it didn't matter. Did it? Whatever it took to keep her talking, he'd play along, even with an imaginary mermaid. They could deal with the rest later. "Where is this mermaid?"

"Half-Moon Bay."

"*You* were at Half-Moon Bay? In *this* storm?"

Something shuttered in her eyes. She turned her face abruptly away from him.

"No!" *Don't turn from me. Not now.* "It's all right, Kamilah. Look at me. Tell me, baby, what's wrong with the mermaid?"

Those huge dark eyes lifted slowly to once again meet his. "She's hurt. You have to help before the sea takes her away again."

"Yes," he said, desperately trying to second-guess his child. "Yes, of course I'll help. I'll go find her."

Hope lit Kamilah's eyes making them once again dance with life. It made David's heart soar. It made every molecule in his body sing. "But listen, Kamilah, you must stay here, in the palace, with Fayha', okay? The storm is much too dangerous for you."

Her little fists clutched at his shirt. David tried to move but Kamilah's grip tightened, balling the fabric. He realized then that she wasn't convinced he'd actually go. She wasn't sure if she could trust him. *Like she hadn't been able to trust him to save her mother.*

A maelstrom of emotion crashed through David. He sucked in a deep breath, hooked his finger under her chin, lifted her face gently. "Listen to me, Kamilah, I *promise* to look for your mermaid. If she's hurt, I *promise* I'll help her. I won't let you down, baby." *Not this time.* He'd do anything to keep that sweet little voice talking. Whatever it was out there in that storm that had cracked her open, he'd find it. And he'd make damn sure it stayed on his island.

"Come here. Give me a hug." He swooped her up into his arms, felt her warm little body close to his. He felt her tiny hands creep up behind his neck and hug him tightly back. Warmth flooded him. Hot tears spilled down his face. For the first time in nearly two years he had found a connection. He was sure his heart would burst with the sheer joy of it.

With new fire in his blood, David set his daughter down. He had a storm to brave, a mermaid to find. And he had a little girl to get reacquainted with.

The wind was ten times more powerful on the battered beach of Half-Moon Bay. Froth whipped off the surface of the sea in fat globs, and bullets of hot rain beat against his face.

David squinted into maelstrom. What had disturbed Kamilah? What had she seen?

Then he saw it. A pale form among the debris. The symmetry of the shape was unmistakably human. And female. *Kamilah's mermaid!*

He kicked his stallion into a gallop along the packed wet sand. The form remained motionless as he neared. David dismounted, crouched down beside her.

She lay among scattered debris, limp as the pieces of broken jellyfish that had washed up with her. David pressed his fingers against the cold skin of her neck, searching for a pulse. She was alive. Barely. He quickly assessed the scene.

She was naked from the waist up. Her wet hair was almost hip length, and it tangled like amber seaweed about her upper body. She had the most perfect breasts he'd ever seen. Small with dusky coral-tipped nipples scrunched tight. Torn green fabric swathed her legs.

He glanced up at the perilous, churning ocean, the waves thundering over the outlying razor-sharp reefs. It was an absolute miracle she hadn't been sliced to ribbons.

He carefully moved the strands of hair from her face, looking for injury, and his breath caught. She was utterly exquisite. Her slanted eyes were closed, fringed with long amber lashes. Her honey-brown skin glistened with rain. But below the cosmetic appearance of a healthy tan, she was deathly pale. He could see why. A gaping gash split the skin on her temple. It had been washed bloodless by the sea.

He rolled her gently over toward him. There were more cuts, angry ones, down the left side of her torso. And a jagged wound on her left forearm, also bloodless from time in salt water. As he assessed her injuries, a rogue part of his brain noted she wore no wedding band, no engagement ring. A primal male awareness quickened the pace of his heart.

Thunder exploded above him and he winced. Lightning forked over the horizon. The wind shifted suddenly, thrashing in frenzied circles as if delirious at the prospect of even heavier weather. A solid wall of blackness begin to swell out over the water. It rose like a monstrous gray-toothed maw, filling the sky, sucking in everything in its path. And it began rushing in a towering, screaming wall toward the island. It was the brunt of the electrical sandstorm and it would hit any second. He had to risk moving her. Thank God Dr. Watson was still on the island. The foul weather had stopped him from flying out to Khartoum this morning.

David yanked the curved dagger from his waistband, slashed the fabric binding her legs. He ripped off his shirt, carefully slid his hands under the woman, winding the wet fabric around her. He then lifted her limp and unconscious form up onto his horse's back, praying she didn't have a back injury because this movement sure as hell would seal her fate if she did. But he had no choice. She would most certainly die out here if he tried to go for help first.

He mounted, gathered her in close to his naked chest and kicked his stallion forward. The horse bolted, stumbling wildly up the dune, eager for the shelter of home. David bent low over the woman, shielding her from the worst of the violent weather. His concentration was on speed, yet a part of him was acutely aware of the stinging sand and slashing rain on his bare back—and how the painful sensation contrasted with the soft feminine swell of the woman's breasts, of her smooth wet skin against his naked chest.

And even as he raced for his palace, deep down in his heart, David Rashid he knew he was in trouble.

Chapter 1

*W*here was she? Her eyes flared open. Dim light sliced through to the back of her brain where it exploded in a burst of sharp pain. She scrunched her eyes shut tight again.

She could hear an unearthly sound, like wounded banshees or a screaming wind. She couldn't make sense of it. She thought she could hear surf crashing far away. Like the drums of gods or rolling thunder. Or maybe it was just the dull thudding of her heart, the sound too loud inside her skull.

She tried to move her head, but it hurt. *Everything* hurt. Her whole body pounded with rhythmic pain as if her veins and vessels were too small and too fragile for the angry blood that was being thrust through them.

She tentatively tried to open her eyes again. Through her lashes she could make out shapes, shadows. Quivering. Firelight? Candles? An exotic scent stirred in warm currents of air. She couldn't seem to find focus. It was all a blur, so very foreign.

A wedge of panic rammed into her heart.

Then she sensed a presence. Someone standing over her. Her heart stalled. With a bite of fresh urgency, she forced her eyes open wider, trying to pull the dark shadow that loomed over her into some kind of recognizable form.

It was a man, staring down at her. A severely beautiful man with dark skin, sharp, angled features, raven-black hair and piercing blue eyes. Eyes that bored right into her soul.

Danger!

Her chest constricted. Her heart hammered up into her throat. She knew that face from somewhere. It set every alarm bell clanging. She tried to swallow, to calm herself, to breathe. She concentrated on the man's face, mentally cataloguing his features, desperately trying to find a match in her brain, to understand why he was supposed to represent a threat.

He was big, tall, with a wide chest and powerful forearms covered with dark hair. His wrists were broad, and his fingers, she noted in a distant part of her brain, were long and exquisitely shaped. His skin was an exotic mocha brown, a sharp contrast to the startling indigo of the eyes that bored into her, through her.

His brow was prominent over his eyes giving him a predatory look. In fact, everything about him was predacious, save for his mouth. His lips were full and elegantly sculpted, rescuing his features from the severity of harsh angles and planes, giving him a smouldering male sensuality, an air of refined yet dangerous aristocracy.

Her eyes moved slowly down the length of his body. He wore a loose-fitting and very white *galabiya* that offset the dusky tone of his skin. It was cinched at the waist by a brocade belt and into that belt was thrust an ornate *jambiya*. Her brain cramped. The world spun around her. A *galabiya?* It was the robe worn by most Saharan desert tribes. And the *jambiya?* Only Arabs carried the traditional curved dagger like that. But those intense blue eyes were *not* those of an Arab. *Who was he?* Where on earth was she? Confusion and fear tightened twin fists around her heart.

He was profoundly attractive, powerful, but he was also an enemy. Not on her team. She had to be careful, guarded. Her life depended on it. She knew this somehow. But how did she know all this? Why? A wild terror scrambled through her brain. What *did* she know?

Her eyes flicked nervously around the room. It was lit by lamplight, a kerosene lamp. That's what the smell was. That's what made shadows flicker on the whitewashed walls. A wooden fan turned slowly up on an exceptionally high ceiling. The room was furnished with artistic, antique-looking pieces of dark burnished wood. She noted the ornate arch over the heavy wooden door at the end of the room. The whole effect was high-end North African...or perhaps Moorish. Her heart stuttered into a crazy panicked beat. She didn't recognize a thing. She had absolutely no idea where she was. She tried to sit up.

He restrained her instantly, placing a hand firmly against her shoulder. "It's okay, relax, take it one step at a time," he said.

She stilled at the deep gravel tone of his voice. He had a British accent, yet it was underlaid with the low and sensual gutturalness of Arabic. His hand was warm on the bare skin of her shoulder, and his palm rough. She realized then that she was covered by only a white cotton sheet. Under it she was utterly naked. Alarm mounted, swamping any attempt at rational thought.

"Don't touch me." She warned, her voice coming out in a raw croak.

He withdrew his hand instantly. "As you wish. But take it easy. You've been unconscious."

"Where...where am I?"

"You're in my home on Shendi Island."

"Where's that?"

"The Red Sea, off the coast of Sudan. Shendi is a private island. I own it. My name is David Rashid."

"The Red Sea?" Her words came out in a panicked and painful rasp. Why was she anywhere near the Red Sea? The wind was making a terrible howling sound outside. She could hear it banging, tearing against shutters. It muddled her mind. She couldn't think.

Concern shifted into his eyes as he stared down at her. And that distressed her. If he was worried, she too had reason to be.

She held his gaze, fighting her fear, determined to show some strength. "Why am I here?" she demanded.

"You took a bad knock on the head. We found you unconscious on the beach. You're very lucky you didn't drown."

Drown? Knock on the head? She reached up, tentatively felt her brow where it throbbed dully. Her fingers detected a neat line of stitches along her temple just below her hairline. Alarmed, she fingered the length of what must have been a nasty gash.

"You have more cuts," he offered. "Down your left side, and along your arm."

Her eyes shot down to her forearm. More rows of tiny black stitches. Swelling. Blue-black bruising beginning to show. "What happened to me?"

"You washed up on the beach in the storm. We need to know if you were on a boat, if there were others with you. We have a search party out but have found nothing so far."

Confusion shrouded her brain. She tried to marshal her thoughts but couldn't. Her head hurt terribly. "I...I don't know..."

"That's okay." He lifted his hand to touch her shoulder again, thought better of it. "Give it time. It's probably the concussion. Let's start with your name."

She opened her mouth to say it, but she couldn't. It wouldn't come. Terror ran hot through her veins. Frantically she searched her brain, but she couldn't locate it. She couldn't remember her own name. She couldn't seem to recall anything. How she got onto the island. Where she'd been. Or why. The storm. Others on a boat.

Absolutely nothing.

His eyes sharpened again, cutting into her with laser intent as he waited for her to speak. Her mouth went dry. She clutched the sheet tight around her chest as if it would somehow shield her from the sheer horror at her predicament. The wind rose to an awful howl. Shutters crashed somewhere.

He was still watching, still waiting. But something else was shifting into his features. Pity. He felt sorry for her. And that made her feel infinitely worse. It also made her angry. She hated pity.

"If you tell me your name," he said, "once we get our communication system up and running again, we can let someone know that you're all right."

She remained silent. She had absolutely no idea who might be looking for her.

"I'm sure there are people worried about you."

She drew in a shaky breath, said nothing.

A crease deepened across the smooth skin of his brow. He studied her face, his blue eyes analyzing, stripping her down to her mental core, making her feel more naked than she already was under the crisp sheets.

"You don't know your name, do you?"

"Of course I do."

He arched a brow, waited.

"I…my name is…it's…" It still wouldn't come. She couldn't find it. She felt it was inside her head somewhere, lurking in a file folder in her brain. She just couldn't find the tab that identified the folder so that so she could grasp it, pull it out.

He touched her arm again.

She jerked back reflexively.

But this time his hand remained on her arm. "It's all right," he said, his voice suddenly incredibly gentle. His hand was warm. The roughness of his palm against her skin spoke of a man who spent a great deal of time outdoors. For some reason this grounded her. This time she found some small comfort in his touch. This time she didn't pull away.

"Just relax, I'll get Dr. Watson."

"Doctor?"

"He tended to you most of the night." He smiled into her eyes. "I took the graveyard shift so he could get some rest. I'll send for him."

Panic swamped reason. "No." She jerked away, fresh energy and determination surging through her system. She struggled into a sitting position. She clutched the sheet around her torso and swung her legs over the side of the bed. "I don't need a doctor. I'm fine."

She *would* be fine. As soon as she got moving. As soon as she got blood flowing back into her brain. Then it would all come back. Her name, everything. She was sure of it. "Where are my clothes?" she demanded.

He angled his head, tilted his dark brow, a hint of amusement lighting his intelligent eyes. "You haven't got any."

"What?"

A smile ghosted his lips. "You washed up on the shore as naked as the day you were born…apart from some torn green fabric wrapped around your legs."

She stared at him, mortified. "Who brought me up from the beach?"

"I did."

"How?"

"On my horse."

Oh, Lord. She closed her eyes, tried to find a center in the gray swirling blankness of her brain. She had to get moving. It was the only way. She was sure of it. Once she moved she'd be fine. She forced herself off the bed and onto her feet, clutching the sheet tightly around her body. Her legs felt like lead, her feet were as heavy and about as cooperative as dead stumps.

She took a step, and the world spun wildly. She wobbled, grabbed the edge of the bed, steadied herself.

He grasped her elbow. "You shouldn't move so quickly."

She jerked away from him. "I said don't touch me." She took a determined step toward the thick-looking bedroom door. Then another. But her body wouldn't behave. Her steps turned into a wild, flailing stumble, and the whole room spun. She swayed as a dizzying kaleidoscope of black and bright closed around her. She felt her legs collapse under her. Everything moved in slow motion as she sank to the floor, the sheet pooling embarrassingly at her feet as she went down.

He moved quickly, catching her head an instant before it thudded onto the cool tiles. She was vaguely aware of his callused hands against her bare torso, the brush of his forearm over her naked breast as he lifted her from the ground.

Then everything went black.

David yanked on a thick, tasseled bell cord. His housekeeper appeared almost immediately.

"Fayha', get Dr. Watson, please. Tell him his patient surfaced briefly. I think she's sleeping now."

Fayha' dipped her head in silent acquiescence, closed the door gently behind her. David turned to the mysterious woman lying in his bed, all the while listening for the approach of Watson's heavy footsteps in the stone corridor.

She looked like a wax sculpture in the golden glow of the kerosene lamp, a surreal angel. She was in her late twenties, he guessed, possessing an unconventional and exotic beauty, with high defined cheekbones, elegant arched brows and almond-shaped eyes fringed with thick amber lashes. She was tall, her muscles long and lean. But above all, it was those eyes that had undone him. They were closed now. And that made him feel a little safer.

But when they'd flared open he'd been stunned by the hugeness of them, the deep emerald green. And when she'd found focus and stared up into his own eyes, he'd been rocked by the depth he'd seen in them.

A man could drown in eyes like that. Eyes the color of the ocean.

Then a thought slammed him up the side of the head so hard and sudden he sucked in his breath. Aisha had drowned in an ocean that color. While he was diving, taking personal pleasure in the beauty and depths of a coral reef. He'd left her and Kamilah alone, up in the boat.

David swallowed against the hard knot of pain, of love and loss and irrational guilt. That was almost two years ago. The memories should be a little easier now. But they weren't. A part of him didn't even want them to be. A part of him relished the sharpness of the pain they brought him, as if hanging on to the hurt would preserve his love for his dead wife, as if it might absolve his guilt in some way.

He didn't deserve easy memories as long as Kamilah still suffered. And he didn't deserve to dive in waters like that, ever again. Which is why he hadn't. Not once since Aisha's death.

The woman in his bed moaned softly, jerking David's attention back to the present. He felt himself bracing for the incredible green of her huge eyes.

But she didn't wake. Her breathing settled back into a soft and regular rhythm, her chest rising and falling under the Egyptian cotton sheet he'd placed over her. Her hair was dry now, full of wave and curl. It fanned out about her face over the white pillows, the fiery color of a Saharan sunrise.

Her neck was sleek, elegant in the way it curved down to her collarbone. His eyes followed the lines of her body down to where the sheet rose gently over the swell of her pointed breasts. He thought of the soft and heavy weight of those breasts, naked against the palm of his hand, against his bare chest. He thought of the dusky coral nipples. David's mouth went dry. Unbidden heat spilled low into the pit of his stomach.

He wiped the back of his hand hard across his mouth in shock. This was sick, to be aroused by an injured and barely conscious woman. A woman who couldn't be more vulnerable if she tried. But by God she was desirable, in an unattainable and otherworldly kind of way.

Kamilah was right. If he'd had to conjure up the image of a mermaid in his dreams, this would be it.

A smiled tugged at his lips. Maybe he had more in common with his daughter than he dared admit. His smile deepened as he allowed his thoughts to go. Because in his dream the mermaid too would be naked with perfect coral-tipped breasts, waist-length amber hair, bewitching green eyes and an emerald-green tail.

He mentally shook his head. This was ludicrous. His thoughts and emotions were bouncing all over the place. This woman was real. A normal human being. And what might have passed for a tail was a swath of tangled green fabric. Still, he couldn't shed the deepening sense of unreality.

He reached out, tentatively touched her cheek, almost to prove to himself she was not a figment of his imagination.

She murmured again.

He jerked his hand back. His breath snared in his throat. His heart rapped a light and steady beat against his ribs. The lamplight quivered, teased by invisible fingers of warm wind that had found their way through cracks in the shutters.

He felt edgy. Finding this woman on his beach had totally unstrung him.

She groaned suddenly, wrenching her head from side to side, wincing from the obvious pain and discomfort the movement caused her. Instinctively he reached out and smoothed her hair back from her forehead. "Shh, it's okay," he soothed. "You'll be all right. You're safe here. There's nothing to hurt you here."

She stilled, as if listening for his voice.

"You're safe," he whispered again.

Her eyelids stopped flickering. The tension in her features eased. He'd managed to quell her angst, and that satisfied something primal within him. He began to move his hand away but was arrested by the silkiness of her hair against his skin. It was impossibly soft.

He lifted a long strand, let the curl twist around his fingers. And inside he felt a sudden, aching, vast and indefinable emptiness. His eyes flicked down to her left hand. There was definitely no sign of a ring, no tan line, nothing to indicate a ring that may have been lost to the storm. A hot thrill of promise speared through his chest and into his belly.

He jerked back, startled by the sheer power of his own physical reaction. He sucked in a deep breath, dragged both hands forcefully through his hair and told himself in no uncertain terms that he was only looking for clues to her identity.

But even so, he couldn't deny the spark of interest that had flared deep within. Even as he tried to quash it, he could feel the small, hot, ulcerous burn of it. He had a sinking sense it wasn't going to heal anytime soon.

The thought made his mouth dry, his head hurt. It was as if the freak storm had invaded his very brain, whipped up his normally razor-sharp and logical mind, clogging it with the rain-soaked sand.

The door banged open behind him. David just about jumped out of his skin. He swiveled around. Dr. James Watson stood there, medical bag in hand, his gray hair still slightly disheveled from sleep.

"I didn't hear you coming," he growled, furious at having been caught unawares. David Rashid was *never* caught off guard.

The doctor's wise gray eyes studied him silently, knowingly, irritatingly. "Sorry, David. Didn't mean to scare you." Watson jerked his chin toward the door. "Wind just grabbed it from my hand. Fayha' must have a door open somewhere. There's a bloody gale blowing down the corridors."

Watson closed the heavy door carefully behind him and ambled into the room with his customary air of casual authority. "So she woke up, did she?" he asked as he set his big black medical bag down on the nightstand and opened it. "How was she?"

David gave himself a mental shake, banishing unbidden images of mermaids and wedding bands to the farthest reaches of his mind. "She seemed fine. Apart from the fact she has absolutely no idea who she is, what happened to her, or how she got here," he told Watson. "Doesn't even know her name. She got up, tried to walk and went out like a light."

The doctor nodded, feeling for her pulse. He timed it, his face furrowed in thought as he focused on his watch.

David paced the room. Through the slats in the louvered shutters he could see the sky beginning to brighten. He glanced at the clock on the bedside table in surprise. It was almost 5:30 a.m. He hadn't slept a wink since he'd tucked Kamilah into bed.

Watson rested the woman's wrist back on the covers and joined David near the window. He kept his voice low. "Her breathing and heart rate are back in regular range. So far everything is looking normal."

"What about the amnesia?"

"It's not uncommon to experience some memory loss after a blow to the head. It may last seconds, days, months. It could even last years."

"Could it be permanent?"

"Possibly. She might never remember the accident that brought her here."

David studied the doctor's face. "But there's something else worrying you."

Watson pursed his lips. He glanced at the woman then back at David.

"What is it Watson?" he pressed.

"The retrograde amnesia, that's consistent with head trauma, with organic damage." The doctor chewed on the inside of his cheek, a furrow deepening along his forehead. "But the loss of sense of self…" He shook his head. "We really should get her to a hospital for a CAT scan. Maybe fly her into Nairobi, or north to Cairo. In the meantime, she'll need to stay under constant observation. And—"

But before the doctor could complete his sentence, their patient groaned. They both spun around.

Her lashes flickered against her cheeks.

David tensed, once again anticipating those incredible eyes.

Outside the wind was suddenly silent. The storm had finally died. Only surf boomed over distant coral reefs. Yellow dawn sun seeped through the louvered shutters, throwing patterns on the tiled floor as the sun peeked over the distant horizon.

Then her eyes flared open. She stared straight at David and blinked like a confused and trapped animal. Something snagged so sharply in his chest it clean stole his breath.

She looked so lost. So vulnerable.

She was straining to pull her whole world back into focus.

Lancaster's hulking frame filled the doorway of the Khartoum hotel room.

O'Reilly glanced up from his laptop. He stilled instantly at the somber expression on the big man's face. "Bad news?"

"Still no sign of her." Lancaster dragged his powerful hand over his brush cut and stepped into the room, momentarily blotting the early-morning sunlight from the window.

"And Gibbs?"

"Got picked up by a Sudanese fishing vessel last night. He's pretty bashed up. Damn lucky to be alive. He says he saw her go under, says there's no way she could have come out of that alive."

O'Reilly swore bitterly under his breath. "What the hell do we do now?"

"We find her. Dead or alive. We need to be damn sure either way."

O'Reilly turned to the window and stared out at the African city skyline. "If we go looking for her, if we send search parties out with guns blazing, Rashid's gonna find out."

"Then we do it another way, and we do it real quiet. And we kill any information before it gets out, starting with the embassy."

O'Reilly nodded. "If he finds her first..." He paused. "Rashid is a dangerous man," he said very quietly.

Lancaster studied him in silence. "Yes. But if crossed, *she* is one dangerous woman." His eyes narrowed. "And right now she is a loose thread we can't afford."

Chapter 2

"This is Dr. James Watson." David introduced the large gray-haired man to whom he'd been talking in hushed, guarded tones.

Why the secrecy? What were they hiding from her? Unfocused panic skittered through her system.

The doctor came over to her bedside. His smile was warm. "How're you feeling, Sleeping Beauty?"

From anyone else, the trite comment would have annoyed her, but she didn't mind it from this man. He seemed genuine enough, and he had the comforting look of experience in the deep lines of his weather-beaten face. "I...I've been better," she said, her voice still coming out raspy. Her tongue felt too big for her mouth, and her lips were dry and cracked. The skin on her face felt tight.

"I want you to follow this light with your eyes," Dr. Watson said, moving a pencil-thin flashlight across her field of vision. She followed the movement.

"Looking good." He clicked off the light, stepped back slightly and studied her face. "I hear you're experiencing some amnesia."

She tried again to recall what had happened, how she'd ended up on the beach of a Red Sea island in a terrible storm, but she couldn't. With a horrible, sinking realization she realized she still didn't have a clue who in the world she was.

"The most important thing is not to panic," he said.

Yeah, right. She swallowed, wincing at the raw pain in her throat. David moved instantly to the dresser, poured water from a jug into a glass, brought it to her.

She raised herself slightly on one elbow, accepted the glass from him and swallowed greedily. But before she could drain the glass, he grabbed it from her. "Whoa, take it slow."

She felt as if he'd snatched a life source from her. Her eyes flashed to his. "I'm thirsty," she challenged.

His eyes held hers, the ink of his pupils blackening his irises as he watched her face. "Too much, too fast," he said slowly, too slowly, his voice low like heavy mist in a dry and rocky canyon, "and you'll only feel worse. Trust me, I know thirst. I know the ways of the desert."

Trust him? Instinctively she knew she shouldn't. But she couldn't break his gaze. She couldn't tear her attention away from the smouldering male interest in his eyes. Her heart began to beat faster. Her breathing became more shallow. And with utter shock, she realized her body was warming under the intense heat of his gaze. She was reacting physically to the thirst in this powerful man's eyes.

He stepped slowly back from the bed, his eyes still holding her prisoner, even in retreat.

"I'd like to ask you some questions if that's all right?" The doctor's voice snapped her back. With sheer relief she turned her attention fully to Dr. Watson.

"Do you know who this is?" He gestured to David as he spoke.

She hesitated, unwilling to look at David, afraid to snare his gaze again, mortified at how he made her feel inside. Lord, she sure wished she *did* know who he was, why she was feeling these things about him. "Of course I know who he is. He's David Rashid. We...we met earlier. He...he said he brought me up from the beach." *Naked.*

"Very good. You're able to form new memories since your accident. That means no anterograde amnesia. Now let's see what you know about the past." He paused, thinking. "Okay, tell me, do you know who John Lennon was?"

"Of course."

"Churchill?"

She let out an exasperated breath. "Yes. I know who Churchill was. And Hitler. I know my history. I know about World War II. I know when the Berlin Wall came down. I know when Mandela was released. I know..." *that David Rashid is smuggling weapons-grade uranium.*

She froze. Her heart cramped tight and then hammered hard against her chest. Oh God, where had that come from? Heat flushed into her cheeks.

"Your parents?"

The doctor was talking to her, but her mind was suddenly blank.

"Do you know who your mother is? Your father?" he pressed.

She squeezed her eyes shut, trying to remember something about her childhood...*anything* about her childhood. But there was nothing. Just a black hole. She sucked in a shaky breath. "No," she said softly, opening her eyes, still trying not to look at David. "I don't know who my parents are."

"Can you recall where you went to school? To university? Your job?"

She shook her head.

The doctor was chewing on his cheek, his brow furrowed in thought. She could feel the heat of David's concentrated gaze on her. It confounded her thinking further. Unsettled her. She needed clothes. A hairbrush. Maybe then she'd feel less vulnerable.

"Do you remember where you grew up?" This time the question came from David.

She sucked in a breath and turned slowly to look into his face. She felt a flush rise in her cheeks again the instant his eyes caught hers. She fought the warming sensation, forced herself to scrutinize his features, to find a match in her brain. Why did she think he had anything to do with nuclear weapons? What did uranium have to do with anything at all? Where in heavens had that thought come from? She tried to dig it out of her memory. But it was gone, a wisp of smoke in the breeze. Had she fabricated the notion? Maybe it had been born of a confusing nightmare she'd had as she'd slept in his bed. She didn't trust anything about her mind right now. Or her body. And that scared the hell out of her. She didn't want to show just how frightened she was.

"This is ridiculous," she said. "If I can remember the Beatles, if I can recall historical events, why don't I know how I came about that information? Why don't I know where I went to school? Why don't I know who the hell I am? It just doesn't make sense." She felt tears burn behind her eyelids, which only frustrated her more.

"Give it time," Dr. Watson said. "I'll run a few more tests later. Meanwhile," he said, clipping his black bag shut, "try to relax. No use worrying about what you don't know, now is there?"

Oh, yes, there was. She angrily sniffed back the thick emotion rising in her chest.

"You're British," David offered, his voice a little softer.

"Is that a question?" she snapped.

The hint of a smile tugged at his finely sculpted mouth. It only served to irk her further. Her belligerence, given her absolute vulnerability at the moment, obviously amused the man.

"It's a suggestion," he offered. "Your accent is English. You sound like you're from the U.K. Maybe you came on a diving holiday? Not many tourists come to the Sudanese region otherwise. Unless of course you live in the area. Or you're working here, with an aid organization, maybe?"

"*Those* are questions." And they made her deeply uneasy.

"Does any of it seem even remotely familiar?" he asked, a twinkle in the indigo of his eyes.

She closed her eyes, shutting him out. "No."

"Well…do you dive?"

Her eyes snapped open. "I don't know!"

"You *do* know where the Red Sea is?"

"Of course I know where the Red Sea is. I'm not brain dead. I just can't remember who I am." Frustration clipped her words.

David opened his mouth to speak. But Watson's hand restrained him.

"It's perfectly normal to feel frustrated," said the doctor, eyeing first David, then her. "Things will probably start coming back as you begin to feel better. For starters, you could probably do with something to eat."

God bless the doctor.

"Of course," said David. "Forgive me. I'll get Fayha', my housekeeper, to bring you some breakfast. Anything in particular you like?"

"I…I…" She racked her brain. "Dammit, I don't know!" She struggled into a sitting position, clutching on to her sheet.

Something shifted suddenly in David's eyes. He was

watching how her hands clutched the sheet over her breasts. "Don't worry," he said, his voice deeper, the Arabic accent suddenly stronger. "We'll find out who you are. We'll put word out as soon as we have communication up and running again. We'll contact the embassies in the region and the Sudanese Ministry of Interior. You can't get into this part of the world without a visa, and you have to register with authorities once you arrive. If you came to Shendi from Sudan, there'll be a record. We'll also put word out in Saudi Arabia and Egypt in case you were on a dive trip that originated from one of those countries. Someone will know who you are."

"Great," she muttered. "I sure as hell hope so."

"And once you've eaten," said Dr. Watson, "I'll come back and run a few more simple tests. In the meantime," his eyes shifted to David, "I need to pack for Khartoum. I have to leave this afternoon if we're going to get those medical supplies to the Ba'ar mine before the end of the week."

David nodded and Watson made for the door.

She panicked. The doctor was going to leave her alone with *him.*

"Are you a neurologist?" She called after Watson in an unfocused attempt to keep him in the room.

The doctor paused, turned calmly back to face her. He indulged her with his warm and generous smile. "No, I'm an internist. But I do have some basic neurological and psychiatric training. I'm in David's employ," he explained.

"Employ?"

"Watson works for Rashid International, my company," said David. "He sees to my employees in remote areas, and you're damn lucky he was still around when you washed up."

Rashid International. Something pinged faintly in the back of her brain. There was something familiar about the name... as if she had a role to play with the organization. But that wasn't possible…because then surely David and Watson would know who she was, wouldn't they?

A noise outside in the passage interrupted her thoughts. David heard it, too. He stilled, listened. And a grin spread slowly across his face. "Kamilah?" he called out. "Is that you lurking out there?"

The silky, dark head of a child peered around the heavy door. Huge chocolate-brown eyes stared straight at her. They were the eyes of a beautiful and nervous deer, she thought as she studied the girl. She had velvet coffee-brown skin, and her hair, the same blue-black as David's, hung thick below her slight shoulders.

"Ah, as I suspected." David held his hand out to the child. "Come on in, sweetheart." He turned to face her. "This is my daughter, Kamilah. She discovered you on the beach. I believe she saved your life."

She looked from David to Kamilah and back. Saved her life? This child?

Kamilah stepped cautiously into the room.

A band of tension strapped tight across David's chest as he watched his daughter edge toward the woman in his bed. Kamilah had not uttered another word since he'd brought her "mermaid" up from the beach, in spite of his best efforts to reengage her verbally.

At first his heart had sunk. But her eyes had looked deep into his, giving him a rare window into her little soul. And in her eyes he'd read gratitude. That look alone had shifted the ground beneath his feet. And her small hand had held his so very tight when he'd brought her to see the "mermaid" in his bed once Watson had stitched her up.

And when he'd kissed Kamilah's soft dark head goodnight, she'd smiled, hugged him as if her little life depended on the contact. It had all been a precious slice of pure sunshine in a world that had been way too gray for way too long.

But still, he couldn't shake his feeling of unease as he watched Kamilah venture up to the woman's bedside. He watched his daughter's eyes widen in awe at the sight of the golden woman in his bed.

"Hello, Kamilah." The woman's voice was suddenly soft. Melodious.

"I guess I owe you a very big thank-you," she said. "How on earth did you manage to find me in the storm?"

She waited, expecting Kamilah to answer.

The room went dead quiet. Expectancy hung thick in the air. David felt the muscles in his neck go stiff. Would she speak again?

His daughter edged even closer to the bed. It had been a long, long time since David had seen such confidence in his baby. For the past two years, she'd all but coiled up in front of strangers. He tried to swallow against the odd mix of sensations in his throat. Would she speak in front of one now?

"I…I was waiting for you," Kamilah said so softly David thought he might have imagined the sound.

"Waiting for me?"

Kamilah's dark head nodded. "For a long time."

Emotion exploded instantly into David's chest. She'd spoken to a stranger! Just like that. When for the past two years she hadn't been able to utter a word to *him*. A curious cocktail of relief and resentment began to churn in his stomach.

"You were *waiting* for me?" the woman asked again, confusion knitting her brow. Her eyes flicked up, met David's. He could see the unspoken question in them. But he couldn't move. He couldn't say a thing. She scrutinized him, then she turned her green eyes on Watson. He said nothing, either. Neither of them were willing to break the spell.

The woman turned her attention back to Kamilah, obviously aware that something was playing out on a much deeper level. "Well, I'm very grateful that you found me," she softly.

And with those few words, she notched up a resenting respect from David. In spite of her injury, in spite of her memory loss, she had enough presence of mind not to call Kamilah on her statement. She'd simply gone with the flow.

David watched as Kamilah's eyes slid in wonder down from the woman's face to where her legs raised the Egyptian-cotton sheet. Then his daughter tensed visibly.

"What is it, Kamilah?" the woman asked.

Kamilah's eyes shot up to the woman's face, then back to the unmistakable shape of legs under the sheet. And David knew. He knew *exactly* what was worrying Kamilah. The woman didn't have a tail.

He had to do something, say something. He cleared his throat. "Kamilah…feels, uh, she believes that you should have a tail."

Everyone stared at him. He cleared his throat again. "You're…you're supposed to be a mermaid. With a tail."

The woman's almond-shaped eyes widened. Her jaw dropped. David's stomach balled into a knot. He had no idea what the woman might say, what words it would take to crush his child. He was petrified Kamilah would once again derail when she discovered the woman was not a real mermaid.

"A tail?"

David nodded. "Yes."

She studied his eyes, trying to read him, trying to guess his game, then she turned slowly to face Kamilah. "Should I have a tail, Kamilah? Please don't tell me I should have a tail. Have I totally lost it?"

Watson chuckled heartily, cracking the tension. "Well if you had a tail it's gone now, so yes, I'd say you lost it." The doctor continued to chortle merrily at his own joke.

David didn't find it at all amusing. He knew what this meant to Kamilah.

The woman sensed it, too. "But *you* seem to think I should have a tail, Kamilah?"

The little girl nodded, her face deadly serious.

"Hmm." Then the woman smiled. A warm smile. Like sunshine. It reached right into her emerald eyes making them sparkle with the morning light. And it made a dimple deepen in her one cheek. David stared, struck once again by her unbalanced beauty, by how white her teeth were against her soft tan. She'd been exquisite in repose, but the animation in her smile brought her beauty to full life. And it was dazzling. But it wasn't only her physical appearance that intrigued him. She possessed a latent confidence, and right now she was in control of this bizarre situation in spite of her loss of identity, in spite of the fact she was stark naked under that thin sheet, a fact he couldn't seem to erase from his mind.

Bemused, he watched as she placed her hand gently over Kamilah's. "You know, sometimes it happens when mermaids come on land," she said softly. "Sometimes they lose their tails in exchange for something else…like legs." She tipped her head conspiratorially closer to his daughter's, and lowered her smoky voice to a whisper.

"And, Kamilah," she said. "You do have to remember that sometimes things are not quite what meet the eye. You've always got to keep an open mind, because one can never be sure when it comes to the magic of fairy tales." She smiled again. "But I think you know that, don't you? I think you know all about fairy tales."

No one spoke. Tiny dust motes danced, glistened in the shafts of yellow sunshine sneaking through the wooden slats that covered the window.

"What's your name?" Kamilah's little whisper sliced the silence. David released a whoosh of air he hadn't realized was trapped in his lungs. His heart tripped back into a steady rhythm. His child was coping. She was going to be okay.

The woman studied his daughter carefully, looking deep into her eyes, as if seeing something there that he, a mere mortal, a mere father, didn't have the power to see.

"Kamilah," she said. "I don't have a name. Not right now, anyway. I can't remember it. I got a bad knock on the head, and I can't seem to remember where I came from."

Kamilah nodded solemnly, as if she understood completely, as if mermaids not only lost tails but that it was quite common for them to lose their minds when they got washed up out of the sea. Then his child turned suddenly and stared expectantly up at him.

David swallowed, taken aback by the spark of urgency in his child's eyes. He wasn't sure what she wanted. "What is it, Kamilah?" he asked.

His child waited, eyes eager.

"Kamilah?"

She said nothing.

Why wouldn't she speak to *him?* Why did *he* have to try and second-guess everything? What did she want from him?

Watson nudged him. "She wants you to come up with a name, Rashid."

"What?" His eyes flashed to the doctor.

"Give her a name," urged Watson. "She wants you to give the mermaid a name."

Kamilah nodded, her liquid eyes intent.

David felt suddenly cornered. He scrambled through his brain, trying to find some moniker for the mysterious woman. He couldn't.

Kamilah waited. Everyone waited.

Why was this suddenly his responsibility? He swallowed, cleared his throat. "Sahar," he said finally.

Everyone in the room looked at him. "Sahar," he said again, as if the repetition would somehow make it more real. Still the silence hung heavy and awkward. It was as if he now needed to explain his choice.

But he couldn't do it. Wouldn't. It was suddenly too personal, his choice too intimate. Because Sahar meant awakening. Dawn. A new beginning. And he'd chosen it because of what she'd brought to his daughter. This woman had made his precious little desert flower come alive again, long after she'd all but withered on the vine.

And she had hair like a Saharan sunrise.

The woman's eyes studied him from across the room. Something strange and unreadable shifted in her features. "Thank you," she said softly. "That's a beautiful name."

David shrugged. He felt awkward. This whole damn situation had knocked him off balance.

But he was rewarded with a brilliant smile from Kamilah as she nodded in happy agreement. David's heart torqued in his chest at the rare sight of warmth and animation in his little girl's face. He'd done something to make his baby happy. He'd taken another tiny step on the complex road he traveled with his daughter. And despite his portfolio of international achievements, nothing made him feel more proud, more worthy.

The woman, Sahar, turned to Kamilah. "Now, sweetheart, do you know where a mermaid could possibly find something to wear…and maybe a hairbrush?"

Kamilah hesitated. Then she spun on her heels and charged from the room, brushing David's legs as she ran past him into the hallway.

It was in that very instant that David knew *exactly* where his daughter was going.

"No!" he yelled, spinning around. "Wait! Kamilah!"

Watson grabbed his arm, held him back. "Let her go, David. She needs to do this. She needs to move on. You both do."

David clenched his jaw. His heart pounded in his chest. His hands felt clammy. He could feel the woman's eyes appraising him. And he suddenly felt exposed. Humiliated by his own irrational outburst.

He jerked free of Watson's hold, stormed from the room. Furious, he marched down the passage, his riding boots clacking loudly on the stone floors.

"Fayha'!" he barked. The sound of his voice bounced off the thick stone walls, resounded under the arches of his palace. "Fayha'! Where are you?"

His housekeeper came scuttling from the direction of the kitchen. "Sir?"

"Help Kamilah," he ordered. "I'm going for a ride."

"Where is she?"

"In—" he hesitated "—in the room. The room with her mother's things."

Fayha''s eyes widened.

"Just do it." He swiveled on his heels and headed for the stables. But inside he knew. *He* should be the one helping Kamilah. *He* should be with her in that room, going through Aisha's things. Working through the past, putting it away properly. But he couldn't. He just couldn't make himself go in there. He hadn't so much as opened the door since he and Kamilah had returned to Shendi Palace. He'd had his staff move all of Aisha's possessions in there after the funeral.

At the time, he hadn't been able to throw or give anything away. He loved his wife too much for that. At the time, he'd felt that getting rid of her things would be like trying to excise her memory.

And now…well, now it was two years later. What good

would it do either of them to dig into old memories now, to touch Aisha's clothes, to feel the silk of them, to smell her lingering fragrance on them?

His eyes burned.

Holding on to memories was one thing. Physically digging up the past quite another. He'd said his goodbyes. He'd come to terms with the fact she was gone. He had no need to go digging into the past, and neither should his daughter. They had to look forward. Not back.

This was all Sahar's fault.

David clenched his fists, gritted his jaw, strode angrily through the courtyard toward the stables. There was dust and sand everywhere, piled in miniature dunes and stuffed into every conceivable crevice. The whole bloody world had been turned on its head by the freak storm.

And by what it had blown in.

He shoved the stable door open, felt the soft and familiar give of pungent hay. It helped ease his mind. He made directly for Barakah's stall.

But even as he led his stallion out, deep down, David knew what was really irking him. It was the fact his little girl had responded to a total stranger. She had spoken words that had flowed so naturally from her mouth you'd think she'd never been mute. She had quite simply come alive. Because of a stranger washed up with the wind and rain.

After all he had tried to do for Kamilah, after all this time, a mysterious woman had simply blown into their lives and made it happen in the blink of an eye. It should have been *he* who'd broken through his daughter's shell. He *needed* that victory, dammit. He *needed* to know his daughter had forgiven him. Totally.

The woman had deprived him of that.

Resentment began to snake through him. But braided with

the bitterness he felt toward Sahar was a thread of gratitude for her having cracked open Kamilah's shell. And there was a third thread in that complicated braid. One he preferred not to think about. Because it forced him to face the fact that she had not only awakened his daughter, she had stirred something frightening and powerful in *him*. She'd made something come alive and burn, slow and deep inside his soul.

Trouble was, he didn't want to feel this way. He didn't want to feel this insidious burning in his gut, this low, raw longing for a woman with no memory. A woman who was surely going to leave Shendi, abandon Kamilah as soon as she figured out who she was.

David gritted his teeth.

It was best she left, sooner rather than later. Before Kamilah got too attached, he wanted her gone from his island.

David led Barakah into the storm-washed morning. In the distance the rising sun glimmered off the ocean surface, making it shine like hand-beaten copper. The color filled his mind. And as he mounted his stallion he could think only of how the color resembled Sahar's long sun-kissed curls, the way the gold and copper shades contrasted with the startling green of her haunting eyes. And the way her skin had felt against his.

He swore softly in Arabic. He needed her gone all right. He couldn't begin to feel these things for a woman who had another life, perhaps even another man. He *wouldn't* allow Kamilah to be hurt.

With a spurt of anger, he kicked Barakah into action. He needed a tough workout. He needed to clear his head. And by the time he returned, he expected his technician to have restored communication on the island.

Then he would set to work, find out who the devil this woman was and where she had come from.

Then he'd send her right back where she belonged.

Chapter 3

Sahar listened as David Rashid's angry footsteps faded to a distant echo. Confusion shrouded her brain. She lifted her hand to her forehead. Why in heavens did she know the meaning of the name he had just given her? Did she know Arabic? Or just the meanings behind Arabic names? And why did she feel honored, touched, by the name David had given her? Was it because of the raw look she'd glimpsed in his eyes as he'd spoken it? Or was she trying to read meaning where there was none?

Watson misread her confusion. "Your head hurting?"

"Uh…no. I…I'm just trying to remember."

He smiled. "No need to try and rush the process. The body is a wonderful thing in the way it can heal—and protect itself—but you must give it time."

Time. She didn't have time. Why did she feel she was running out of time?

"I'll come back once you've got some clothes on and had something to eat. We can do some more tests then, okay?"

She nodded, watched the doctor make for the door. "Dr. Watson," she called out. He halted, turned around.

"About Kamilah…the mermaid thing?"

He hesitated. "The child hasn't spoken a word in two years," he said. "Not since the death of her mother."

"What happened?"

"Aisha Rashid drowned in a boating accident not far off the coast of this island." He smiled sadly. "David took a huge gamble coming back here. Returning to Shendi was a final bid to bring life back to his child. He's done everything within his power to try to get Kamilah to speak again. Nothing worked until now—until you arrived."

"Me?"

He nodded. "That's right. Kamilah Rashid had not spoken in nearly two years—until she found you on the beach."

"And she…she really thinks I'm a *mermaid?*"

"The fact that she thinks you're a fantasy creature is key," he said. "You've helped bridge the gap between her silent, private world and the real one."

"So…so why is her father so angry?" The range of unguarded emotion she'd seen cross David Rashid's face in the space of a few beats of a heart compelled her to ask.

A broad grin creased the doctor's sun-browned face. "Ah, a couple of things have got his goat, I suspect. Rashid likes to be in control. *He* wanted to be the one to make his daughter well again. Now he's faced with a mermaid who's done the trick for him." Dr. Watson chuckled. "You've wounded the man's pride, but don't worry. He'll be fine once he's licked his wounds. He always is. I'll be back later."

Sahar watched as the doctor closed the heavy door behind him. She was desperately grateful to have some time alone.

She needed to think. She swung her feet carefully over the side of the bed and stood slowly, not wanting to repeat the fainting episode. The tiles were cool under her bare feet. She steadied herself against the bed, waiting for a momentary dizziness to pass. Then she wound the sheet neatly around her body and moved over to the long oval mirror nestled into a tall dark-wood closet at the far end of the room.

She hesitated, almost afraid to look. Then she sucked in air and stepped squarely in front of the mirror. She stared at the person reflected in the glass.

The eyes that stared back were her own. Logic told her that. She stepped closer, touched the reflection with her fingertips. There was something vaguely familiar about her image. It was as if she was looking at someone she'd crossed paths with once or twice before. But she couldn't place where or when.

She studied the face. It was a face she was comfortable owning. It felt like her. But how? How did she know what it felt like to be her?

Was she a tourist? Somehow she didn't feel like one.

Could she dive? She thought she probably could.

Slowly she unwound the sheet and studied the rest of her body. She had no jewelry. No necklace, rings, bracelets or earrings. No clues. Nothing at all to give her away.

That didn't feel right. Something was missing. The sensation niggled away at the back of her brain. And with a start, she realized she was fingering her left hand, exactly where she'd wear a wedding ring…if she had one. She frowned. Why did she feel as if it was missing?

She ran her hand gently over the cuts and bruising down the left side of her torso.

Had she been on a boat when the storm hit? Were there others who hadn't survived? Damn, damn, damn. For the life of her she couldn't recall a single thing about how she got to this island of David Rashid's. She scooped up the sheet in frustration, wound it tightly around her body and stomped over to the shutters. She flipped the catch and threw them open wide as if to cast clarity on her situation. But the harsh flare of yellow sunlight exploded against her eyes. She scrunched her face tight in painful reflex.

As the stab of pain slowly subsided, she became cognizant of the sun's rays. With her eyes still closed, she lifted her face to meet the light. The warmth on her skin offered a basic animal comfort. She breathed in deeply, feeling tension slowly begin to dissipate as she allowed the warmth to soak through her.

It dawned on her then—she was like a primal creature. No clothes. No identity. No past. Only the present. Only the sensation of warmth on her face to give her a feeling of being alive, a feeling of belonging in the world. This sensation was the closest she could come to a sense of home, of who she was. Because beyond that, she'd been reduced to nothing.

She didn't know if she had a family or if she had kids, though she guessed not—the idea seemed too foreign. Perhaps she had a lover, someone who right now was worried sick about her. Did she have a job? A house? An apartment? Did she have a cat or a dog?

Is this what it felt like to start from scratch? To have a blank slate and a chance to do things over? Because it sure as hell didn't feel like fun. It felt formidable. And claustrophobic, as if she was hemmed in by an invisible fortress.

Panic started to grip again. She pressed the palm of her hand against her stomach, trying to force calm on herself. The doctor had said she might feel like this. He'd said she would also likely experience anger, denial. That was normal, he'd said. But what in hell was normal about this? What in hell was normal about a stranger giving you a new name? A name that means dawn, new beginnings.

The distant sound of hooves thudding on packed sand registered in her brain, yanking her mind back into the room. Her eyes flicked open. She shielded them against the harsh glare of the sun with her hands and searched for the source of the sound.

The sight that greeted her clean stole her breath. Through the arched window, the sea gleamed a brilliant turquoise in the distance. Waves rolled relentlessly toward the shore and broke in long ribbons onto a beach of pure white sand, spraying spumes of white spindrift into the wind.

The beach turned gradually into shades of cream, amber, orange and ochre as the land curved in sweeping, undulating hills toward her. Then the sand gave way to rich vegetation closer to the castle walls.

She blinked. *Castle?*

She leaned out of the window. Yes, she was in some kind of Moorish-style castle. Walls, several stories high, ran off in either direction from her window. Arches were cut into them at regular intervals. At the end of the one wall, the building veered off into another wing and at the end of that she could make out a square tower with turrets along the top. In other parts, the roof was angled over the walls and covered with thick irregularly shaped tiles baked reddish-ochre by the sun.

The sound of the galloping hooves that had alerted her grew louder, echoing off the palace walls. She leaned even further out the window, searching for the rider. Then she saw him.

He came around the far wing of the castle and headed at breakneck pace across the sandy ridge on a huge and powerful white stallion. Her stomach muscles tightened automatically at the sight. David and the horse formed a dark and powerful silhouette against the glare of the sea. He rode with a fierce and reckless abandon. Bareback. Like a wild desert warrior born with the beast between his legs.

He and the creature on which he was mounted looked as untamed and dangerous as the Sahara itself.

How did she know that? Had she been to the Sahara? Her hands tensed on the thick stone windowsill.

As he reached the edge of the ridge, his horse reared up, hooves pawing the air. Her breath caught in her throat. But he moved naturally with the stallion, steadying him effortlessly. Then he reined in the horse and headed down the ridge. She could see the sheen of exertion glisten on the animal's white flanks and the blue-black glint of the sun on David's hair. Even from this distance she could see the powerful strength in the man's coffee-skinned forearms.

He kicked his horse into a gallop and she could feel the rapid, rhythmic pounding of the hooves echo right through her chest as he disappeared down the far edge of the ridge and headed into the hills that sloped toward the sea.

She tried to lean even farther out the window in an effort to catch one last glimpse. But he was gone. And she felt a small and inexplicable slip in her gut.

She stepped back into the cool of the room, suddenly aware of her quickened pace of breathing, the heightened rate of her pulse. Who *was* this man? She forced her brain to think. He said he headed up a company, Rashid International. A sinister sensation crept up the back of her neck. Maybe she had a role to play, something to do with him and with his company. Something subversive. She could sense it in the murky shadows of her mind. Fear began to edge in.

She tried to swallow, to fight down the fright demons. She couldn't allow fear to take over. She had no one in the world to turn to right now. She had to get a grip on herself. She had only herself.

The door banged open behind her.

Instantly she spun around.

But it was only Kamilah, a shy grin on her little face, her arms piled high with silky garments.

With shock, Sahar realized her hands were raised in front of her, her legs tensed for a kick, her whole body, every muscle, was primed to attack this child. Shaken by her instinctive aggression, she pressed her hands firmly down to her sides and forced a smile. "Kamilah, you startled me."

Kamilah entered the room and began to lay her armload of garments out on the bed. Sahar forced herself to relax. She moved over to the bed and fingered the sheer, exotic textures. "These are beautiful, Kamilah, where did you get them?"

Kamilah looked down at her feet. "They're my mother's," she said softly.

Sahar froze. "Oh, Kamilah, I couldn't possibly wear your mother's clothes."

Kamilah's big brown eyes lifted slowly up. Sahar could read the hurt in them. She crouched down to the child's height. "Kamilah," she said. "It's not because I don't like them. I think they're the most beautiful dresses I've ever seen. But I'm not sure your father would be happy if he saw me wearing these clothes. And I really wouldn't want to upset anybody."

Kamilah's bottom lip trembled slightly. Sahar was at a loss. The poor child seemed to desperately need this. She sighed. "Okay, how about I just try one dress on, then?"

Kamilah's face lit up. She immediately reached for a silky green dress and held the garment out to her.

Sahar took it from the child. "You think it'll fit me?"

Kamilah nodded.

Sahar held the fabric against her face and turned toward the mirror. Kamilah had made a fine choice. The jade-green silk picked up the dark flecks in her eyes. She moved closer to the mirror. But as she did, a bright-white light stabbed through her head. She gasped. Her hand shot to the neat line of stitches under her hairline. It was as if she'd seen something. As if dark glass had cracked and let in a painful bright shard of memory. A memory that had something to do with the color of this jade-green silk. Something more than just the color. But as sharp and fast as it had come, it was gone.

Sahar's heart pounded. She carefully set the dress back onto the bed. She couldn't possibly put it on. She had to find a way out of this without upsetting Kamilah.

But before she could speak, the unmistakable sound of galloping hooves once again thudded into her brain. *The Arabian horseman—David Rashid.*

She spun around and peered out the window inexplicably hungry for another glimpse of the man on his stallion.

She saw him coming back up along the ridge at a hell-bent pace, spurts of red dust shooting up behind the stallion's hooves, the horse's mane and tail flying free with the wind of speed. Her breath caught once again at the primitive image of the powerful man astride his white horse.

"That's my daddy," said the small voice at her side.

Sahar released her breath in a whoosh. "Wow, he sure can ride. What a beautiful horse."

"He's got lots of horses. That's Barakah, his stallion. He's just broken him in." Pride for her father had burst out in a spurt of words that left the little girl looking shell-shocked at the sound of her own voice.

Sahar chose not to comment, to go with the flow as if nothing was unusual. "You're kidding? He's totally in control. That stallion must be a devil to ride, but your dad makes it look like he was born on the horse."

Kamilah shrugged.

"So, *was* he born on a horse?"

A smiled struggled across Kamilah's lips. "Kind of."

Sahar crouched down again. "How so?"

"My…my daddy, he used to ride with *his* daddy, Sheik Omar bin Zafir Rashid, when he was very little, in the desert. That's where he learned how."

"Sheik? Your grandfather's a sheik?"

The little girl nodded.

"And does he live here, too?"

She shook her head. "He's dead now. Like my mummy. He was the leader of a nomad tribe in the desert. Now daddy is the sheik."

Curiosity quickened through Sahar. Somehow, instinctively she'd known David Rashid was connected with the Sahara. And the fact he was titled slotted into her brain like a missing puzzle piece. "So is *that* where your father is from? The Sahara desert?"

Kamilah nodded.

"But he's also got a bit of an English accent."

She nodded again.

"So he's from two places? From England *and* the desert?" She felt a twinge of guilt at pressing the child like this for information on her father, but she couldn't help herself.

The child smiled shyly. "Yes, and he's been teaching me to ride. Horses and camels, too."

"Your daddy must be very, very proud of you."

Kamilah shook her head solemnly. "He's upset with me."

"Oh, sweetheart, why on earth would he be upset with you?"

"Be-becau-because I…I can't talk." She stumbled over her words, suddenly self-conscious again.

"Oh, honey," she bent down, took Kamilah's hands in her own, "you *are* talking. Beautifully. Listen to yourself."

Tears pooled along the rims of the child's big eyes. "I…I can talk to you…but…I…I can't talk…to my daddy. Or…or anyone."

"Because I'm a mermaid? Is that why you feel you can talk to me?"

"Yes," she said in a tiny voice. "Because I knew my mommy would send you from the sea."

A swell of emotion choked Sahar's throat. "And that's why you were waiting for me? You knew your mother would send you something from the sea, because that's where she went?"

Tears spilled from Kamilah's eyes and ran in a sheen over her smooth brown cheeks. Sahar took the child's shoulders in her hands and looked into her eyes. "Kamilah, have you been able to speak to *anyone* since your mother died?"

She shook her head.

"No one at all?"

A sob shuddered through her body. "I…I…I had to…I had to tell my daddy you were on…on the beach. I *had* to speak or the sea would take you away."

"And you haven't been able to speak to him again, not since you found me?"

She shook her head. Another sob racked through her little body, and fresh tears streamed down her face.

"Oh, honey, come here." She drew the little girl into her arms and hugged her tight. She nestled her nose into Kamilah's hair. She could smell the apple scent of the child's shampoo. She could smell sunshine in her clothes.

And in Sahar's heart an unbidden sense of responsibility swelled. She hugged tighter. She wanted to tell Kamilah she wasn't really a mermaid. But she didn't know what she was. She had a fictional name. No past. No future. She wasn't a real person. Not in this child's eyes. Not in her own eyes. She was a one-dimensional fabrication with no sense of self. A half person. A fairy tale.

And the notion made her feel suddenly so very alone and desperately lost. As lost as Kamilah probably felt.

As much as Kamilah seemed to need her, Sahar also needed this child. She needed this connection, this hug, this human touch. It somehow grounded her in the frightening mental blankness of her world.

The child probably needed her own mother for all the same reasons. To feel grounded. Whole. Loved.

She *had* to help this little girl, whatever it took. Right now this child was the one thing that linked her to some sense of purpose.

She felt Kamilah's little hands stroking her hair. A hiccup of emotion tore through Sahar's chest. Even in her own state of distress the child was offering comfort. She was a deep little thing. Intelligent and full of silent, lonely agony. Kamilah's subconscious had cooked up a mermaid story to help explain the inexplicable—why the people you loved most had to die. The fantasy somehow helped justify the tragedy to the child. And perversely Kamilah now thought Sahar was one of the mermaids sent up from the sea by her mother to help her. A gift from the ocean in exchange for all the ocean had taken away.

And with that realization, Sahar vowed to herself that no matter what it took, she would do what she could to help Kamilah. She would *be* that gift from the ocean.

And hopefully, by the time she got her memory back, by the time she figured out who she was and where she belonged, Kamilah would be beyond the need for fantasy and mermaids and she'd be ready for her to leave Shendi Island.

"Kamilah, look at me, honey."

Kamilah's tear-streaked face gazed up at hers. "Listen to me, Kamilah. I'll make you a promise. I will help you find your lost voice if you will promise to help *me* find my lost memory."

The little girl's lips began to tremble.

"Is that a deal, sweetheart?"

Kamilah nodded, swiping at her tears with her little hand, smudging them across her face. Then she flung herself back into Sahar's arms and clung tight. "Please," she whispered, her little breath warm against Sahar's neck, "please don't ever…ever go away…like…like my mummy. Please don't ever go back to the sea."

"You think she's *faking* it?" David's hand tightened around his glass. He had to get a grip on the irrational anger, the strange swirl of unidentifiable emotions that tightened around him when he thought of Sahar.

"No, I'm not saying that."

David slammed his glass onto the table. "Then what are you saying, Watson?"

The doctor eyed him silently. "Why don't you sit down, David."

"I'm comfortable standing." He waited for Watson to continue.

"Okay, all I'm saying is that her amnesia appears to be psychological in origin."

"Meaning what, exactly?"

The doctor sipped his mint tea, ice chinking against the glass. "Meaning I think she needs a shrink. Her vitals are fine. I ran several basic memory tests and apart from the loss of personal identity and personal history, I can detect absolutely no other retrograde or anterograde dysfunction—no signs of organic damage."

"So it's all in her head, then?"

Watson smiled. "I forgive you the pun, Rashid."

David was not amused. He waited in irritable silence for the doctor to continue.

"She appears to have a dissociative disorder, most likely stemming from the trauma. It's probably some kind of coping mechanism. She really needs a specialist for me to be one hundred per cent sure, David. I don't want to jump to conclusions."

"You think she's mentally cutting herself off from her accident?"

"It's possible."

"Or faking it."

The doctor sighed. He set his glass down, pushed it to the middle of the table, leaving droplets of condensation in its wake. "It's always difficult to tell."

David dragged his hands through his hair. This mind business was so damned awkward. He'd been through all this with Kamilah. It had taken him months to come to terms with the fact the accident had shut his daughter off. A part of him always believed Kamilah held some control, that if she really wanted to, she would speak. That she had the choice.

He'd dealt with anger. Denial. He'd even come to a kind of acceptance. Yet a mad part of himself couldn't let the thought go that perhaps Kamilah was punishing him for not having managed to save Aisha.

Specialist after London specialist had not been able to help either of them. That's where Watson had come in. He'd helped David come to terms with the fact Kamilah did not hold control over her speech. That she was trapped in a psychological prison.

And now this woman. More mind games. He liked things up-front. Direct. Straightforward. He blew out a breath of pent-up air, reached for his tea, swigged. "Okay. So what you're saying is medical attention is not urgent."

"Not life-threatening urgent, but a good idea."

"Fine." He set his glass down. "My tech says the sat-phone system should be up again by tomorrow morning. In the meantime, when you get into Khartoum this evening, you get Sahar's details to the British Embassy and to the Ministry of the Interior. Hopefully they'll get bulletins out via Interpol, newspapers, whatever, and she'll be identified within the next few days. Her relatives can then come and get her and take her to a specialist in her hometown…wherever that is."

Watson drained the last of his tea, plunked the glass down and stood. "Good enough. I'll stop by and see the ambassador this evening. In the meantime, little things like a familiar scent or sound could help jog her memory. Once she grabs on to a particular thread, the whole lot could come cascading back in one go."

"Yeah, let's hope that happens sooner rather than later."

"It could be traumatic if it happens all at once, David. She'll need someone to help her through it."

"Yeah." David checked his watch. "The chopper should be ready. I'll see you out."

The doctor hesitated.

"What now?" David asked, words more clipped than he'd intended.

"Why the anger, David? The woman's helpless. It's not her fault."

"Ah, don't you go pulling the shrink stuff on *me* now, Watson."

"You're worried about the mermaid thing, about Kamilah."

David sighed deeply. He studied Watson's lined face. The man was his friend. He meant well. He had no right to take his frustration out on the doc. "Yes," he said. "I'm concerned about her grasp on reality, on her unnatural attachment to this woman." *And his own alarming physical attraction to her.*

"Kamilah has started to speak, David. You've both reached a major milestone. Things can only go forward from here."

"Kamilah thinks the woman's some kind of fictional creature. *That's* the only reason she spoke."

Watson chuckled heartily. "Mermaid, schmermaid, whatever Kamilah thinks, it broke through her mental barriers. Use it, David. Use the tools that have been placed in your hands."

David gave a derisive snort. "The *tool* I have been handed, Watson, is an unexplained woman coughed up by the sea in a freak storm. Why can't my life be simple?"

Watson grinned broadly. "Because you're not a simple man, Rashid."

David smiled in spite of himself. "Seriously, Watson," he said. "The woman will be gone in a few days. Where will *that* leave us?"

The doctor tilted a bushy white brow. "Us?"

"I mean Kamilah, where will that leave Kamilah?" His verbal slip shocked him. And it must have shown in face. Because the doctor angled his head and scrutinized him knowingly. "She's a beautiful woman, David."

"What the hell has that got to do with it?" he snapped, his voice harsher than he'd intended.

The doctor raised his hand in mock defeat. "Okay, okay. But any red-blooded male can't help notice she's one hell of a woman."

"And probably attached," he said in spite of himself.

Watson's weather-beaten face cracked into a grin. "Ah, so you *did* notice, Rashid. There is hope for you yet."

"She'll be history as soon as her memory returns. The sooner she goes, the better. I don't want Kamilah any more attached to the woman than she already is."

And *he* sure as hell didn't want to feel any more attracted to her than he already was.

The doctor nodded, the twinkle still in his eyes. "Word about our beautiful amnesiac should start circulating by this evening. People like her don't go unnoticed, David. Especially in a place like Sudan. We'll know soon enough."

David watched the doctor waddle off with his characteristic uneven gait. Damn him. That all-knowing gleam had never left Watson's perceptive eyes. Not once. He'd noted David's blatant attraction to Sahar, and that just made David angrier. He'd thought he'd at least demonstrated outward control of his libido. That his male interest was so obvious irked the hell out him. It meant Sahar had likely seen it, too. And that gave her a power he didn't want her to have.

Because David Rashid *always* made sure the balance of power was in his hands.

Chapter 4

David took his brandy out onto the tiled terrace that overlooked the lagoon and the ocean beyond. The sky was devoid of cloud, the air sultry and the black heavens peppered with stars.

Dinner with Kamilah had been really special. Just the two of them. She hadn't spoken to him again, but she'd engaged him with her eyes. Watson was right. It was progress. And he was going to hold on to that.

He allowed himself to relax. Cradling his drink, he watched the pale light of the moon shoot silver ribbons across the oily black sea with the rise and curl of each wave. In the calm of the lagoon below, his yacht swayed gently with the rhythm of the incoming tide. He could hear the distant chink of the halyard against the mast.

Having the occasional drink was one of the few Western luxuries he allowed himself. Being born of an English mother and Arabic father, being raised half his life in the desert, the other half in the hallowed halls of British aristocracy, he'd found himself torn between two cultures—a man with one foot in an ancient world and one in the new. His detractors saw this dichotomy as a weakness. But David had made it his strength, in business and in life.

He took a sip of his brandy, the fire of it burning down his throat. He felt its warmth diffuse through his system. He exhaled softly, stretched out his legs.

"It's so peaceful."

He jolted, almost choking on his drink.

"It's hard to believe there was a violent storm only hours ago."

He turned to look at her. She stood in the arched doorway. The lamplight from the dining room behind her set a halo of soft fire to the amber-gold of her hair. It was tied back loosely with a piece of ribbon, but fine tendrils escaped and wafted ever so slightly about her face in the warm, salty breeze. Her eyes were darkly luminous in this light. An oversize white muslin shirt hung to her thighs. On her legs she wore soft white muslin pants. She had oversize leather thongs on her feet. *Watson's clothes?*

He swallowed against the tightening in his throat. He'd expected—no, dreaded—seeing her in Aisha's clothes. And here she was in Watson's garb. And in spite of the getup, she remained ridiculously sensual and feminine, in the way of a woman confident and secure with her sexuality. That in itself was insanely arousing to David. He couldn't seem to find his voice. All he could do was stare at the shape of her body under the sheer African fabric, silhouetted against the lamplight. It made him recall her perfect breasts, the tight coral tips.

His pulse rate kicked up, and his breathing became light and shallow. This woman had a confounding effect on his body. He cleared his throat. But his voice still came out low and gruff. "Those clothes?"

She smiled. "The doctor's. May I join you?"

"Why are you wearing Watson's stuff? What happened to the clothes Kamilah brought you?"

She stepped out onto the patio and into his personal space. "It didn't feel right," she said. "I didn't want to upset anyone. I told Watson how I felt, and he gave me free access to his closet." She looked down at the garments and grimaced playfully. "I'm afraid this is the best I could come up with. Couture à la doc."

He couldn't help but smile. She'd floored him. Her sensitivity and tact, especially given her circumstances, made him feel like a brutish clod. He'd been so self-indulgent he hadn't begun to think about what she might be going through.

"You look great," he said. And he meant it.

"Thanks." She came up to his side. He felt his nostrils flare in reflex as she neared, drinking in the fresh, clean scent of her.

"You didn't join us for dinner." The banality of his statement belied how he'd felt about it. A part of him had hungered to see her again. Another was relieved when she hadn't shown. And then, when she still didn't appear, he'd felt slighted, even irritated.

"I ate in the servants quarters," she said simply.

"Why?"

She smiled at him, that dimple deepening in her one cheek. He couldn't take his eyes off the way her lips curved. He noted that one side of her smile was a little higher than the other. It gave her a mischievous look, as if she held some hidden secret, as if she was toying with him.

"I didn't want to interrupt your private time with Kamilah." She hesitated. "Dr. Watson told me about her…about her problem."

He stared at her in stunned silence, a grudging respect rising in him.

She came even closer to his chair. He felt the hairs on his arms rise, warmth stir in his groin. His body was powerless in her presence. Entranced, he watched the way the pale moonlight played across her exotic features.

"How was dinner…I mean with Kamilah. How was she?"

He was taken aback by her question, the intimacy of it. This was Rashid business. "Special," he said.

She waited, eyes watching him.

"She didn't talk to me, if that's what you want to know."

Her brow raised at the brusqueness of his tone.

He felt a pang of guilt, a need to elaborate. "She…she was there in a way she never was before." He grinned in spite of himself. "She even laughed at my silly camel jokes."

Sahar smiled. But it wasn't the same smile he'd seen before. There was a haunted look deep within her eyes, a look that betrayed her outward control. It was the look of someone adrift. Lost. Even a little afraid.

She was doing her best to appear relaxed, confident. She was looking beyond herself, beyond her own tragedy, caring about him and Kamilah. But he'd glimpsed the truth inside. She was hurting. Guilt knotted in his chest.

"I'm glad I found you," she said. "I've been looking for you all over the place. This palace is like a maze." Her voice curled like silk ribbon through him, tightening around his insides.

"You were looking for me?" She needed him. That pleased the primal male within.

"I wanted to ask you if…if you've had any contact from the mainland yet…about me?"

The question jolted him to his senses. He coughed, recalling his manners, stood up, pulled out a chair for her. "No, I'm afraid not. Communication is still down. Take a seat. Would you like a brandy?"

"No, thanks, I'm fine. I need to work on keeping my mind

clear if I want to remember anything." She sat with fluid grace but he could hear the disappointment in her tone at his answer.

"When I hadn't heard from you, I guessed there was no information. I kept telling myself you'd come and tell me the minute you learned something." Her eyes flashed up to his. "Right?"

Oh, God, she'd been waiting all day, anticipating word. And all he'd been thinking about was how to get rid of her, how to stop her impacting his personal life. And here she was being considerate of him, being tactful by not wearing Aisha's clothes, by not interrupting his dinner time with Kamilah. She'd even waited until the last possible moment in the day before coming to find him, although she'd been dying for some news, some clue to her identity.

The knotted ball of guilt in his chest tightened. "Of course I'd tell you right away," he said. "Hopefully we'll know something tomorrow. My tech reckons he'll have the satellite communication system up and running again by morning."

"It was downed in the storm?"

"Yeah, the sand out here gets into everything. We use a fixed satellite system which means the phones inside the palace can be operated just like landline sets. Only trouble is the radio antenna unit and junction box need to be mounted outdoors with a clear view of the sky. That means it's vulnerable to sandstorms."

She tensed suddenly. Her eyes widened, then the line of her mouth flattened. She turned abruptly away from him, shutting him out.

A frown cut into his brow. What had he said? He studied her profile. She was hugging her arms tight to her stomach, staring out over the inky ocean. What had caused this rapid shift in mood?

Perhaps she was wondering what befell her out there in the dark void, what had happened to the people she may have been with. Something snagged in his chest. What *had* she been through in that storm? Something so traumatic that it had shut off a part of her brain, made her dissociate from herself? Was what she experienced anything like the mad, awful terror that had gripped him as he'd watched Aisha, bleeding, being sucked down by the waves? Had she, too, known that huge hammerheads swam like shadows between the reefs underneath?

If Watson was right, her memory loss was only a temporary buffer against pain she might yet have to face in the next few days. Did she even have any idea that her amnesia was psychological? Would it help to tell her? Or would it only cause more distress?

She put her hand to her temple, pressed down on the stitches.

"You okay?" he asked.

She shook her head. "No. I mean yes. I'm fine. I…I just got a feeling."

"You remembered something?" He leaned forward.

"I…I don't know. Maybe." She forced a smile and abruptly changed the topic. "You're a very lucky man to own such a slice of paradise, David. This place is truly beautiful."

"Yes," he said, his eyes holding hers. "Very beautiful."

She faltered at his loaded words but held his gaze. The jasmine-scented air grew warm and thick between them. She swallowed and then turned away, but not before David had glimpsed the flare of female interest in her eyes.

"Do storms like that happen often out here?" she asked, her voice smoky, thicker. Her obvious physical reaction to him did wild things to his body. Heat simmered in his belly. His throat went dry. He told himself this was ridiculous. To even begin to think of her in this way was a fool's game. She was vulnerable. She wasn't able to make rational decisions in her state. And she probably had a lover waiting for her somewhere.

He cleared his throat. "No," he said. "Storms like that are rare. And when they do come, it's usually without the rain." He angled his head, caught her eyes. "And without mermaids."

She laughed. The sound caught him by surprise. Husky. Rich. It socked him right in the gut. But even though she laughed, David noted she was rubbing her arm nervously. Inside she was still loaded with angst. He wondered if it would help if he tried to prompt her memory. And a part of him couldn't help thinking about the possibility she could be faking this. "What do you know about the Red Sea?" he asked.

"Nothing really…I think."

"Seems strange how you washed up out of a sea you know nothing about."

She stopped rubbing her arm. "You make it sound like you don't believe me."

He took a long, slow sip of his brandy, studying her face carefully. She didn't shy away from his scrutiny for an instant.

"No, I believe you," he said finally. "What would you stand to gain by faking something like this, anyway?"

"That's a rhetorical question, right?" Her words were markedly clipped. "I can't believe you'd even begin to think I was malingering."

"Right," he said, noting her use of the word *malingering*. Watson had used the same word in a medical context. That didn't necessarily mean a thing. But still, it alerted him, put him on guard. David was not a man who trusted easily. He'd never have gotten where he was now if trust had come easy. He'd learned as a child out in the desert that you always had to watch your back. And he'd gradually learned that the more powerful a man became, the more people tried to tear him down.

No. For David Rashid trust was a very rare commodity. For him trust was hard-won.

But his suspicion had offended her. She glared at him, fire snapping in her eyes. Even though he'd upset her, he was pleased to see her energy back. He could deal with anger. He couldn't deal with the haunting loneliness he'd glimpsed a few seconds ago.

"Believe me," she said in a low, cool tone. "I have no desire to be stuck out here on some lump of land in the Red Sea with a man who doesn't believe I can't remember who I am." She pushed herself up from the chair. "If you think for an instant that I'm enjoying any part of this, you're dead wrong. It sucks. And I can't wait to get off this bloody island."

He grabbed her wrist as she turned to go. "I'm sorry," he said, looking up into her eyes. "That really was uncalled for. It's just such a strange thing to have happened. And I can't even begin to imagine how it feels to have no sense of self. I do apologize."

She glared at the hand that restrained her. But he wasn't going to let go until he got through to her. "Will you forgive me?" He smiled slowly, deliberately, aware he was turning on the famous Rashid charm.

He felt her relax under his fingers. Male satisfaction spurted through him. His charm had effect on her. She was not immune to him. He released her arm. "Please sit."

She acquiesced, but a sharp wariness lingered in her eyes. He felt compelled to chase it away. "I should be doing more than apologizing," he said. "I should be thanking you for allowing my daughter to speak again."

Her eyes softened. "Dr. Watson told me she hasn't spoken in nearly two years, not since the death of her mother." She hesitated as if unsure of her ground. "I'm sorry for your loss, David," she said. "I'm sorry for what you and Kamilah must have gone through."

The muscles of his neck constricted. He shouldn't have opened this door. He didn't know what had possessed him to do it. He looked away. "It's in the past," he said.

She had enough presence of mind not to press him. They sat in uneasy silence, watching the pull of the moon on the ocean, keenly aware of each other's presence.

"David," she said suddenly.

His eyes shot to hers.

"I...I want you to know that I'll do whatever I can to help Kamilah."

"Why?" The word came out too terse.

"Because I feel somehow responsible. I..." She wavered. The light of the moon caught the glisten in her huge green eyes, giving her away. She swallowed. "I don't know how to explain it but I feel like I have a connection, that I can somehow relate to her...to what she's been through."

David wanted to reach out, to touch her pain, to share his own. Instead he slammed down the doors. "You'll probably be gone by tomorrow night," he said brusquely.

Hurt flashed through her eyes. She turned her face away from him. "Yes," she said softly. "I hope I *will* be gone by then." She got up and left.

And he let her go.

He cursed silently in Arabic and swigged back the last of his drink, relishing the angry burn down his throat.

It took all Sahar's control not to run. She walked calmly over the terrace and back into the palace. But once inside, she pressed her back hard up against the cool stone wall and scrunched her eyes tight, willing hot tears of frustration away. She was shaky, an absolute mess of conflicting emotions. She knew *exactly* how David Rashid's satellite communication system worked. The realization had hit full-blow between her eyes the instant he'd begun to explain it to her. And she'd gone stone-cold. Some remote part of her brain had recognized that how his communications system functioned was somehow vitally important to her. *But why?*

She shivered. The more snippets of recollection she got, the more ominous her whole situation seemed. She felt there was something really big she was just not grasping. But the more she tried to grab hold of those elusive feelings, the further it all seemed to retreat into the murky shadows of her mind. It made her feel vulnerable, as if an unidentified enemy prowled in the peripheral darkness of her brain, closing in. And Sahar knew that whoever she was, she *hated* feeling vulnerable.

And on top of it all, she was attracted to the man in the most basic way. He stirred things inside her she didn't want to begin to think about right now. Not when she didn't know if he was supposed to be an enemy. But even though David Rashid set off every warning bell in her system, an instinctive female part of her wanted to ease his pain, help him connect with his daughter. And she'd tried to do just that. She'd reached out to help. And she'd been burned by rejection.

Despite Sahar's best efforts to quash the rising tide of emotions, a sob escaped her. It shuddered up through her body, and the pent-up frustration spilled hot down her cheeks.

David was furious with himself. He shouldn't have let her go like that. He jerked off his chair, stormed across the terrace, swung into the dining hall. And froze.

She was pressed up against the wall, head back, eyes closed, a shimmering trail of tears down her cheeks.

His throat closed. He'd done this to her.

"Sahar," he said, his voice thick.

Her eyes flared open. She gasped, tried to turn away. He lunged forward and grabbed her arm. She stilled. He reached up, cupped her jaw, turned her slowly to face him. But she wouldn't look him in the eyes.

"I…I didn't want you to see me like this," she whispered.

"Oh, God, Sahar, I'm so sorry. I didn't mean—"

She pulled loose. "Don't. It's nothing. It's me. I'm just tired. I need sleep. I…I guess I get emotional when I'm tired." She forced a weak smile. "See, I'm learning something about myself."

"Sahar," he said firmly.

Those huge green eyes looked into his. Bewitching, mesmerizing eyes, filled with a shimmering ocean of emotion. He felt himself pulled inexorably toward her, he felt his lips move closer to hers. So close he could feel the warmth of her breath against his mouth. It took all his strength to hold back. To not press his lips down on hers. "Sahar." His voice came out rough and deep. "I meant it when I said thank you…for helping Kamilah."

She stared silently up at him, her lips parted. The look of hurt and frustration in her eyes tore at his heart. He moved a stray gold tendril of hair from her face, hooked it behind her ear. "In the desert," he said softly, "rain is a gift directly from the gods. There is nothing more spiritual than rain in the desert. Because it not only brings life, it *is* life."

He cleared his throat. The look in her eyes had forced him down this track. And he could no longer turn back. "You blew in with the rain, Sahar. And like the rain you brought the life back to my child. You awakened her. And me. That's the reason behind my choice of name. *Sahar.* It means dawn, to awaken. A time of new beginnings. Of growth. Life. I want you to know that. I want you to know why I chose it."

Time stretched as she stared up into his eyes, a range of unreadable emotions crossing her face.

"It's a beautiful name, David," she said finally, her voice

thick and husky. "Thank you." She looked away. "I wish it really was mine. I mean, to keep…forever."

And David suddenly felt sick. Because nothing about this woman in front of him could be forever. It was simply a matter of days before she was history. He'd do well to remember that fact. But right now trying to send her away seemed about as logical as trying to stuff the rain back into the clouds, as trying to roll the morning sun back into the night.

"I…I really should go to bed," she said. "Good night, David. And thank you for your hospitality, for your help." She turned to go.

He watched the sensuous sway of her hips as she walked the length of the dining hall, her spine held stiff, her chin held high, her luxurious reddish-gold hair rippling across the small of her back. He swallowed against the thickness in his throat. He hadn't been any damn help at all. He'd been suspicious, resentful and ridiculously turned on by this woman.

He'd been focused only on himself and Kamilah and how this woman was rocking their boat. Not on her anguish, her loss. And he could kick himself for the way things had gone tonight.

"Night, Sahar," he whispered as she slipped through the doorway into the corridor.

But there was no one to hear him.

O'Reilly peered through the dim blue haze of smoke. He spotted Lancaster at the far end of the bar. He made his way through the crowd, edged in next to him. "You'll never guess who dropped in on the ambassador's little soiree this evening."

"Who?"

O'Reilly glanced over his shoulder, leaned forward and dropped his voice so that it was drowned by the bar racket. "Rashid's very own Dr. James Watson."

Lancaster's body stiffened. "And?"

"They have her. On Shendi Island."

"Jesus, you've got to be joking—she survived the storm?"

"You betcha. And get this, she claims to have amnesia. According to the doctor, she has no idea who she is. Apart from that, she's fine."

Lancaster threw his head back and roared with laughter. He stopped almost immediately. "What did the doctor want from the ambassador?"

"Rashid sent him. Our sheik is trying to find out who she is. He wants the ambassador to get the word out."

"Kill it."

O'Reilly grinned. "Already done. Rashid will never be the wiser." O'Reilly motioned to the bartender to bring him a whiskey. He took a swig, then paused. "What if...I mean, what if she really can't remember? What if she's *not* faking?"

Lancaster studied his drink. "Then we're safe. In the meantime, we wait to see if she makes contact. If she doesn't, we pose as loving relatives, go in, neutralize her. If she does make contact—" Lancaster grinned devilishly "—then, partner, we're back in business."

Chapter 5

Soft yellow light seeped through the louvered shutters, throwing stripes of shadow onto the whitewashed walls. She blinked in confusion, then her heart sank like a stone. It was dawn. She was still on Shendi. She still had no memory of her identity.

The thought paralyzed her for a moment. She lay staring at the bars of shadow on the wall. They only served to drive her situation home. She was trapped. Imprisoned inside her own damn head, on a remote island with a man who scorched her insides every time he turned his laser-blue eyes her way. A man who might be dangerous—if only she could remember why.

A man who had named her Sahar.

Frustration burned her eyes. How in hell did one deal with this? Then she thought of Kamilah.

Kamilah understood something of the prison she was in.

Maybe that's why she felt she could identify with the child. If the little girl could cope, so could she. She closed her eyes, willed away the panic.

Everyone had their own pain, she told herself. It was all relative. Besides, today she might learn who she was. Today word might come from the embassy in Khartoum. Things could start looking up. She *had* to stay positive.

She shoved the covers back, sat up. She needed a run to clear her head. Maybe once she got blood pumping through her cells that darn gray matter would start functioning properly again.

She pulled Dr. Watson's clothes over the simple white underwear Fayha' had given her, then slid her feet into Watson's oversize thongs and slipped out of the heavy oak door into the long, cool hallway. She paused. Fayha' had shown her how to navigate two of the palace wings yesterday, but it was still a confusing labyrinth to her. Like her mind.

She turned to her left and wound her way through stone passageways and mosaic courtyards thick with the scent of jasmine and the hum of bees, searching for the archway that would lead her down to the strip of sugar-white beach she'd seen from the window yesterday.

The phone on his desk beeped. David's head jerked up from his papers. The sat system was operational. It beeped again. He stared at the phone. Watson perhaps? At six in the morning? Maybe he had an ID on Sahar.

It beeped a third time. David's muscles tensed inexplicably across his chest. And he realized a part of him wasn't quite ready to find out who she was. He picked up the receiver. "Rashid."

"David, it's Larry Markham. I've been trying to get hold of you for two days."

Relief slid through him at the sound of his lawyer's chipper voice. "Markham. We had a storm take our system down. We've been incommunicado until now. Everything okay at the London office?"

"All's fine. I just wanted to let you know I'm going to fax through those papers you wanted prepared. As soon as you okay them, we can have Tariq sign them. It'll put him in control of the second uranium mine and the last northern Azar oilfield."

"Thanks. Have you made the extra adjustments to the trust?"

"Done. In the event of your death, Tariq will retain management of those mines, but he'll remain under the control of the board you appointed. Your plans for Azar will stay in place no matter who takes the helm of Rashid International."

"Good. Send the papers. And, thanks, Markham." He hung up and his fax machine started to hum. David stretched, cricking his back into place. He stared at his phone again. He should call Watson. He should find out what happened at the embassy. He checked his watch. No, too early. And right now he needed his ride.

But as David strode toward the stable compound, he knew he was only postponing the inevitable.

And he really didn't want to think about why.

Sahar slipped the thongs off her feet and stepped onto the sand. It was already warmed by the morning sun. She curled her toes into the fine grains, savoring the sensation. She shaded her eyes and scanned the bright strip of beach. Nothing but sand for miles. Waves crunched rhythmically against the shore, ridges of swells feeding them from behind. She felt her spirits begin to lift.

She began to run. And her spirits soared as the salt breeze

played with her hair and blood pumped through her system. She picked up her pace, ran faster. Harder. The muscles warmed in her body. Her breath rasped at her throat. And she felt free. Truly free.

She ran even faster. And it felt as natural as breathing. She began to almost feel herself.

The notion brought her to a screeching halt. *Herself?*

But as fleetingly as it was there, it was gone. Nothing but the dull thud of blood in her head.

It was as if her body, her cells, had a physical memory. Her body remembered motion, how to run. And she'd listened to it intuitively. Her body had craved this feeling of release from the minute she'd woken up. But in her mind, she hadn't registered she was a runner. Or why. She'd simply moved instinctively. But the physical action itself had jolted her brain, given her a glimpse. Maybe she could do it again. Maybe there was another physical motion that could knock something free in her brain.

What else did her body know that she didn't?

David halted Barakah up on the ridge and patted his muscled neck. They were both damp from the exertion of the ride. He drew in a deep breath, surveyed the ocean below. He loved this spot. Here he felt above everything, as if nothing could touch him.

Then he saw her.

His heart bucked, kicked into a light, steady rhythm. She was running on the strip of sand below the ridge. He leaned forward on his horse, mesmerized by her fast, fluid, natural motion. Her waist-length hair fanned out behind her, whipped by the sea breeze as she ran. It caught the morning sun, glinting with gold and copper light. The skin on her arms glistened with a sheen of moisture.

He whistled softly under his breath. For a mermaid she sure knew how to move on her legs.

Then she stopped suddenly and bent over, bracing her hands on her knees, catching her breath. Intrigued, David watched as she stood up again and raised her face to the sun. She stood like that for a while. Motionless, hands at her side.

It made him wonder what she was thinking.

Then she began to move. He watched as she placed her palms together between her breasts, as if in prayer. She then moved her hands up along her body until she held them high above her head, palms still pressed together. She stepped forward with one leg and leaned into a lunge, her hands still held in perfect symmetry above her head.

She was doing some sort of yoga, as if in salutation to the morning sun. She turned her body sideways, bent at the waist. Then she faltered. Her movements became a little more tentative as if she were slowly recalling a sequence.

She crouched suddenly. Then lurched into a leaping spin as her leg kicked out to full length at her side.

The muscles in David's stomach tensed at the sudden and aggressive, yet exquisitely fluid movement.

Entranced, he watched as she continued her sequence, each kick and thrust of her arms flowing with fluid grace into the next. She looked like a golden warrior, balletic in her fighting sequence. Where in hell did she learn that? he wondered.

Then she stopped, looked around as if confused. She moved up to the high-tide line, searching for something among the scattered storm debris. She picked up a piece of flotsam, discarded it, hunted for another. Then she found what she was looking for. A long, slim and flat piece of wood, about as wide as her arm.

Holding it with two hands, wielding it like a sword, she began to swing it in front of her. Rhythmic. Fast. Sparring with an imaginary foe. Faster. Harder. But even as her speed mounted, each thrust of her weapon remained clean, smooth.

She was in control every inch of the way, perspiration gleaming on her skin.

A smiled tugged at the corner of his mouth. She was a phenomenal athlete. It didn't surprise him, given the state of her body. Just the thought of her naked warmed him inside.

"Come, Barakah." He nudged his horse toward the steep path that led down to the beach. "Let's go and see what's gotten our mermaid so worked up this morning."

The beach was empty when he rounded the ridge and came through the grove of palms at the bottom. Puzzled, David scanned the area. She'd been here only seconds ago. Then he saw the neat pile of clothes on the sand. Doc Watson's clothes. David's eyes shot immediately out to the waves breaking along the shoreline.

She was there, playing in the waves. He watched as she moved into a swell with long, smooth strokes. It crested into a wave. She turned at precisely the right moment and rode the wave in as it broke, her hair streaming around her in the water. She ducked under the foaming surf, popped out behind the froth and headed for another swell.

She was playing in the ocean like a young seal, showing none of the fear someone who'd recently survived a boat wreck might. David shook his head. The woman was an absolute enigma.

He watched as she rode another wave in. A smile quirked along his lips and he felt his heart lift at the sight of her playful spirit. It made a part of him want to play too. He shook his head mentally. He couldn't recall having felt this way in years.

She caught yet another wave, and he marveled at the way she was toying with the power of the swells, the force of nature, becoming one with it. It excited him. He could relate to it. He nudged his horse forward, watched hungrily from the shadows, the feeling mounting within him that this woman was some kind of wild and kindred soul.

She kicked out of her final wave and swam to shore. He watched her emerge from the turquoise water. Droplets caught the sun and slithered down her flat, tanned belly. She raised her arms and slicked her hair back, the movement highlighting the firm swell of her breasts.

Barakah moved under him, making him conscious of the heat in his loins as he watched her stride up the beach, her chest rising and falling from the exertion of her exercise, the sleek muscles of her thighs shifting under smooth wet skin.

As she came closer he could see the darker shade of her tight nipples under the wet, white underwear she was wearing. It hid nothing. His eyes slid down her body, drawn by the darker delta between her thighs.

His pulse quickened. His mouth went dry. His stallion stirred again, restless under him.

David swallowed and shifted on his horse, conscious of the beast between his thighs, of his own searing heat as his body responded involuntarily to the sight of the woman nearing him.

But he stayed in the shadows, just feet away from her.

She went straight for her piece of wood. With her back to him, she stooped, picked it up, swung it around...to face him. Barakah spooked, reared up violently. David grabbed the reins.

Sahar cried out in shock, dropped her piece of wood.

His stallion reared again at the sound of her cry. David felt himself slip. He clenched his thighs. "Whoa. Steady, boy, steady." He struggled to calm his massive horse. Then he coaxed Barakah gently out onto the beach and into the sunlight.

Sahar glared at him, hands on her hips, her eyes wide, breathing hard. "What the hell!" she demanded.

He grinned, couldn't help himself. He jerked his chin in

the direction of her weapon. "You planning on killing some-one with that stick?"

"You were *spying* on me?" she accused, furious spots of color flushing her cheeks.

"Last I recalled," he said lazily, holding a tight rein on Ba-rakah, "it was my island and I was free to go where I willed."

Her jaw clenched and she held her ground, feet firmly planted in the sand. David had expected her to lunge imme-diately for the protection of her small pile of clothes. She didn't. Neither did she back away as his massive stallion ap-proached. Instead she pulled her shoulders back, thrust her chin forward. Even in that simple, yet very revealing, wet un-derwear she was as proud and regal as a lioness.

"What were you doing with that stick?" he asked. "Some kind of martial art?"

She faltered. "I…I'm not sure. I was trying to remem-ber…until *you* interrupted me."

He couldn't stop his eyes from sliding slowly, brazenly, down her awesome body.

She didn't flinch under his scrutiny. Instead she caught his eyes, held them, defying him to look away from her face. He forced himself to hold her gaze. But her challenge excited him, it shot a jolt of heat to his groin. His stallion pawed at the ground, the movement making him exquisitely conscious of his hot, pulsing desire. And for a moment he couldn't speak, couldn't breathe even. He was pinned down by the dare in her eyes, by the dark hum in his body. The world around him seemed to slow to a standstill. The sound of waves break-ing along the shore receded to a dull white noise in his head.

His horse snorted again, jerking him back to his senses. He sucked in air sharply, trying to pull his scattered thoughts to-gether. Seeing her standing like that in her underwear had sent his brain and blood south.

"It was perhaps a mermaid fighting sequence?" he offered, provoking her further.

She pulled a face. "Yeah. Probably."

Right. It was more likely some fitness routine picked up in a swanky London gym. Despite her lack of any worldly possessions, Sahar carried herself with obvious breeding and grace. He suspected her life, once she figured out what it was, was well-heeled. She'd probably acquired her perfect biscuit tan aboard upper-class yachts and on the shores of exotic beach resorts. Yet there was something else about her that was innately earthy.

And something that told him he wouldn't want to confront her in a sword fight.

Although he was practically born with a *jambiya* in his hand and could wield a scimitar with the best Arabian horseman, he suspected she just might match him in that department. That only deepened his curiosity. Who *was* this woman? He was quite simply drawn to her, like a proverbial moth to a flame.

He leaned forward, slowly massaged Barakah's neck. "Want a ride home?"

"Home?" Her eyes widened like a child's. "You got news from Khartoum?"

Guilt bit at him again. "Sorry. It was a figure of speech."

Her features fell. She nodded silently, studying the form of his horse.

"I'm sure word will come soon," he offered, hoping at the same time it wouldn't. He wanted just a few more hours with this compelling woman. Because right at this instant he liked the way she made him feel. She'd made the blood flow hot in his loins in a way he'd forgotten was possible. And it made him feel powerful. Alive. It made the colors of the world seem brighter. It made him feel like a king.

She lifted her huge green eyes to his. "He's stunning," she said. "I heard you'd just broken him in."

"Yes."

"All primal power," she said, moving closer. From his vantage point David looked down into the valley of her breasts. She laid her palm flat on his stallion's flanks and rubbed him as if testing his muscle, his strength.

To David's astonishment, Barakah held steady under her touch, obviously reading her surety. The woman was confident around horses. And too bloody confident in her underwear. This was going to be his undoing. He couldn't take his eyes from the depression between her breasts, the way droplets of sea water clung to the fine blond hair there, drying into soft clusters of salt. He moistened his lips. He could imagine slowly licking that salt from between her naked breasts as he watched those exquisite nipples tighten. He could almost taste the salt. His vision began to narrow at the hot and delirious thought of it.

"Yes," she said, her voice shattering his illicit thoughts through his brain in a kaleidoscope of sharp shards.

He blinked, momentarily confused. He cleared his throat. "Yes, what?" His voice came out thick and rough.

"Yes, I'd like a ride home," she said, her eyes studying him intently.

"You're not afraid?"

"Of what? You?"

He shifted. She had to have seen the raw stamp of arousal on his features. And now she was toying with him. Or was she?

"My stallion," he said. "You're not afraid of Barakah?"

"No," she said simply.

"You're experienced, then."

Her eyes flashed to his and she raised a brow.

"I mean, with horses."

She gave a slow, sly smile. Damn she *was* toying with him. "I guess I know a thing or two." She stroked the stallion's neck. Then she angled her head, catching his eyes with a mischievous twinkle in her own. "He looks like one hell of a challenge, though."

David swallowed. She wasn't only toying with him. She was flirting. She was turned on. He could see it in the hardening of the nipples under that darned thin fabric. It spiked his blood clean off the Richter scale. "You afraid of *anything?*" he asked, his voice coming out an octave lower.

She held his gaze. "I guess I'll have to find out."

"Barakah's no easy ride," he warned. "And there's no saddle."

"You make that sound like a dare, Rashid."

He smiled slowly. "Maybe it is, Sahar."

"I don't believe I turn down a challenge."

"A woman after my own heart." He held out his hand, palm up. "Come on, then."

"Wait." She spun around, her hair fanning out behind her. It was almost dry already and the salt had plumped the curls, making her mane wild and full. With her back to him, she bent over to retrieve the pile of clothes. Her movement was so fluid he didn't have a chance to turn away. Even if he had wanted to.

He was held transfixed by her smooth back, the neat ridge of her spine, the way her panties skimmed her firm rump. He became insanely aware of the way her buttocks separated into two tight globes; of the neat gap at the apex of her thighs.

Blazing heavens. He blew out a hot breath, turned quickly to stare over the ocean as she slipped back into Watson's clothes. He couldn't do this. He couldn't have this woman, for all the reasons he'd mentally checked off last night. They were still just as valid. She had another life that could come back and bite them all, that could hurt Kamilah. And him. And her. In spite of her rebellious streak, she was vulnerable, even if she wasn't admitting it to herself. She wasn't in a position to make decisions like this. And it was up to him not to abuse that. He clenched his teeth.

"I'm ready."

He was not. He turned to face her. She was holding her hand out to him. He reached down, grabbed her arm and swung her up fast and hard. Too hard.

He bit back a curse. He hadn't meant that. His vigor had been born of sexual frustration. But she moved fluidly with his brusque momentum, straddling her legs over the flanks of his horse and slotting comfortably in behind him. She slid her arms around his waist. "Ready."

And he knew he was sunk. He swallowed hard at the sensation of her legs splayed open against him. He nudged Barakah forward and instantly he felt the tense and flex of her inner thigh muscles around him as she moved with the rolling motion of the horse. This was going to kill him.

He sucked in a gulp of air and urged his powerful stallion slowly back up the ridge, allowing both the horse and the woman to get used to each other.

Barakah topped the ridge and immediately strained against David's control in a desire to charge across the hills for home as they did each morning. He held the beast in, allowing only an incremental increase in speed. Sahar moved with surprisingly fluid ease behind him. He kicked up the pace—she handled it. He gave the stallion even more rein, freeing him to gallop.

Her arms tightened around his waist, the wind pulled at his hair and she laughed behind him. It kicked his spirits sky-high. He let loose, holding nothing back. And they sped with reckless abandon over the hills. Sahar moved as if she was one with his body. He moved as if he was one with his horse. And for an instant they *were* one. A most intimate union. Man, woman and beast. David felt a wild spiritual freedom. His heart sang. The horse's hooves thudded on packed dirt, his mane flying free.

Sahar knew in her deepest being she had never experienced anything like this with a man. She knew it not with her mind but the very molecules and cells of her body.

She'd never dreamed, when she'd seen the dark Arabian horseman silhouetted against the sea, that she'd be straddled behind him like this. One with him and his stallion. It was sublime. She felt the wind pull at her hair, draw tears from her eyes. And she clung with her thighs to the hard and powerful man between her legs, the sensation deliriously wild and intimate.

They raced along the ridge and over the hills, the sea gleaming aquamarine in the distance, the castle looming ahead. Sahar knew she'd have to wake up eventually. But right now she was existing merely in the moment. She was living a dream. A fairy tale. And a part of her did not want to wake from it.

Breathless, exhilarated, blood pumping, they came to a halt in front of the stables. David slid down from the horse, held his arms up to her.

She stilled.

He stared up at her. Silent for a moment. There was a blaze in his eyes she had not yet seen. An unspoken connection. His hair was tousled by wind and he was covered in fine desert dust. So was she. She swung herself off the stallion and into the steely strength of David Rashid's arms.

For a second he held her there, aloft, his eyes smouldering. They were at a crossroads. Her world stood still. She became conscious of nothing beyond the hot breathing of the horse, the rhythm of blood in her veins, the heavy-lidded intent in David's eyes. And a scorching ribbon of desire unfurled slow and deep inside her.

He brought her slowly down to him, drawing her closer into his chest, toward his exquisitely sculpted lips. He let her feet touch the ground. And his hand ran roughly up the back of her neck. He forced his fingers up into her tangled mass of hair. He tilted her face sharply up to his and he pressed his lips down hard onto hers.

Sahar's vision swam. Her knees buckled. Her lips opened under his aggressive firmness and his tongue slipped hot into her mouth. She felt herself go faint. He deepened his kiss as he slid a hand down the hollow of her back to the base of her spine. He pulled her pelvis sharply up against his thigh. Sahar gasped, her mouth opening wider. She could taste the salt of his skin, feel the roughness of the dark stubble on his jaw, the hard heat of his chest against hers.

Her body thrummed. Ached. With exhilaration, with need. Nothing existed beyond this moment. And in his arms she felt the way she had felt in the ocean. Natural. Wild. A primal being. She kissed him back, hungrily, trying to feed an unidentified need deep within.

Then he jerked back, releasing her instantly.

Stunned, Sahar blinked into the sudden sharpness of the sun. Why had he dropped her like that?

Then she saw. A little figure, in the far distance, barely distinguishable, was skipping along the path that led down to the stables.

"Kamilah!" His voice was hoarse. There was raw shock in it, as if he'd been caught off guard doing something illicit. As if the fact he was doing it at all rocked him to the very foundation of his being.

Sahar swallowed, still stunned. "She…she couldn't see us, David. She's too far away," she said, out of concern.

He turned on her, his face like hard granite, a blackness in his eyes. All trace of the man she was with a second ago was gone. The look on his face ripped the ground right out from under her, and her heart sank like a cold stone. "David?"

He glared at her. "This is *exactly* what was not supposed to happen!" He whirled on his heels, grabbed Barakah's reins, stormed off toward the stables.

Sahar reeled. She felt as though she was flailing in air. She watched his powerful form disappear into the stable buildings.

She sucked in a shaky breath and pushed her mess of hair back from her face. Reality began to seep back into her brain. He was right. She'd been a fool. They had both been crazy. Overpowered by the moment they had slipped across a line. But neither of them had any idea what other life might await her. *Who* might be waiting for her.

But whatever life she'd had, she knew for certain she'd never had a man like David Rashid. A deep loneliness seeped into her, but she shook it off. There could be no tomorrows for her. Not until she figured out who she was. It could be no other way.

She turned her attention to watch the dark little figure coming down the path.

Kamilah came to a halt in front of Sahar. Puzzled, the child looked from Sahar to the stables, to where her father had disappeared. A sadness slid into her eyes.

Sahar bent down. "Were you looking for your daddy?"

She nodded, still staring at the empty stable door.

"What did you need him for, sweetheart?"

Kamilah hung her head. "I guess he has to work again," she said softly. "He always has to work. He never has time to play with me."

She stroked Kamilah's cheek. "I think your daddy's got a lot on his mind. He's a busy man."

"I guess so," she said quietly. "But he used to play before mummy died. He wasn't so busy then."

And with those few words, Sahar got a whole picture. While Kamilah had cut herself off from her father and the rest of the world through the loss of her voice, David had cut himself off in his own way. He'd turned to work. He'd lost the ability to connect with his child.

The idea made her heart squeeze tight inside her chest. It was all so tragic. A father and a child who loved and desperately needed each other, but who couldn't find the way to each other. They stood on either side of chasm not even knowing they needed a bridge. And Sahar felt something surge through her. A need to help build that bridge.

She hooked her finger under the child's chin. "I tell you what, since your daddy is so busy, how about you play with me?"

A smile crept cautiously along Kamilah's mouth.

"Deal?"

Kamilah nodded, slipping her little hand into Sahar's, her warm fingers clutching tight. And Sahar's heart blipped at the sensation. Because in that instant she just knew she didn't have a child of her own somewhere. She just knew.

A part of her was beginning to feel like there really wasn't anything special waiting for her anywhere in the world.

At least she knew how to play. It was all she really could do right now, exist in the moment, for the moment.

And wait to see if her memory returned.

She tugged Kamilah's arm. "Come on, then. How about a game of tag?" And the two of them raced around the side of the palace.

Chapter 6

David stared blankly at the papers his lawyer had faxed him, unable to focus. He clicked a button on his computer, and the screen crackled softly to life, but he couldn't concentrate on that, either.

He'd showered, changed, but his insides still churned. It was as if he was in shock. He couldn't erase Sahar from his mind; the way he'd connected so intimately with her on his horse. He couldn't pinpoint exactly when it had happened. There was no clear line demarcating black and white. But at some point he'd slipped over the invisible boundary and been swept so completely into the moment that he'd forgotten the past...and the future. It had only been the moment—on that horse with her wrapped around him—the primeval sensation of just being. Man and woman. Fully alive, vividly and vitally so, in a world that was warm and free.

He blew out a shuddering breath.

He'd never felt anything like it in his life. He clenched his fist around a pencil. It snapped sharply. Startled, he looked down at the broken thing in his hand. The connection between them had snapped just like that, the second he'd seen Kamilah in the distance.

And as much as he wanted Sahar, the very last thing he wanted to do was hurt his child. Because when the time came for Sahar to leave, it would kill them both.

He had to stop this. It was too much of a gamble. She could leave anyday. Any minute. It could happen the instant the phone on his desk rang.

David rubbed his brow fiercely, then reached for the phone—and stopped himself. Surely Watson would ring if he had news. *Damn.* He couldn't even pick up the bloody phone to see if they had an ID on her yet. He *wanted* her to be Sahar. Not someone else.

He slammed the pencil shards onto his desk, turned to his computer, forced his mind to function and began to review the latest production report from the Azar uranium mine.

Things were looking good. Britain and France were snapping up all the yellowcake he could produce. He started to scan the numbers. But they blurred, her image once again shimmering in his mind.

He smashed his hand onto the desk. He couldn't take this. She lingered in his senses like opium. He needed to wipe his mind clean, but it was impossible.

He sat back in his leather chair, closed his eyes. And once again he could feel her long, sun-browned legs around him, the wind in his hair, the movement of Barakah under them.

She was so different from Aisha.

Aisha had been soft and dark, sweet and gentle, raised with a strong religious influence. She'd been bright, sensitive, creative. A wonderful advisor and a friend. Yet she'd deferred everything to him with a soft feminine subservience that had boosted his male ego. She'd stood by his side with a quiet luminescent beauty at social functions in London society. She'd carried herself with grace, walking the strange cultural lines of Azarian tradition. She'd been a perfect asset. A gentle lover. A wonderful mother. He never thought he could want anything more.

Until Sahar. This was a shock to his system. She challenged him in a way Aisha never had. She matched him. Her femininity was as strong as it was sensual. Her grace was that of a lioness. Fluid. Powerful. Proud.

And dangerous.

Because she'd snared something within him, made him lose focus. David Rashid *never* lost focus. Doing so meant making mistakes.

He gritted his teeth, jerked up in his chair, grabbed the phone and punched in Watson's number. The doctor answered on the second ring.

"Watson, any news?"

"Rashid, I was just about to call you."

David's stomach tightened. "You have word?"

"Not a bloody thing. It's too weird. The British ambassador here even volunteered to check in with the other embassies in the region for us, but so far, nothing. She's a complete mystery."

A quirky mix of relief and anticipation rippled through him. "The ambassador found nothing whatsoever?" he asked, just to be sure.

"Nope. It's the darnedest thing. No one has ever heard of this woman. No one has reported her missing. There's been zip from the dive operators, the embassies, the Ministry of Interior, the airlines. Nothing from the Interpol databases. It's like she never officially set foot in Sudanese territory."

"You mean she's *un*officially in the country?"

"Well, that's the question, isn't it?"

"Maybe she came down from Egypt on one of their dive tours."

"That's just it, David. The ambassador says his staff has checked everything, even the embassies up there. It's like she doesn't exist."

A dark thrill quirked through him. He couldn't begin to define it. Didn't want to.

"Women like her don't go unnoticed, Rashid." The doctor chuckled. "Maybe there *is* something to Kamilah's mermaid theory."

"Yeah. Right." She was an enigma all right.

"Or…" The doctor hesitated. "Maybe there's something *else* going on here."

David detected the subtle shift in Watson's tone. "What do you mean?"

"I don't know. Maybe I'm just being paranoid, but a part of me gets a sense someone over here in Khartoum might be hiding something."

"Such as?"

"Such as who she is."

"Why on earth would you think that?"

"You know me, Rashid, I'm the born conspiracy theorist. It's nothing I can put my finger on. Just a feeling."

David frowned. Watson might be a conspiracy theorist at heart but his instincts were solid as rock. Still, David couldn't begin to imagine why someone would try to hide Sahar's identity. "I think the African sun is getting to you, Doc," he joked. "Let's wait a couple of days to see what comes up, now that the word is out about her. When are you heading into Azar?"

"I've got the supplies I need. I'll be up at the new mine in about two days to set up the clinic. And, Rashid—"

"Yeah?"

The doctor paused. "Watch your back."

David laughed dryly. "Why? The mermaid's going to stick a knife in it?"

Watson was silent.

The image of Sahar fighting with her stick on the beach filtered into David's mind, but he shook it off. "Seriously, Watson, even if someone is hiding something, what can the woman do?" *Apart from unhinge me physically and mentally.*

"I'm just saying be careful, that's all."

David hung up and stared at the computer screen. He couldn't afford to think about Sahar now. Not in any way. He had work to do. He brutally shoved his thoughts aside and turned his attention to his work.

He leaned forward, his interest finally back where it belonged. But laughter drifted through his open windows, shattered his thoughts.

He cursed softly, lifted his head.

The melodious sound floated up to him on the warm breeze. A woman laughing with a child. The muscles around his heart tightened reflexively.

He got up, moved to the window, rested his hand on the cool sill. Sahar and Kamilah were chasing each other on the grass below the patio. A smile snared the corners of his mouth. They were playing tag, he realized. Intrigued, he leaned farther out the window and once again watched Sahar move. There was nothing self-conscious about the way she was charging about after his little girl. She was utterly free, unfettered of any inhibitions. His smile broadened. It was probably because she didn't know anyone was watching. And once again he was a voyeur. He wanted to keep it that way. He leaned back into the shadow lest she see him. He didn't want them to stop. Not yet.

Kamilah shrieked with utter childish delight, and he felt a heavy burden lift from his heart. His eyes moistened. This is what *he* should have been doing with Kamilah these past two years. Playing. He should have been tumbling on the lawn with his daughter, allowing her to be a child instead of bouncing her from specialist to specialist in an effort to solve her problems. Maybe the answer had been in his own hands all along.

Sahar tagged Kamilah and the two of them rolled like puppies in the grass. The sound of his daughter's infectious chuckle gripped him by the throat. It burbled from deep in her stomach, erupting like a bubbling brook.

It was a sound he hadn't heard in almost two years. Laughter hadn't rung through the halls of the Rashid household in all that time, and his heart lifted in sheer empathetic joy at the sound of it.

He forgot his need for hiding. He leaned forward, pushed the window open wider, hungry for more. He chuckled softly to himself. Sahar was still in the doctor's muslin clothes, still covered in dust from their ride. She was running barefoot, Watson's oversize thongs discarded on the grass. Her hair was a glorious wild tangle, her eyes alive with laughter, her cheeks flushed with exhilaration.

She was like something from another world. Her dusty attire reminded him of a desert traveler, at ease with few possessions, content in the arms of nature's awesome power. It was something he related to. Wholeheartedly.

It was that very sense of purity, of man alone against nature, that had kept driving him back into the harsh ways of the desert for most of his life. It was the clarity he found out there, the brutal honesty, the essence of life that drew him into the oceans of sand and endless horizons.

Out in the Sahara man was stripped to the bare-bone

basics. Hunger and thirst was a constant. And the focus was on the present. It was harsh. But it was true.

And as he watched her, he began to understand how she'd managed to suck him into the moment earlier in the morning. It was because it was a state he'd so often aspired to. It was the very thing that kept drawing him back to the wild open spaces of his beloved Sahara. And now he'd glimpsed it in her.

He wondered, though—would she be this free once her past came to reclaim her? Would she lose that unabashed magic when she found her place in the pecking order of the civilized world again, when she discarded Doc Watson's old garb and once again donned the lush silks and tailored linens he had no doubt she was accustomed to wearing?

He chewed on his cheek, wondering what she'd look like in silks and gold. Would the clothes and adornment change how he viewed her? Maybe if she dressed in the couture to which she was accustomed she might actually remember more about her past, about herself.

Again Kamilah chuckled. Sahar laughed heartily in response, the sound of it rich, enticing.

He could feel it inside him.

His smile deepened. And on impulse, he swiveled, reached over his desk, picked up the phone and punched in a number he hadn't called in a very, very long time. It was the number of a high-end boutique in Cairo. And as he waited for the sales clerk to pick up, he felt just a little playful. The sensation caught him off guard—and it felt good.

Sahar and Kamilah took refuge from the midday heat in the shadows of one of the palace courtyards. They sat on an intricately carved marble bench, sipping the iced mint tea Fayha' had brought them. While they sipped they listened to the soft tinkle of water spouting from the mouths of ornate stone lions that reared up around the fountain in the center of the enclosed garden. The air was heavy with sensual warmth and the heady scent of flowers.

The palatial surroundings seemed surreal to Sahar. She felt like Alice, slipping through the looking glass of her old world into the alternate reality of a Middle-Eastern fantasy. She was sure that any minute she'd wake with only a massive bump on the head to show for it all. She wiggled her toes in the jasmine-scented air, not sure if she actually wanted to wake up. Because this dream came complete with a dark and dangerously seductive Arabian prince. The memory of their morning ride began to stir her blood once again. She couldn't believe how she'd let herself go.

She laughed at herself. What a twit. Of course she'd slipped into the moment, because that's all she could do. She only had the present. No past. And therefore no future to contemplate— at least not until she had an identity. She'd be crazy to let herself go like that again. Besides, she still had the lurking sensation of danger when she looked into his face. But that only intensified his mystique. And despite the fact he set warning bells clanging in her brain, she knew if David Rashid so much as looked at her with those smoldering eyes again…she laughed nervously.

"What are you laughing at?" Kamilah asked.

Sahar glanced down at the little girl sitting companionably at her side. An old leather-bound book rested on her lap.

"I'm laughing because I'm a silly fool in a crazy dream," she said. "And if I don't laugh about it, I'll cry." Sahar nodded toward the book in Kamilah's lap. "What book is that you're reading?"

Kamilah lifted it, pushed it reverently into Sahar's hands. Sahar read the title and smiled softly. She fingered the embossed lettering. It was an old copy of Hans Christian Andersen's *Little Mermaid.*

Kamilah's liquid brown eyes watched her intently, waiting for reaction. "It's my favorite," she prompted.

"It is?" She was amazed at how Kamilah had opened up after their game of tag. It had broken down yet another barrier, and the child was almost talking with ease.

"It was my mother's. She used to read it to me a lot. Do you know the story?"

Sahar thought about it. "Yes, I do, actually. If I remember correctly, it's about a little mermaid princess, the daughter of the sea king. She was the youngest of five sisters and the prettiest of them all."

"Six," Kamilah corrected. "There are six sisters."

"Oh. Okay. Well, the youngest of the six mermaids, then. And she was not only the most beautiful, she also had the loveliest voice on earth. She fell in love with a human prince and she desperately wanted a chance to be on land with him. But," said Sahar, "before she could get legs and go on land she had to sacrifice her voice to a wicked old sorceress. And then, because she didn't have her voice, she had to try and make the prince love her without using words."

"So you *do* remember that." There was a strange mixture of curiosity and accusation in the little girl's statement.

"Kamilah, I know it's strange. I find it very difficult to understand myself. But I do remember a lot of things, just not who I am, or how I came to learn the things that I do know. I haven't the slightest idea when I read Andersen's *Little Mermaid.* I just know that once upon a time I did. Maybe *my* mother read it to me."

The dark eyes studied her with brooding intensity.

"Why is that story your favorite, Kamilah?"

The little girl fiddled with her fingers in her lap. "'Cause my mummy liked it and she used to read it to me."

Sadness clogged Sahar's throat. She stroked Kamilah's silky hair. "I guess you are like the Little Mermaid, too, huh? Because you also lost your voice." Sahar smiled tenderly.

"I guess." Kamilah sat silent a while. Then her eyes flashed up to Sahar's. "Do you think the ending in the book is happy?"

David made his way along the corridor. He needed to find Fayha' and inform her that Tariq would be dining with them tonight. He stepped out to cross the courtyard when he heard Kamilah's and Sahar's voices. Instinctively he froze in the shadow of a mosaic column.

They were just feet from him, sitting on a marble bench facing the fountain. Kamilah's little face was turned up to Sahar's. Sahar's wild hair cascaded down her back, the sun bouncing off glinting gold highlights among the auburn. They looked like a painting, a Madonna and child. He was held transfixed.

Then he heard his daughter's clear little voice over the sound of the tinkling fountain. She was asking Sahar if she thought the ending of a book was a happy one.

"Hmm, that's an interesting question," he heard Sahar say. "I guess it depends on how you look at it. What do *you* think?"

Kamilah pulled her legs up onto the bench, wrapped her arms around her knees. "The Little Mermaid didn't get to marry the prince."

"No, she didn't."

"Because the prince got confused," said Kamilah. "He mistook the Little Mermaid for someone else, and he fell in love with that person instead. I don't think that part is happy."

David leaned closer, greedy for the sound of his daughter's little voice, the sound of the words she'd had locked up inside all this time. For almost two years he hadn't had a window into his daughter's soul. And now here she was, opening up to Sahar. And he was getting a glimpse. But at the same time, a perverse jealousy twined itself around his heart. He wanted it to be *him* on that bench with Kamilah. It *should* be him.

"But even though the mermaid lost the prince, she did get her own reward," offered Sahar. "She sacrificed herself for her love, and for that she got a chance to have an immortal soul, which mermaids don't ordinarily have."

"I know," said Kamilah, her voice suddenly incredibly sad. "But I think she should have gotten the prince."

David's fists balled. An ache swelled in his chest. He wanted to step out into the bright sun, claim his place alongside his child. But he couldn't move. He was afraid he'd break the magic, stop the talking. He watched Sahar take his daughter's hand. "Kamilah," she said gently, "when the Little Mermaid threw herself into the sea, she started an incredible journey on her way to getting an immortal soul. She became like a piece of sea foam and she could float around the world bringing happiness to good children."

Kamilah's head drooped a little. "I know," she said resignedly. "When the Little Mermaid visited the good children, she was invisible. They never knew she was there, watching over them." Her eyes flashed suddenly up to Sahar's. "But *I* knew that if the child was very, very, good, she would get to see the mermaid one day. That's why I went down to the beach every day to wait. I thought maybe my mummy would send one to me. To be my friend…and to be daddy's friend."

The words grabbed David by the throat. He couldn't breathe. Is *this* why his daughter had insisted on going to the beach every day since they'd arrived back on Shendi? He hadn't had a clue. How could he not have known this? How could he not have been there in a more profound way for his child?

"So you waited at beach where you found me?" asked Sahar. David could hear the tenderness in her voice.

"Yes," said Kamilah. "I waited at Half-Moon Bay because it looks just like the beach in the book where the Little Mermaid used to watch the prince."

David watched in dumbstruck awe as Sahar tilted Kamilah's chin and looked down into the child's eyes. "Kamilah, you *do* understand that I am not really a mermaid, don't you?"

He stilled, waited for his daughter's response, petrified.

Kamilah silently studied Sahar, head to toe. Then she pursed her lips. "What *are* you then? You haven't got any clothes and you haven't got a house and you haven't got a memory. You *gotta* be a mermaid. I *want* you to be a mermaid." Her voice quavered. "'Cause if you're not…you will go away. I don't want you to go away."

Every muscle in his body strapped tight. *This was enough!* He had to stop this. Here in front of his eyes was the perfect example of why he couldn't let this continue. Because it was going to kill his daughter when Sahar left. They would all be back at square one. He *had* to step in, tell Sahar to back off.

She could stay on his island but she was to stay *away* from his daughter.

Sahar put her arm around his daughter's slight shoulders and hugged her close. "Oh, honey, right now I also wish I could be your mermaid. But you know what, whatever I am, *whoever* I am, something in the stars allowed you and me to meet. Something made me wash up on that shore while you were waiting. And for whatever reason that happened, we can give this story of ours its *own* happy ending, okay?"

Kamilah looked up at her.

"Is that a deal, Kamilah?"

David tensed.

"Yes," his daughter said. "I like happy endings."

"We all do, Kamilah. We all do."

David was furious. Sahar had no right making promises she couldn't keep. Happy endings were for fairy tales. This was reality. Reality had no promises of ever after or happiness. His nails dug into his palms, and he took a step forward. Then he went rigid as he heard her next words.

"Would it help you to talk about what happened to your mother in that accident, Kamilah?"

David's stomach churned violently. What in hell did she think she was doing?

Kamilah looked up at Sahar. "Do you want to hear it?"

"Sometimes it's good to talk about difficult things," she told his child. "Because then you can share the unhappiness with someone else and it can make things easier to bear. And sometimes it helps to get it off your chest because if you hold it inside too long, it can really hurt and make you feel sick in many different ways."

His little girl nodded with a wisdom beyond her years. When she spoke her voice was crystal clear and it ripped out his soul. "We were in daddy's boat, at the reef. We had gone diving—"

No!

He could not listen. Would not.

He did not want to hear the accusation come from Kamilah's own lips. For two years he'd lived with it in her eyes. He could not hear the words. Not now. Not ever. *Damn this interfering woman to hell!* He spun on his heels and stormed off in search of Fayha'. He'd get Sahar later, give her a piece of his mind. She'd gone way too far.

Sahar felt the muscles in her chest tense. She wasn't sure if she was doing the right thing, but she sensed deep in her gut that this was what the child needed. To talk. To put into words what she'd bottled up inside for two years.

The Sheik Who Loved Me

"Mummy stayed up on the boat with me while daddy went under the water," Kamilah said. "And when daddy was deep under looking at the fish, there was a bang and a funny smell and then the boat caught fire. My mummy rushed for the extinguisher, but the end of the boat exploded. The explosion hurt mummy and the boat tipped up on the one end and we started to go under really fast. We both fell into the water and mummy was bleeding." She shuddered. "A lot."

Sahar's jaw clenched. She could almost see it. She could *feel* it. As if she'd been there.

"I was far away from mummy," said Kamilah. "She was way off to the other side of the burning boat and the waves were coming in between us. Daddy came up when he heard the explosion. He came up in the middle of us. I could see mummy going under the waves but she yelled for him to save me—" Kamilah choked "—to save me first." Tears streamed down her face.

A shiver chased down Sahar's spine. The blood drained from her head. She hugged the child tight. She could literally feel the water sucking at her, see the little girl going under behind the huge swells, taste the burning salt in her own throat, the claws of terror. Her body went cold. It was as if *she* was there. As if *she* was remembering. Something from long, long ago. But she couldn't pull it from the void.

"Daddy got me and he swam and put me on the beach. He went back for mummy." Another shudder racked her little body. "He was too late. She'd gone under already. He really tried. He tried so hard. I could see him. He went under and under and under and he was coughing and he was crying and screaming at the sky, and I was so scared and sore from the cuts and the bleeding and the fire." Another sob choked her little body. "Daddy tried so hard…but…the…the mermaids took her."

Sahar felt tears streaming down her own cheeks. She held Kamilah very tight. She stroked Kamilah's hair. "It's okay, baby, it's okay. It's good to talk about it. It's good to get it out. Because then you can deal with it. Your mummy did such a wonderfully brave thing. You must be very proud of your mummy and your daddy. Very proud."

Kamilah sniffed and rubbed her nose. "I am proud of them."

And as she spoke, Sahar's heart cracked. This family had been through an awful tragedy and it had barely begun to heal. She kissed Kamilah softly on the top of her head. And once again she vowed not to let this child down. Or her father. She would do what it took to help the two of them. Because somehow, buried deep in her memory, she sensed she knew just how this kind of tragedy could tear a family apart. And how, without help, the wound might never mend. And it would continue to destroy.

But she had to promise herself another thing. She had to resist the powerful physical attraction of David Rashid. Because until she knew who she was, who might be waiting for her, she could not possibly begin to think of a relationship at that level.

Chapter 7

David worked until the sun was in its zenith and the air thick and shimmering with heat. He knew Kamilah would be resting at this hour, along with most of his staff. It was the right time to confront Sahar.

He was clear about what he intended to tell her. Quit with the mermaid fantasy stuff and stay away from his daughter. She could be gone within days. He expected her to keep to herself until then. If she was going to be on his island, she'd best know her boundaries. And his.

David searched his palace, but he couldn't find her anywhere. His frustration mounted along with the heat. Anyone in their right mind was under shadow, grasping for respite from the oppressive noon heat of early summer.

Even the birds had gone quiet.

But Sahar was not resting in her room. She wasn't in any

of the courtyards. She wasn't in the massive pool, cooling off under the fountains that splashed into it.

The last place David looked was the kitchen. There he found Farouk, the only member of his staff not taking a siesta. Farouk didn't have a problem with the heat. He was busy cleaning the kitchen countertops.

"Have you seen Sahar?" David asked him.

The man's toffee-colored skin gleamed with perspiration. He wore the traditional head cloth of the Azar nomads. Farouk wiped his brow with the loose edge of the cloth. "You mean the woman from the sea?"

Irritation spiked. "Yes, where is she?"

Farouk tipped his head toward the wide, arched doorway that led outside. "She's in the kitchen garden."

"In *this* heat?"

"She asked if she could help." Farouk shrugged. "I told her it would be better when the shadows grow long. The sun is very hot today. But she said she needed to do something useful. She said she was tired of just sitting around, so I gave her a job."

A hesitancy sneaked in under David's resolve as he made his way to the door.

"*Sahar.* It's a good name," Farouk called after him. "Shendi has come alive since she arrived."

David didn't answer. He stepped out into the herb and vegetable garden that lay off the kitchen and a wave of heat slammed into him, knocking the breath right out of his lungs.

The garden was enclosed by tall stone walls and crisscrossed with paved pathways. It was a marvel in this climate and made possible only because of the sweet water pumped from the deep wells on Shendi. Creeping thyme filled the cracks between the paving stones. Vegetables burgeoned from beds and were identified by seed packets propped up on sticks.

Little stone benches rested against the walls under trees heavy with ripe fruit.

She was at the far end of the garden, bent over, jabbing a trowel into the moist earth, her back to him. An oversize straw hat, battered and crumpled, shaded her head. Watson's hat. She'd tried to tame her wild curls into a thick braid that hung down the center of her back, but soft spirals of fine hair floated free in the rising heat currents. The sun caught the amber and gold fire in the strands.

David walked quietly up to where she was hunched over, angrily thrusting her trowel into the ground, forcing it to yield up monstrous carrots. As she uprooted them, she tossed them with a clunk into a large blue enamel bowl at her side.

She'd changed out of the dusty muslin clothes but another oversize shirt covered her lean frame, also one of Watson's. Pale-blue cotton. It all but covered the khaki shorts she wore. Watson's shorts, bunched in at the waist and wide and baggy over her smooth thighs.

She was doggedly refusing to wear anything of Aisha's. She was more than going out of her way to respect his feelings.

Guilt niggled at him and his resolve wavered further. Suddenly nothing seemed simple. What was it that he was going to demand of her? Keep out of his business? His life? Stay away from his child? It suddenly seemed unreasonably harsh. He swallowed. The midday heat was making his mouth dry, his head thick. It didn't usually affect him this way. Heat was a familiar thing in his life. But there was nothing about this situation that was familiar.

David stood silent, watching her, trying to find his focus, listening to the hum of bees and clicking of tiny grasshoppers among the vegetation. Her garden tool scrunched against soil as she stabbed at the earth. Her movements were snappy in spite of the temperature. Her body language screamed frustration. He watched as she tossed another bright-orange carrot into the bowl with a clunk. The livid color was in stark contrast to the verdant green of the leafy tops that hung over the side of the deep-blue bowl.

David stared at the colors, the contrasts. Everything seemed unusually bright, his senses extraordinarily heightened.

He wiped his brow. It must be the sun, he thought.

He glanced at the sky. The sun was at its zenith and there was not a wisp of cloud in sight, not a hint of breeze in the air.

He turned his attention back to Sahar. Her hands were covered in soil. She was fully engaged in her task in the same way she'd been engrossed in her game of tag with Kamilah. He found this deeply alluring.

She unearthed another carrot, tossed it in with the others. The bowl was almost full now. Still David didn't speak, couldn't. He was fascinated. There was something so earthy, so organic about the vignette in front of him. Something basic and honest and life-affirming about the way she was digging in this time-old garden that had fed generations before them.

He cleared his throat.

She gasped, spun around, stared up at him, lips parted in surprise. "David, you startled me!" She rose slowly to her feet, trowel in one hand, carrots in the other.

There was dirt on her knees. The brown smudges drew his eyes down the length of her lean, tanned legs.

"Do you always sneak up on people like that?"

He dragged his eyes up from her legs, along the length of her body, to her face. Her features were dappled by the shade of her straw hat, her wide eyes an impossibly luminous and bewitching green in this light.

"I've been looking for you," he said, stepping closer. He could smell the musk of freshly turned earth. And he could smell her. The heat was lifting her fragrance into the air. Citrus. Warm. And female. His nostrils flared reflexively.

She angled her head to get a better line of sight from under the battered brim of her hat. Up close he could see a fine sweep of almost imperceptible gold freckles across her nose, her cheeks flushed from the kiss of the sun.

"And now you've found me." She smiled, hesitantly. "What did you want me for?"

Oh, he wanted her all right. Right now. Right here. He moistened his lips, trying to find focus. But he couldn't quite get his mind back on track. Her skin was slick with the soft sheen of perspiration. Mesmerized, he watched as a small bead of sweat shimmered down from the hollow of her throat toward the valley between her breasts. His eyes followed the droplet as it slithered down into her shirt. He felt a sudden dizziness. It was the sun, he told himself. The heat.

His eyes slid slowly back up to her face. She was watching him warily from under the brim of her hat, like a wild cat in the shadows. Time seemed to hang still, warped by the waves of heat. The buzz of the bees grew louder in his ears. His focus shrunk to another tiny jewel of perspiration that traveled like a tear from the side of her eye. David watched the glistening drop slide slowly down the subtle swell of her cheek to dangle precipitously on her jawbone. She sensed it, swiped it away, leaving a smudge of dirt along the side of her chin.

He reached out reflexively and wiped the dirt from her jaw. Her breath caught sharply in her throat.

His hand stilled. "You've got dirt on your face," he explained, his voice thick.

Her mouth tightened. "Thanks." She turned away from him, dropped back to her knees, tossed the carrots she was holding into the bowl, jabbed angrily again at the earth.

She was cutting him off. That's what he wanted, wasn't it? So why did it sting?

"Why were you looking for me?" she asked as she dug.

"I need to talk to you about Kamilah."

She glanced up at him.

"Why don't you come inside? We can talk there, get a drink."

"We can talk here," she said bluntly.

He blinked. He hadn't expected resistance. People seldom resisted his will. David crouched down beside her and reached for a carrot, as if asserting his ownership, his control over everything including the vegetables in this garden. He dusted it off against his pants, crunched his teeth into it, watching her as he chewed.

Something shifted again in her features. She turned abruptly away from him and concentrated on unearthing another root. "What about Kamilah?" she asked as she turfed the carrot into the bowl.

"I want you to stop with the mermaid nonsense."

She went dead still. Then she turned slowly to face him, her eyes narrowing. "What *nonsense,* exactly, David?"

Again he moistened his lips. The heat of the sun beat relentlessly through the fabric of the shirt on his back. A trickle of sweat ran down under his arm to his waist. "It's hot as hell out here," he said. "You'll get sunstroke. Come, let's go inside."

She didn't budge. "*What* nonsense?" she insisted.

He blew out a hot breath of frustration. Well, if she wanted this on her terms, her choice of turf, she'd get it.

"Kamilah has been through a lot, Sahar. I don't want to go into all the details because it's *not* your affair. This is Rashid family business, and I expect you to keep out of it. I want you to stop filling her head with fairy-tale garbage. Life isn't like that. There are no happy endings. I don't want you filling her head with unrealistic expectations."

Her jaw dropped. She stared at him. "You were listening to us?"

"It's my island. My palace."

She glared at him in silence.

He shifted uncomfortably. Another trickle of sweat traced around his underarm, slid slowly down the length of his waist.

Still she said nothing.

Irritation simmered under his skin. "Do you understand me, Sahar? You're welcome to remain on Shendi until your memory returns, but you are *not* to interfere in my life."

She jerked to her feet. "*Your* life?"

Her reaction startled him. He looked up. *Mistake.* Her legs were astride, feet planted angrily into the ground. He was uncomfortably conscious of a gap between the hem of the wide, oversize shorts and those smooth, long thighs. Fixated, he stared at the opening. Something hot and slick slipped low in his belly. He felt his blood rush from his head.

He quickly stood up, seeking the advantage of height, forcing his brain back on track. But it only made him dizzy.

"This is not just *your* life, David. I don't know if you've noticed but you've got a little girl who desperately needs to share what she's been through. She *needs* to talk. Have you even considered the fact that *you* may the one who's been blocking her efforts to reach out?"

She was lecturing him? How dare she? "Sahar—" His voice came out in low warning. But she refused to back off. She was on a roll and she was going to have her say.

"You're all cramped up with your own damn anger, David. You're so busy wallowing in your own guilt that you can't see what your child needs. I saw how you shut her out this morning. She came down to the stables to be with you. She was reaching out, David. And you snubbed her."

"*Damn you, woman,*" he snarled, grabbing her wrist. He

wrenched her toward him. It silenced her instantly. His fingers tightened like a cuff, digging into her skin as his eyes bored angry into hers. "How *dare* you? I love Kamilah more than anything in this damn world. She's all I have left. I've hired the best specialists, the most expensive tutors. I'd move heaven and earth for her—"

"David," she interrupted, her voice suddenly soft, caring, so gently feminine that it knocked him completely off stride. "Kamilah doesn't need heaven and earth. She doesn't need specialists. She just needs *you*. She needs her daddy. She needs to play. She needs to be a child."

His throat constricted around his words. Because he knew she was right. Her presence on Shendi had shown him that.

"She just needs you to hold her, David. Is that really so hard?"

His fingers tightened around her wrist. But she didn't flinch. She just stood there probing his soul with those haunting eyes, getting right inside his bloody head. She was scrambling his radar. He was primed for a fight, and she'd come at him sideways, knocking his knees out from under him with her soft voice and liquid eyes.

And words of truth.

He wanted to lash out at her, hurt her for doing this to him. He wanted to pull her to his chest, kiss that incredible mouth, plunge himself between her legs. But he didn't dare move. Because he wasn't sure what in hell he *would* do. So he held dead still. Too close to her mouth, to her beautiful breasts. So close that the scent of her filled his nostrils, his mind, drugged his senses.

"Why the anger, David?" she asked softly.

That's what Watson had asked him. He sucked in a shuddering breath.

She reached up, placed her palm against his cheek. The simple gesture cracked him. It took all his control to hold back the bank of emotion that exploded painfully behind his eyes. God, this woman was splitting him right open. She'd ripped back his barriers and exposed him. And now her simple touch was blowing salt into his wounds. He clenched his jaw and held on desperately to the volatility heaving inside him.

She moved her body closer to him. "Let me help you, David," she whispered.

"Why?" his voice came out hoarse.

"Because I can see your pain." She hesitated. "Because I've ridden with you on a horse and I know that inside is a man aching to be free again. Free like you felt on that stallion… with me."

She was unreal. She could see right into him. How could she possibly know the depth of what he'd felt on that horse? Where in hell had this woman come from?

Shocked, he pulled away.

As much as he wanted to take her into his arms, to believe in her, to make this journey with her, he couldn't.

He took another step back, sucked in air. He couldn't do this. She was going to leave. Anyday. Any second. Watson may have information on her right this instant. There might be a message waiting in his office that would take her away before nightfall.

"Sahar, just keep out of it. I don't need your help."

Hurt flashed through her eyes. She bit her bottom lip. He could see why. It was beginning to tremble. She was trying to stop it.

His heart twisted. She had her own pain. "Sahar—"

She looked abruptly away. But not fast enough to hide a fat tear that slid down her cheek trailing fine dust after it.

Great! Now she'd switched tables on him! What was a guy to do? "Sahar?" He stepped forward.

She wouldn't look at him. She held up her hand, shook her head as if warning him to back off.

He'd done it again. He'd pushed her too far. There was something so innately resilient about her that it kept surprising him when he hit her sensitive spot. She seemed too outwardly strong to hurt. But inside she was lost. And instead of offering comfort, he was doing his damnedest to chase her away. He was lashing out at her because of the way she clouded his mind. Because of what she did to his body. And if he was truthful, it scared the hell out of him. He was used to being in control at all times. He was *not* used to *this*.

"Sahar—" he took her elbow firmly "—come sit in the shade."

She acquiesced, allowed him to lead her to the stone bench under the fruit-laden tree. She seemed suddenly spent. The energy that had quivered around her was gone, and that threw him. He felt like a cad for having done this to her. She was probably exhausted, drained. She'd been through a terrible accident. And on top of that, she'd been physically going at it all morning, running, swimming, riding, playing tag with Kamilah and now jabbing a trowel into the earth under the fierce heat of the North African summer sun.

She slumped onto the bench in the shade. He sat down beside her. They both remained silent. As if afraid to take the next step in the bizarre game they seemed to have been thrust into.

"That came out all wrong," he said finally. "I'm sorry."

She swiped at a tear, leaving a smudge of dirt across her face. "It's okay, I…I totally understand."

How could she possibly understand?

She took Watson's battered old hat off, exposing the bruised look in her eyes. She swiped her damp brow with the tail of her shirt. It only streaked the dirt from one place to another.

"I should be the one apologizing, David. I can see I'm making you unhappy. It's not my intention to hurt you or Kamilah. I only wanted to help. I *needed* to help. I can't explain it." She smudged another tear across her cheek. "I'll go. I'll leave Shendi. I'm an uninvited guest and you've been good to me, and I thank you for that. But I'll leave in the morning. Dr. Watson left me his mobile number. I'll call him and ask him to help me find a place…somewhere…maybe Khartoum…while I try and figure out who I am."

Oh, boy. He felt like camel dung now. She hadn't asked to be washed up onto his beach unconscious. She hadn't asked to be placed in this predicament. Hell knew what she'd been through in that storm, what she may yet have to face when the nature of her accident began to reveal itself.

And Kamilah? She'd be devastated if she found Sahar gone in the morning. Damn, this was a double bind. This was precisely what he'd been trying to avoid in the first place. Hurting Kamilah. Allowing himself to *feel* something for this stranger.

Because suddenly she wasn't a stranger anymore.

She was Sahar. She was digging up carrots in his vegetable garden, riding with him on his stallion, telling him how to be a father, stirring feelings in him that were fit for sin.

When exactly had this started to happen? He blew out a breath.

This woman didn't play fair.

She didn't play by the rules.

He placed his hand on her knee. "Sahar, I want you to stay."

Her eyes slanted up to meet his. More tears pooled in her lower lids. Her hand fidgeted at her side.

"I want you to be my guest. Consider this an official invitation." He did his best to smile warmly, but inside he was a mess of conflicting, uncertain emotion.

"David—"

"No." He placed two fingers against her lips. "Enough. I apologize. I've been an abominable host. I want you to stay on Shendi. But I also want you to remember one thing. When you leave, Kamilah will be devastated. I just want you to consider that, when you interact with her. I guess that's all I was really trying to say."

She took his hand from her lips, held it in her own. "I know she will be sad. She told me. But I was hoping we'd have managed to work through the mermaid thing by the time I left, that she'd be ready for me to leave. But maybe you're right, David. I shouldn't have interfered. In her life or yours. But I couldn't *not* help. Maybe it is best if I do go now."

His stomach swooped out from under him and his pulse quickened. "No, Sahar. I can't let you go." It was too late. As much as he wanted her to leave, it was beyond him to actually let her go. He just couldn't. And even if he could, what kind of man would that make him? Sahar had amnesia. She was helpless. She had absolutely nowhere to go and not a possession to her name. "Give me a chance to be a better host, Sahar." He attempted a laugh. It came out a little hollow, a little desperate. "I haven't even shown you around my home." He cupped her jaw, tilted her face to his. "What do you say, Sahar? Will you stay? Be my guest? For as long as you need?"

Sahar hesitated, snared by the intensity in David's eyes. But more than anything it was the deep sincerity, the honesty and integrity in his voice that held her. This was a man struggling to do what was right. And she could only respect him for that.

Besides, she had nowhere to go. The thought of being nameless and alone in a place like Khartoum terrified her.

"Yes," she said softly. "I'll stay. Thank you, David."

David exhaled, ran his hands through his hair. "Good. That's settled then. *Now* can I give you a tour of my home?"

A shaky smile tugged at her mouth. "Yes." She said, swiping at the last of her tears, trying to pull herself together. "I'd be delighted."

He stood, thrust his shoulders back in mock gallantry, grinned like a pirate and held his hand out to her, palm up, steady as a rock. "Come, then."

She reached out, placed her hand in his. He closed his fingers around hers. And inside she felt as if she'd found a bridge, steady and dependable, one that would somehow get her to the other side.

Wherever that was.

Chapter 8

"My father bought this place when I was a child," David explained as he took Sahar's arm and led her into the enormous main hall.

She stared up in awe at the stained glass dome high in the centre of the curved ceiling. The midday African sun streamed though it, picking up hues of oranges, ochres and greens, imbuing the vast room with a cathedral-like quality. Except the architecture couldn't be further from the cathedrals she knew. "It looks Moorish in design," she said.

"You're right. Moroccan inspired," he explained, pushing open thick double doors at the far end of the room. "Shendi Palace was built by an eccentric French general in the early 1800s. He'd served for years in Algiers, Morocco and Mauritania before the jinns got him."

"Jinns?"

David grinned, a sharp twinkle lighting his eyes. "The evil

spirits of the desert." He tapped his finger against his temple. "The heat, the thirst, endlessness of the Sahara, it can drive a man crazy. The locals say that's when the jinns come and get you."

"So the general went a little loopy?"

"That's the story. He took early retirement and moved out here onto Shendi. He bought the island because of the unusual springs of fresh water. He dug the wells that feed these gardens, and in designing the palace, he copied the Moorish architecture from the areas he'd come to love, combining it with whatever other North African influence inspired him."

"It's absolutely stunning…eclectic," she said, studying the mosaic work in one of the recessed alcoves.

"Eclectic is the word. In some ways Shendi Palace is symbolic of North Africa itself. So much of this part of the world is a fascinating and often uneasy blend of past cultures, Arabian, African, colonial, each one trying to erase traces of the previous one, going all the way back to the Kingdom of Sheba and beyond."

The sudden deepening of his voice, the guttural catch in the honeyed gravel tones, forced her to look up.

He was staring at her. His face had changed. A sharp and fervent energy had shifted into the granite of his dark features. His eyes flashed dangerously.

Sahar swallowed. A tingle of foreboding trickled down her spine at the mood in his eyes. North Africa and the Sahara was something David Rashid obviously cared passionately about. The palace, the Africa he described, they were like the man himself, she thought. He too exuded a timelessness, as if the spirit of ancient warrior tribes, the wild and exotic spice of desert leaders, still shaped his thoughts. Yet his barely leashed and feral energy was veneered with the fine cultural sensibilities of British aristocracy.

David Rashid was a mystery in more ways than one. It

made her curious about his personal history…and more than curious about why she was feeling this shiver of portent down the back of her neck.

She cleared her throat, trying hard not to shy away from the hooded intensity of his indigo eyes. "Kamilah said your father was a sheik."

"Kamilah *said* that?"

"Yes."

His jaw hardened. He turned away from her, grabbed a brass ring and flung open a heavy wooden door to another room. He strode ahead of her into the vast chamber.

She caught up with him. "Does that make *you* a sheik then?"

He stopped, swung around to face her, the lines bracketing his mouth hard. "I am Sheik David bin Omar bin Zafir Rashid. I am the oldest son of my father. According the customs of my father's people, I now bear his title."

He paused, his eyes boring into hers. "But it means nothing." He swept his arm out in an expansive movement, dismissing the subject. "This is the hall where the French general used to host his famous balls."

Sahar was more interested in studying the face and architecture of David Rashid than the room. "Why do you say it means nothing?" she pressed.

His eyes probed hers, as if he were weighing her up, deciding her worthy of the information. "It would take time to explain. Come." He took her arm, urged her through enormous double doors to another enclosed courtyard, this one with a long, black marble pool sunk into the center. The pool was flanked by columns and surrounded by arched walkways fragrant with exotic blooms. Elaborately carved fountains splashed water into the pool causing ripples along the shimmering black surface. The pool looked darkly cool under the white-hot sky. Sahar could not see below the surface. She looked from the pool up into David's eyes. The reflection of the water rippled like wet ink through them. She couldn't see below the dark surface of this man either. But she wanted to. She *needed* to.

"I have plenty of time," she said, forcing a soft laugh. "More time than I know what to do with right now."

He stilled. "You really are interested?"

She looked up into his smouldering eyes. She was interested all right. She was drawn to him by every cell in her body. "Yes," she said. "I am."

He pursed his exquisite lips in thought, his eyes never leaving hers. "All right." He took her hand, drew her to a bench in the shade of the arches facing the pool. He seated himself beside her, eyes focused on the dark water.

"My father, Sheik Omar bin Zafir Rashid, was descended from a tribe of desert warriors that migrated from Arabia and down through Egypt into the Sahara hundreds of years ago," he explained. "The Bedu of Azar. A fiercely proud people. They lived as nomads and hunters, and their lives were ruled by the stars and the seasons. They killed oryx for meat and they traveled from oasis to oasis with their camels and goats. They lived by an ancient code of ethics and were both revered and feared."

He stopped talking, his eyes distant, staring into the waters of the swimming pool as if he could see through them to a distant desert oasis. "They were a noble people, Sahar. But they are no more. I am the lineal leader of a tribe that no longer exists."

"What happened?"

He shrugged. "The world changed. My people and their ways didn't. The desert is dying, and with it an ancient way of life. After years of relentless drought, traditional watering holes have dried up. The oryx are gone. Famine has taken its toll. Camels and goats died. And the Bedu were forced to abandon their way of life, the very existence that made them proud and free. In desperation they were forced toward towns and settlements, and they began to eke out an existence living in shacks on the outskirts of civilization."

David turned to look at her, his eyes glittering. "A once-noble people have lost their culture, the bonds that held their tribes together. They are now scattered, directionless and impoverished, subsisting mainly on supplies of American grain and other foreign aid."

The ferocity in his voice caught her by the throat.

"That is why I say the title means nothing." His jaw steeled, flint sharpened his gaze. "But I will give pride back to my people, Sahar. I will make them whole again. It was my father's dream. And it is now mine."

Sahar stared at him. So this is what drove the man. His raw passion for his people, for the desert, moved her profoundly. "How would you do that?" she asked. "How would give pride back to the Bedu?"

He smiled in a way she had not seen him smile. A smile so powerful it reached right to her heart, took hold of it and squeezed so that she could barely breathe.

"I told you, it is a long story."

"I want to hear it, David." She needed to. It gave her unique insight into the man, to what fired his soul. He possessed a depth, an integrity she had only guessed at.

He took her hand, and his thumb absently stroked the inside of her palm as he stared into the black water. Her insides went shivery, but she could not bring herself to pull her hand away. This man held an enigmatic power over her, something that defied her control. Did he even realize what he was doing to her?

"I spent half my life in the Sahara," he said, speaking into the distance, to a place way beyond the pool, a place that lived in his mind. "My father wanted me to see it, to experience the old ways firsthand. He wanted me to taste the ancient lifestyle of a desert warrior before it disappeared from the face of this earth forever." His fingers laced through hers, tightened. Her heart beat faster.

"My father realized when he was still young that the old ways were going. And he knew the only way to save his people would be to bring the ancient ways of the desert in line with the new world, to give the nomads economic control over their destiny." He paused. "My father made it his goal to be accepted at Oxford. He'd heard the Bedu legends about the black gold, the oil, that lay beneath the sands of northern Azar. And he wanted to learn how to find it. He came back a geologist, armed with both science and knowledge of the ancient ways of the desert." David drew in a deep breath. "He found that black gold, Sahar. After many years, he found it."

For a while they sat silent, her hand still held in his. Sahar looked up into his face. "And?" she prompted softly.

He turned to look down at her, his gaze meshing intimately with hers. "He brought something else back from England," he said. "A British wife…and a son."

"You? And your mother?"

"Some saw it as a sign of my father's betrayal."

"Because she was British?"

"Yes." A bitterness clipped his word. "A foreigner."

"What happened…to your mother?"

"She didn't take easily to the ways of the desert. She was the daughter of British privilege, and to her the desert was simply an adventure that grew tiresome. To my father it was life. My mother began to pine for her home, and my father loved her too much to trap her in a place she couldn't live. He in turn could not leave his beloved desert for a full-time life in England. Their relationship was doomed from the start."

"How awfully tragic."

He drew breath sharply in through his nose. "In the end my mother got ill. She decided to return to her homeland, her people. But she wouldn't leave me behind. I was four. I had been born for the ways of the desert but she took me to England."

Sahar looked up into his eyes. Below the surface of those dark-blue irises, somewhere deep inside this man, lurked a boy, a boy who had been torn between two parents. Two countries. Two cultures. A boy who had shaped this potent man of the present.

He squeezed her hand, gave her a wry smile. "Ever since, I've been divided. For six months of each year I lived in the desert. For the other half of the year I studied in England."

"What happened to your father after your mother left?" she asked.

"He eventually remarried...took an Azarian bride. He had another son eight years after my birth, my half brother, Tariq. Some felt Tariq should have inherited my father's title because he was the *pure* one." David dismissed it with a shrug. "Either way, like I said, it is a title that means nothing."

"Do you get on with your brother?"

His eyes flashed to hers and pierced her with a sudden laser sharpness, with suspicion. He withdrew his hand. "Why are you interested in this? It's Rashid business."

She stumbled mentally at the turnabout. This man had low flashpoints. "Because..." She felt warmth infuse her cheeks. "Because...I...care. About you. About Kamilah."

A muscle pulsed along his jawline. But he said nothing. He waited, watching her face, his eyes unreadable.

"I have nothing else to care about, David. I'm...I'm all alone. Until I find out where I belong."

His eyes softened slightly. He lifted his hand and briefly caressed the side of her cheek. "My brother and I did not get on until about two years ago."

"Why?"

"Tariq felt I was not one of them. Not pure." An anger glittered briefly in his eyes, then was gone.

"He thought he should have been sheik?"

"He thought I should have been dead."

"What?"

David snorted. "Tariq grew up resenting everything about me, Sahar, including my father's affection. You see, my half brother didn't agree with our vision for bringing Azar into the global economy. And because of his radical views, he was cut from my father's will. But that was then. Tariq is older now. Wiser. He is beginning to see beyond his narrow idealist window. He has finally come to accept my views. We share the same goal now, to build the wealth of our people, to marry the ancient ways with the new, using the resources of Rashid International, the company started by our father, the company designed to feed our father's dream."

"What finally turned Tariq around?" she asked.

"A promise." David absently fingered the hilt of the dagger at his waist. "I vowed on my father's deathbed to do everything within my power to heal the rift between myself and Tariq. And I vowed to continue his work to heal his people, the Bedu of Azar. He died with those dreams on his lips."

Sahar noted he said "his" people. Not "my" people. Even in his own mind, he wasn't wholly one of them. David's dichotomy was cleft deep into his soul. And she had a sense that healing Azar, bridging the divide between the ancient ways and the new, would in a sense make this man whole himself. It would make him feel worthy of his title. It would heal the scars of the four-year-old buried deep within the man.

"How did you manage to sway Tariq, David? I mean, a fundamentalist ideology is not something one gives up easily."

His eyes shot to hers. "You're right. But blood can be stronger than ideology. And I never gave up." His exquisite fingers moved absently over the ornate handle of his *jambiya* as he spoke.

He caught her looking. "My father's," he explained, curling his fingers tight around the hilt. "A gift from his deathbed. The symbol of my promise. I wear it always."

She swallowed at the sudden dark and possessive edge in his voice, the way he held his weapon as if he were about to yank it from its sheath. His eyes glittered sharply. She'd hit another of his flashpoints. It made her jittery. Anxiety began to swamp her again for some reason she couldn't identify. She had no doubt that the raw passion housed within the powerful man that was Sheik David bin Omar bin Zafir Rashid gave him the capacity to kill.

What would he do to her if he found *her* to be disloyal? What would *she* do if he turned out to be her enemy? She swallowed, tried to keep her voice light. "So…is…is Azar prospering now?"

"Not quite." He stood up, his one hand still resting on the hilt of his *jambiya*. "There is still much work to do. Come." He held out his other hand. She took it. He led her under the arches and escorted her back into the palace.

"Africa is complicated," he explained. "And in the tradition of Africa nothing goes smoothly." The mellifluous smoothness was back in his voice, the sharp twinkle back in his eyes. "Once all the oilfields were in full production, after my father died, I discovered a source of very unique uranium, something far more coveted than the oil."

David Rashid is smuggling weapons-grade uranium.

The thought speared into her brain. Sahar's chest cramped

tight. She tried to breathe. But this time she couldn't shake the thought. It began to diffuse through her brain like an explosion of ink in water, tainting, suffocating everything.

"And…and what is so special about this uranium?" She heard the catch in her voice.

So did he. He paused, arched his dark brow slightly. "It has a unique molecular structure which makes it very easy to enrich beyond power-station grade."

To nuclear-weapons grade.

Every muscle in her body froze. She stopped in her tracks. He halted beside her. "What is it, Sahar?"

"Ah…nothing. It's nothing." She forced her muscles to move, forced herself to walk. "Go on."

A frown creased his brow. He held her back. "Are you sure you're feeling all right?"

She nodded quickly. "Yes, of course. What happened then?"

"The uranium discovery sparked a coup attempt in Azar," David explained, his eyes searching hers, his frown deepening. "A dissident Azarian faction attempted to overthrow the government. The rebels gained control of the north and my oil fields, stopping a flow of cash into the country. Then they started moving south in an effort to seize Tabara, the capital."

Her mouth went dry. "Wh…what happened then?"

"I fought back," he said, watching her intently. "I hired a private army. I came to an agreement with the Azarian president that I would fund a private military presence on the condition that we would first fight to reclaim and protect my oil fields."

I know this. I know all of this. Every bit of it. She placed her hand to her temple. Maybe she'd read about it in a newspaper, seen it on the news.

The line of stitches under her hairline began to throb with each beat of her heart.

David misread her reaction. "Mercenaries are not all bad, Sahar. There are teams out there who do good. This is one of them. They have pushed the rebels back up toward the Libyan border. In addition, the mercenaries are stiffening and training Azar's own army. They will be able to stand on their own in a way never seen before. I am making my country strong."

She was at a loss for words. All she could do was nod.

"Come," he said, taking her arm. "I'll show you." He led her into another wing and along yet another arched corridor.

Her head pounded wildly. She was dizzy. She could feel the prickle of perspiration along her upper lip. "I…I'm just wondering why you are here, then, on Shendi, if your heart…your business is in Azar?"

"It's a safe home for Kamilah," he said. "England was not good for her, and Azar is still technically at war with the rebels. And while Azar is my dream, Kamilah is still my priority. Shendi is close enough for me to fly into Azar when needed." David opened another door and allowed Sahar to enter ahead of him. "This is my study," he said.

She stepped into a room that was masculine in decor with lots of dark wood and leather and an unmistakable North African stamp in design. The ceiling fan moved slowly up above, stirring soft currents in the warm air.

Sahar caught sight of the huge ochre-toned map on the far wall. A bolt of recognition stalled her heart. She knew instantly *exactly* who David Rashid was. A thousand little loose shards suddenly slammed together into a cohesive picture as sharp as glass. Pain pierced her head. She gasped at the sensation of it.

She knew the map depicted Azar, a country nestled like an inverted wedge of pizza between Chad to the west, Sudan to the east with Libya and Egypt to the north.

She even knew what the different-colored pins stuck into the map denoted. The big blue pins marked the two Rashid uranium mines. The yellow pins were his oil fields. And the clusters of red pins in the north marked the positions of rebel armies that had been pushed back by Rashid money, cash paid to a controversial new mercenary group grabbing international headlines, the Force du Sable, headed by none other than the legendary Jacques Sauvage and the formidable Hunter McBride and Rafiq Zayed.

The room spiraled in on her. Her heart pounded painfully against her chest wall. She groped wildly for the back of a chair.

David's arms shot out to steady her. "Sahar! Are you all right?"

"I…I…I'm fine. Just…a…a bit dizzy."

"It's the heat," he said angrily. "I shouldn't have allowed you to work in the garden. I'll send for Watson."

"No!" She shook her head. "No. No, I'm fine…really."

But she wasn't. She was a mess. Because in the instant she'd seen the map, she'd known that Sheik David bin Omar bin Zafir Rashid was one of the world's wealthiest and most influential industrialists, an enigmatic man with considerable interests in oil, uranium and diamond mines not only in Azar but around the world. She also knew he was a shadowy and mysterious figure who did his best to stay out of the press. But he was a figure who nevertheless fueled the hunger of tabloid journalists who'd touted him as one of the Europe's most eligible men since the death of his wife.

She didn't know *how* she knew all this. But she did. Her mind had somehow taken the bits of information he'd just given her and filled in all the gaps at once, hitting her brain like a bolt of electricity, instantly overloading her circuits. And she reeled with the shock of it.

She tried to force the river of jumbled facts roiling in her brain into some kind of sensible order. But she couldn't.

Somehow she also knew he was smuggling uranium into Libya as well as selling it on the black market to Korea. Uranium for nuclear weapons. Weapons that would be aimed at the U.S. and Britain. He was a bad guy. Her enemy.

She pressed her hand to her head, tried to stop the spinning. How did *she* fit into all this? Who was *she?* Why did she know these things? Had she read it *all* in newspapers, tabloids? Seen it on TV?

She couldn't have read the black-market stuff in papers, could she? Because if it was common knowledge surely he'd be behind bars? A wanted man? She pushed her hands harder against her temples.

But no matter how hard she pressed she couldn't stop the sickening spinning. And as the facts churned through her brain, they swamped in a suffocating flood. She tried to draw in a breath, couldn't. The room lurched wildly. She felt herself sway.

"Sahar, tell me what's going on? You're pale as a ghost." He tried to take her hand.

She waved him off. "I was just remembering…" She clamped her mouth shut. Instinctively. She'd been going to tell him she remembered who he was. But something inside made her stop. Dead. Something told her it was a matter of life and death.

Oh God, why? Would this man kill her if he knew what she knew?

Her stomach heaved. She was going to throw up. She clutched at her belly, bent over. "I…I think I need to lie down for a second." And as she spoke, her knees sagged under her.

David was there in a flash. He caught her, scooped her up, carried her to the door, kicked it open with his foot.

"I'm taking you to your room, and then I'm getting Wat son." His words were clipped, efficient. His boots clacked loudly on the hard stone floors.

"Please no, David. I…I just need a rest. You…you were right, it's the sun, I shouldn't have been out. I'll be fine. Really."

And something cold sank in her stomach as he carried her to her room. Because she knew she had to hide her knowl edge from him. She instinctively knew she couldn't tell him what she knew about him. Because her life…the lives of oth ers depended on it. She just didn't understand why.

David kicked open the door to her bedroom and laid her gently on the bed. The ceiling spun madly. The fan was spin ning, too. Or was it? Maybe it was just her head. She closed her eyes, but still everything swirled in a mad maelstrom of grays and blacks.

David moistened a piece of cloth using the jug on the nightstand and pressed it gently to her forehead. His touch was impossibly tender. She began to breathe easier. She felt the oxygen finally going back to her brain.

"Rest," he said. "I'm going to call Watson and ask his advice."

"I'm okay. Just a bit of sunstroke. I'm sure I'll be one hun dred percent after a rest."

"Here." He raised her head slightly, put a glass of water to her lips. "You must keep hydrated."

She sipped greedily, looking up into his eyes as she did, reading deep concern there.

"I don't care what you say, Sahar, I'm going to speak to Wat son. You might be having complications from the head injury."

Oh, she was having complications all right. He didn't know the half of it. But she couldn't try to think anymore. Fatigue pressed down on her. She lay back, closed her eyes.

David covered her with a cool cotton sheet and stroked her hand as she fell into a deep sleep.

* * *

David closed the door quietly behind him. Sahar had spooked the hell out of him by fainting like that. But she was probably right. It was most likely sunstroke. Still, he'd sound Watson out on her symptoms.

He leaned against the closed door, rested his head back against the wood. And as he relaxed, he began to smile. She was one hell of a character. Stubborn, strong, principled. Intelligent. Sexy as sin. Fun.

Fun? That hadn't featured in his life for two years. Yes, she'd put the word back into his existence. And for the first time in his life he had opened up fully to another human being, about his childhood, his family, his dreams. And it didn't leave him feeling the slightest bit vulnerable. It made him feel good. He'd shared, and it only made him feel stronger. He was able to share with Sahar because he connected with something deep inside her. Whoever she was, surely that would never change?

And she *cared* about him.

For the first time David Rashid dared feel hope. He dared to dream that once Sahar's true identity was discovered, things might not have to come to a grueling halt. That maybe, just maybe, she had a past that wouldn't necessarily tear her away from Shendi. At least not right away. Because he cared for her. A lot. In ways that went way deeper than the heat of raw desire.

That little seed of hope began to grow deep in his belly as he fed it with his imagination. His smile widened, and inside he felt light, exhilarated. Because in some way he felt as if he'd found a friend. And by God it felt good.

In the distance he heard the rhythmic chop of helicopter blades and sobered instantly. He was a fool to think this might last. To even begin to dream it was to set himself up for failure. And he didn't tolerate failure.

He checked his watch, listening to the sound of the chopper grow louder. That would be Tariq. Good. He needed to put his mind to work. The two of them had a ton of business to get through. They only had two days before Tariq left for the mines in northern Azar.

And continuing to build solid relations with Tariq was just as important as rebuilding a nation. David brusquely shoved other thoughts from his mind and went to greet his half brother.

Chapter 9

A soft knocking at the bedroom door roused Sahar from the sleep of the dead. She blinked into the shadows, confused. It was darker, a little cooler. She squinted at the clock. Goodness, it was early evening. She must have slept the afternoon away. And with that realization came the sinking recollection of what had happened earlier in David's office.

The knocking sounded a little louder. She tensed. She wasn't ready to confront David yet. She needed to think. "Who is it?" Her voice came out rough.

Fayha' poked her head around the door. "It's me, Sahar. Are you decent?"

Relief swooped through her. "Oh, Fayha', come on in."

The housekeeper pushed the door open wide, motioned to another young woman who wheeled in a trolley piled high with boxes each tied with a sleek burgundy ribbon and each embossed with the same little gold logo.

"What's this?" Sahar asked.

Fayha' beamed. "Clothes. Mr. Rashid had them flown in from Cairo. They just arrived on his helicopter with Mr. Tariq."

Sahar frowned. "David had *clothes* flown in? For me?"

"A whole wardrobe."

"From Cairo?"

"Mr. Rashid has his pilots fly in supplies weekly from both Cairo and Mombasa…as well as other places if need be. It's how he likes to run things on Shendi."

Fayha' ran her eyes over Sahar and smiled gently. "Besides, it's about time you got out of those old clothes of the doctor's. They need a wash." She gestured to the trolley. "Shall we leave it here in the corner?"

"Um…yeah. Thanks." Her head was still groggy from sleep, her brain still thick with unrelated facts and dark shards of memory.

Fayha' closed the door with a soft click.

Sahar swung her feet over the bed and padded over to the pile of boxes. The labels read Boutique L'Avalle, El Qâhira. She'd heard of L'Avalle, a distinguished and prohibitively priced world-class designer label. She'd also heard that El Qâhira, or Cairo, was the fashion capital of the Arabic world.

Intrigued, she removed the top box, set it on the bed, slid the ribbon off and lifted the lid. She peeled back the pale-green tissue paper and her breath caught. It was the most beautiful green fabric she'd ever laid eyes on. She fingered the texture. It was liquid silk. As she let it slip through her hands it caught different aspects of the light, which made the color shift and shimmer from jade to emerald to turquoise. She'd never seen anything like it.

Sahar held it up to her face, swung around to face the mirror. The entrancing fabric caught the light in her eyes.

But when she moved, the color shifted to a predominant jade green. Once again she stilled, and she had that strange gnawing feeling, like there was something vitally significant about this particular hue of green.

She shook it off, set the gown aside and quickly opened the other boxes. David had thought of everything. There was delicate lacy underwear, sports and workout gear, bathing suits, robes, eveningwear, cool sundresses, shorts, tees, tank tops…all in her size. The man just didn't cease to amaze her.

And she couldn't help smiling.

She felt like a kid at Christmas. She had no idea what she usually wore but she liked what she saw in the boxes. It was a mix of elegant femininity, sleek athletic lines and something a little playful, even a tad daring.

Is that what world-famous industrialist David Rashid thought of her? Or had the boutique owner second-guessed his taste? It didn't matter. Just the idea that he'd thought to do it was intriguing, endearing…intimate. And more than a little titillating. The whole thing sent a crazy spurt of warmth through her.

Then she saw the envelope that had slipped to the floor. She scooped it up, opened it, took out a card the same color as the ribbons on the boxes and embossed with the same gold logo. She read the bold handwriting.

"Join us at nine for a late dinner in the grand dining hall. P.S. Do *not* wear anything of Watson's."

Sahar giggled, her blood zinged. She felt slightly heady, as if she were a schoolgirl invited on her first date with the dark prince.

She almost immediately pulled herself together. This was ridiculous. This girlish reaction wasn't part of her usual repertoire of behaviors…was it?

She sat back on the bed, pushed her knotted hair back from

her forehead. David Rashid was confusing the hell out of her. And it didn't help that her head was a mess to begin with. She stared at the boxes and their beautiful bounty.

So he was famous. And wealthy. And mysterious. Perhaps even dangerous. It didn't necessarily mean he was evil, did it? She'd probably read about him. And if there was anything more sinister, well it was probably simply tabloid gossip and speculation worth zip. She felt in her heart, *her gut,* that he was a good man. A man of integrity and brutal honesty. That was the David Rashid she'd come to know in the short time she'd been on Shendi Island.

And the reason she'd felt so odd in his office, well, that *had* to have been because of the sun and overexertion so soon after her accident, she told herself. And because the heat had scrambled her senses she'd found herself filling in the blanks with dark nonsense.

But deep, deep down, no matter how much she tried to rationalize it all, there remained a sharp biting sensation that wouldn't go away, warning her to be cautious, telling her that being open could be dangerous. That lives were at stake.

And because of that, she knew she wasn't going to tell David about those dark thoughts. At least, not until she knew more.

And what did that make her? A liar? Dishonest?

Ah, what the hell. She jerked off the bed, made for the ensuite bathroom. Whatever it meant, it didn't mean she couldn't take a bath, put on an evening gown and enjoy his company over dinner. She'd just be careful. She'd go with the flow. Because what else could she do? She was stuck in the prison of her mind, and until she had all the facts, she wasn't capable of rational judgment or action. She felt it was now simply a matter of time until her memory returned fully, until she solved this mystery. She was sure of it.

She turned on the taps, and the water gushed from the fish-shaped mouths of brass faucets. Sahar tipped a capful of bath bubbles into the stream of water and watched it froth.

She stepped into the tub, sank down into the fragrant, foaming water, closed her eyes and let the warmth soak deep into her skin. She felt her muscles begin to relax and allowed her mind to go blank. Steam slowly curled up and filled the room, and Sahar felt herself begin to drift into a warm, dreamlike haze. She imagined herself dancing in the beautiful green gown David had bought for her. She was in his strong arms, swirling, twirling under the stained-glass dome. Sahar smiled softly to herself. She could almost feel the motion, see the colors of the fabric of her exquisite gown shifting under the light from emerald to turquoise, to…

Jade!

It hit her like a bucket of ice. She gasped. Her eyes flared open and she jerked upright in the tub, her heart thumping hard. That was it! *That* was why she'd felt there was something so significant about that particular color, that shade of green. *That* was why it had felt so familiar, so right when she'd held the fabric against her skin. Jade…no, Jayde. Her name was Jayde!

Her heart almost tripped over itself in her excitement. She leaped up from the tub, spilling water onto the floor. She grabbed a towel, almost slipping on the tiles. She had to tell David. She had remembered her name! It was Jayde Ashton. Yes, that was it, her last name was Ashton. *She had her name.* And that alone would jog the rest of her memory free in minutes, hours. She was sure of it.

She rushed to her bedroom door and pushed it open. And froze. A bleak coldness descended over her. She couldn't tell David. Not yet. Because Jayde Ashton had something deep and dark to hide from Sheik David bin Omar bin Zafir Rashid. She was now certain of it.

But what, dammit?

She sank onto the bed, towel wrapped around her. She had her name, but she still couldn't make her mind go beyond that. She still couldn't grasp who Jayde Ashton really was and why she knew—and *felt*— these things about David. And she still couldn't explain the sense of ominous portent that grew stronger and more sinister with each snippet of memory recalled.

Jayde Ashton walked into the grand dining hall at five after nine, a thrilling cocktail of excitement and anxiety zinging through her blood. The new gown skimmed her high strappy heels, giving her stride a bold and feminine confidence. She knew she looked damn good. She'd washed her hair and piled it into an updo with tendrils escaping and curling along the nape of her neck. She'd also clamped an exotic copper band around her upper arm and added a choker with a single large amber stone that rested against the hollow of her throat. She simply felt like a goddess.

David sat at the head of a long table of dark wood set with ornate crockery and crystal glasses that shimmered in light cast by two massive antique silver candelabras. He was deeply engrossed in conversation with a man who had his back to her. The man was of remarkably similar stature to David and had the same blue-black hair, only longer. Music, a soft lilting African-Arabic mix underlaid with the gentle rhythm of drums, played in the background.

David's head jerked up as he sensed her presence. The man seated at his side glanced up.

Jayde's blood went ice-cold.

She recognized the stranger's face instantly.

He was Tariq Rashid. David's half brother. He had the same basic bone structure as David yet his face was wider, his skin slightly darker. His nose was a little broader, slightly crooked, as if it had been broken once. And where David's wild and dangerous look was somehow refined with an elegance, this man's was not. He looked rougher, coarser.

Nausea swooped through her stomach, but she fought it off with a forced smile.

Roll with the punches, Jayde. The pieces are coming together. Breathe. Think. Think. How do you know this man?

Although she recognized Tariq, she could read no obvious reciprocal recognition in his coal-black eyes as they studied her with brazen male appreciation. Jayde swallowed her anxiety and approached the table.

Then it hit her. *Lancaster!*

She almost stumbled on her high heels.

Gerry Lancaster, her handler, had shown her a photograph of Tariq Rashid. He'd also shown her black-and-white photos of David Rashid. He'd shown them to her…and agent Michael Gibbs. With David O'Reilly. In the briefing room. On a screen.

She and Gibbs had been sent to spy on David Rashid!

Her breathing faltered. She swayed on her feet. Oh, God, she was a spy. An agent for the British government. She had a handler. It was all coming back. That whole wretched ball of tangled yarn was unraveling in her brain, swamping it, strangling logic. She pressed her hand to her temple. She had to sort it all out. Quick. Before she made a horrific mistake. Dammit, why had she been sent to spy on him?

Because British and U.S. intel had recently discovered Rashid uranium was going into a covert Libyan nuclear weapons program. And some of it was also being sold to Korea in exchange for technological expertise.

Her heart stalled. Time warped into slow motion. Jayde Ashton now knew *exactly* who she was, where she had come from and why she was on Shendi Island in the middle of the Red Sea.

It was true. David *was* her enemy. Her jaw began to tremble at the sheer power and emotion of it all. But she couldn't cry. Not here. Not now. Not ever. Because Agent Jayde Ashton, MI-6, *never* cried.

He stood, came toward her, hand held out.

She clamped her jaw shut, pulled her shoulders back.

The light of the candles glittered in his eyes. His smile was a wolfish slash of white against the darkness of his skin. He took her arm firmly in his hand. There was a proprietary quality in his behavior toward her tonight. His eyes prowled down the length of her body, a predator sizing its prey. She could feel the electrical tingle his heated gaze left in its wake. She held her breath, repressed a shiver.

"You look ravishing." His words growled through her resolve.

"Thank you," she said, trying to swallow fresh, hot panic.

He held her at arm's length, tilted his head to one side, raised a dark brow. "Jade…" he said.

Blood drained instantly from her head. She gaped at him. Oh God. Oh God, Lord Almighty. He knew her name!

"…it's a beautiful color on you. It suits you even better than I thought it would."

Her heart jackhammered. Her mouth went dry.

He reached up, touched his fingers to the stone at her neck. "And amber…" He smiled darkly, a twinkle rippling like ink through his eyes.

Her breath congealed in her throat. Oh God! Amber! Was he toying with her? He couldn't possibly know she'd had a twin sister named Amber. What else did he know? That she was a spy?

"…the colors in the stone complement your hair," he said.

Relief swept through her. *He didn't know.* Unless he was teasing, testing her with loaded words…just to gauge her reaction. She had to change the subject, act normal, buy time, think. "Is…is Kamilah not here?" she asked, anxiety skittering through her belly.

"She's in bed." David spontaneously kissed her on the cheek. "She asked me to kiss you goodnight."

"She *asked* you?"

"Yes, of course." His eyes glistened with mischievous happiness. "I took your advice. We played before dinner. I hugged her a lot. And it's working. She is talking. *To me.*"

Emotion choked her throat. How could this man be bad? How could he possibly be evil. She couldn't believe it. Wouldn't. But…

He sneaked his arm around her waist. "Come. Meet my brother." He led her to the table. "This is Tariq. He's here for two days on business. Tariq, this is Sahar." A wickedness danced in his eyes. "Kamilah's *mermaid,* the one I was telling you about."

Tariq stood, inclined his head slightly in greeting before seating himself again. He didn't deign to smile at David's mermaid reference. He remained aloof, distant. Sahar immediately sensed deep mistrust. The intensity of it only served to deepen her apprehension.

David pulled out a high-backed chair. He motioned for her to sit. She just stared blankly at him, trying to digest everything that had just slithered into her consciousness. Had Gibbs survived the storm? What had happened to *him?*

"Sahar?" Concern shifted into his eyes. "Are you sure you're all right? You still look a little pale."

She mentally shook herself. "Yes…yes of course. I'm fine." She smiled brightly, falsely, and sat in the chair he was offering her.

He bent to push in her seat and as he did, he whispered darkly into her ear. "I see I judged your size just right." His voice chased a quiver down her bare neck, raised the fine hairs along her nape.

She swallowed. "Really, David, you...you shouldn't have. And all the way from Cairo?"

He shrugged. "I fly things in daily. It's nothing. My dress-maker would have taken weeks to make you a full wardrobe." He brought his mouth even closer to her ear. She could feel the warmth of his lips against her lobe. "Besides," he whispered. "Watson's clothes were beginning to look a little tired, don't you think?"

She shivered at the heat of his words against the nape of her neck. She turned her head and looked up, deep into his eyes, searching. For a sign. Any sign that would tell her if he knew who she really was. A sign that would prove to her that he really was dealing in weapons of mass destruction. But in his expression she could see nothing but a dark and visceral hunger...and something else, something that went beyond concern, something that spoke of friendship, happiness. It was a look of...of love. Her heart twisted sharply inside.

"I...I can't thank you enough, David. And you chose so well, I—"

"Shh." He pressed two fingers to her lips, silencing her. "Besides, I had an excellent muse. Now don't say another thing. Consider the clothes a gift in exchange for the life you've brought back to Shendi, to me."

The dinner was lavish and the wine excellent. But Jayde could barely touch it. Her stomach was a ball of knots. It took all her effort to pretend nothing was wrong.

And that in itself was eating her. Because although the forced smiles and hollow platitudes drained her energy, as the evening wore on the deceit began to fit, to feel natural. And that horrified her. Was this who she really was? Was this what it felt like to be Jayde Ashton? A hollow, fake persona?

And all through the dinner, Jayde had felt Tariq watching

her from under his thick black lashes. There was something hidden in his hooded eyes. But whenever she'd sensed those eyes on her, she'd looked up and he'd looked abruptly away. It made her uneasy. And when he did hold her gaze, there was a dark male appetite in his eyes that bordered on threatening and disrespectful.

Although his words said otherwise, Tariq made her feel like she was an intruder in David's castle. And he kept mentioning Aisha as if somehow warning Jayde to step back from his brother's overt attentiveness.

After dinner Farouk brought out coffee, and again Jayde felt the heat of Tariq's gaze. Her eyes flashed up. She was sick of this. She stared at him in challenge.

This time he didn't avert his eyes. He held her gaze and he addressed her. "Your amnesia," he said, "I find it strange."

She kept her eyes locked onto Tariq's. "Why?"

"I placed a call," he said bluntly as he lifted the small espresso cup to his lips. "I have a colleague who is a neurological specialist in Egypt." He sipped, waiting for her reaction, as if trying to catch her out.

Her stomach turned over itself but she refused to show any outward sign of discomfort. "And?"

"According to him, your symptoms are psychological. Or they are…faked."

She reeled, her eyes flashed to David.

David said nothing. He was studying her. She suddenly felt betrayed, hurt…in spite of the fact she was the betrayer in this equation. "You *knew* this?" she demanded of him.

David nodded, placed his hand gently over hers. "Yes. Watson suspected as much."

"And you didn't *tell* me?"

"We weren't sure, Sahar. We decided to try and locate your relatives and take it from there. Since there was no immediate medical emergency, we thought it best you seek psychiatric treatment close to home...once we found out where that was."

She clenched her jaw, pulled her hand out from under his. She reached up, felt the line of stitches under her hairline. She'd thought her memory loss was from the gash to her head. Could it be... No! It couldn't. Her throat closed in on itself. Could it possibly have happened to her...again? After all these years?

"Sahar." David reached for her hand. "Come on, it changes nothing."

"It changes *everything*," she snapped, pulling away. And it frightened the hell out of her to think her memories, her very sense of self, the core of who she was, had been locked away by *her*. And that she alone had held the key to her prison.

Why had she done this to herself again? A mad kind of terror gripped her heart. And why had Tariq even bothered to check up on her? He had to suspect something.

Tariq's eyes continued to bore into hers.

She felt heat rising in her cheeks. She turned on him. "But you, *you* don't think it's psychological, do you? You think I'm faking. Is *that* why you checked up on me?"

Tariq simply shrugged. "Your situation is strange. No one has reported you missing. There is no record of a boating accident. You came out of the sea—" he snapped his fingers in the air "—just like that. And quite frankly, I find that suspicious. So I placed a call—"

"Tariq!" David warned.

Tariq's eyes flashed to David. "I have your interests at heart, David." He turned back to Jayde, leaned forward, his black eyes unwavering, his voice lowering in threat. "Many a gold digger has tried to insinuate herself into his life since Aisha's death."

Jayde jerked up from the chair. "Damn you!" For whatever

reason fate had thrown her up out of the sea unconscious and onto the beach of Shendi Island, this was not it. She did not have to stand for this.

David bolted up, restrained her. "Sahar, relax—"

She pulled out from his grasp. "No, I will not. How could you keep this from me? Is that what you think, too, that…that I'm after your *money?*"

Tariq smiled slyly. Jayde realized she was trembling.

David's eyes pierced hers. The muscle at his jaw pulsed. "I'll tell you one thing about myself, Sahar." His voice was low, fierce. "I don't lie. Ever. And I do *not* tolerate liars. I'd be lying if I said it hadn't entered my head, but—"

She didn't want to hear the rest. She spun around and stormed from the room, not out of the door that led back toward the bedroom wing, but out onto the patio. She needed air, open sky, freedom. The palace was suddenly claustrophobic, a structural maze of a prison that resembled her mental state. And she needed out. She needed right out of this convoluted mess she'd found herself in.

He came after her. "Sahar!"

She ignored him, made her way to edge of the stone terrace, slipped off her shoes and ran down the grass path toward the lagoon beach.

"Sahar!" She heard David call behind her.

She ran faster.

He started after her. But Tariq came swiftly up behind him, grabbed his arm. "Let her go, David. I need to talk to you."

David seethed, whirled around to face his brother. "How *dare* you!"

"How dare I check up on her?"

"You had no right."

"I have every right. We both have a huge amount at stake at the moment. And that woman—" he pointed to where Sahar had disappeared into the dark "—could be more than a gold digger, David, have you considered that?"

"What, exactly, are you trying to say?"

"I don't trust her. She could be working for someone."

He felt his jaw drop. "What in hell do you mean? You think Sahar is some kind of spy?"

"Even if she's not, look how easily she got onto your island, into your home." He jabbed his finger at David. "She got right into *you*, brother. You need to be more careful. And you need better security."

Rage boiled up through David's blood. It took every ounce of control to keep his voice level. "I have adequate security. And if you think Sahar is some kind of spy, you've lost your mind. What in hell's gotten into you Tariq?"

"You're a powerful man with enormous influence, David. And that means you have enemies. There are people, corporations, superpowers, who want to tear you down, take control of the oil fields, the uranium, rob you of your influence in this part of the world. You know it and I know it. And that woman could be faking, working for any one of them. Everything you…everything *we* have worked for could be at stake."

David heard the depth of sincerity in his brother's words. And he felt himself hesitate. That in itself infuriated him. Because he knew as sure as his heart pumped blood through his veins that Sahar was genuine.

He may have doubted her at first, simply because of the weirdness of her situation, because he was a man for whom trust did not come easy. But not now. He didn't doubt her now. Not after he'd seen her with Kamilah. Not after he'd spent time with her, not after he'd gotten a glimpse into her soul. He would *not* let Tariq's paranoia get to him.

"Sahar was injured, Tariq, washed up in a storm. I was there. I saw her. I saw the gash in her head, the cuts and bruises on her body. She was unconscious. No one fakes stuff like that."

Tariq shrugged. "You said it yourself, it had entered your head."

"Of course it entered my head. But that was before—"

"Before what?" His eyes dipped briefly down David's body. "Before you started thinking with…your third leg?"

David cursed viciously in Arabic. He stepped aggressively close to Tariq and lowered his voice to a snarl. "I may not know who Sahar really is but I have seen the person inside. And that person is *true*. I know it here." He struck his fist to his heart. "And from this point on you will stay out of my personal affairs."

Tariq smiled slowly, teeth glinting in the pale moonlight. "You've already slept with her, haven't you? Is she really that good, brother?"

David's anger spiked clean off the Richter scale. His fists balled, the muscles across his neck snapped tight. His hands shook against the force of control it took not to hit his brother square in the face, breaking his nose, just as he had done once when they were boys.

"No," he said through a clenched jaw. "I have not slept with her…*yet*."

He pivoted and stormed off down the stairs to the grass path and into the dark after Sahar, intending to do just that.

David knew it was an irrational fire that seared through him. But burn it did. Tariq's challenge had only solidified whatever he had been feeling for Sahar. Now it was clear as crystal in his head. He wanted her. More than anything in this world right now, he wanted to make her his, to stake his claim, to prove he had every belief that she was genuine and that she had his and Kamilah's interests at heart.

"Watch your back, David," he heard Tariq call after him into the night.

David's heart blipped at the reminder. It was the same thing Watson had said.

"Her name isn't even *Sahar*, it's simply a name you conjured from your head! You have no idea who she is." Tariq's voice taunted him in the dark.

And David realized in that instant how much he wanted her to be just that. His Sahar. The Sahar that belonged to him and to Kamilah and to Shendi Island. Not to another world lost to her memory.

And as it hit him, part of him realized he was a fool, a man made powerless by a bewitching woman with no name, a man wanting desperately to believe in a fairy tale cooked up by his daughter.

He cursed again.

And then he saw her.

She stood on the far edge of the stone pier that stretched out into the lagoon, a siren staring out over the dark water, the moonlight catching the shimmer in her dress.

He halted, caught his breath, stared at her statuesque silhouette.

He had a sense that if he went to her, if he walked out onto that pier, he would be crossing a final line. And if he took so much as one step over that invisible threshold tonight, there could be no turning back. Because this thing simmering between them was too powerful.

He thrust his hands into his pockets and studied the feminine form on the end of the pier, watched the way her hair lifted in the slight salt breeze. She looked so alone out there.

As he watched her, he became acutely aware of the soft susurration of tiny waves that licked and sucked at the white sands of the lagoon shore and he could her the rhythmic *chink, chink, chink* of the halyard against the mast of his yacht anchored off the pier, the soft slap of the incoming tide against its hull.

And he realized he could no more turn back the ocean's tide, the natural pull of the moon on the waters, than he could deny the natural force this woman exerted over his body and his mind.

He sucked the night air deep into his lungs. He had no choice. He had to go to her. He could no more deny his need than a sailor of old could refuse the ancient call of the mythical siren.

He took the first step over that invisible line and made his way down the pier.

Tariq watched David disappear down the path into the dark. He took a sleek silver box from his pocket, opened it, extracted a long cigarillo. He lit it, the flame flaring hot and orange into the dark. He blew out a stream of smoke and swore under his breath. He was troubled—gravely so.

David might have nothing to hide, but *he* did. David could afford to trust. But *he* couldn't. The woman was a professional. He'd stake his life on it. He knew her type. And she knew just how to get to his brother. She'd made him blind. She only had to look at them with those big green eyes and he went soft—not the David he knew. He'd never seen his brother like this, not even with Aisha.

This was different, and it worried him. Innocent or not, a woman like that could change things. Either way, to Tariq she was an enemy. An obstacle. And either way, she had to go. He had two options. Get rid of the woman. Or find proof that she'd been sent to betray David. He had to move fast.

And if she was some kind of spy, how had it been set up? That part puzzled him. Had she been dropped on the beach in the storm? David had said there was boating debris found with her. Had that been planted? Or had there really been an accident? Could there be more debris out there, possibly some clue that might tie her to a foreign government?

Tariq stubbed his cigarillo out in the flower pot. He'd call his men tonight, get them to scour the remote outer islands at first light, see if they could find anything he could use.

David walked slowly, deliberately along the pier toward Sahar, each step swelling the thrilling sense of anticipation that surged through his blood.

As he got closer to her he could see the soft night breeze toying with the loose tendrils of her fiery hair and ruffling the hem of her silk gown about her ankles. His loins tightened instantly in response.

He swallowed. He was already pumped from his argument with Tariq. Anger had heightened every sense in his body, heated his blood to feverish pitch. He moistened his lips, tasted the salt in the air.

And then he took that final step. "Sahar."

Chapter 10

His hand touched her shoulder, and a crack of heat jolted clear through her spine. She clutched her arms tightly against her stomach, against the sensation.

She didn't want him to see her face, to see that he possessed the power to melt her from the inside out, to see that he'd once again managed to push her up to the brink of emotional collapse.

But she wasn't crying, not this time. She was close. But she would not cry. Crying wasn't part of Jayde Ashton's makeup. Tears were a sign of weakness. She was not weak. Just stupid. A naive idiot for allowing herself to fall for David Rashid. For allowing her brain to do this to itself again after all these years.

Doctors had always said it could happen again. That she could slip more easily into a fugue-like state of dissociation a second time around. But in all those years, she had never believed it would happen. She thought she'd made herself too strong for it.

Now she knew different. She had an incurable fissure in her foundation. She had no control over it. And that terrified her.

But what horrified her even more than having slipped into that state again was the way her amnesia had lowered her defences against emotion, how it had torn down the protective walls she'd been building around herself since she was eight years old.

How could that simple blank gap in her mind have allowed David Rashid in like that, allowed her to *feel* so deeply when feeling was a just not part of who Jayde Ashton had become?

And why in heaven was she actually feeling rejected and betrayed by David—her target, the man she was being paid to betray?

What was that about? Where in hell had that come from? He didn't owe her a damn thing. He had every right to be all-out suspicious of her story. Hell, it was barely making sense to her. One minute she'd been setting up a surveillance system, posing as Gibbs's wife on a diving expedition off the coast of Shendi Island. Then the storm…then next thing she knew she was lying in David Rashid's bed with not a scrap of clothing and not a clue how she got there.

Even though she'd been sent to spy on David Rashid, her amnesia was genuine. And the desire, the care that had grown out of it was genuine. Frightening as all hell, but genuine. She'd never meant to get into his and Kamilah's life like this. She would never consciously have done it. And she didn't know what the hell to do about it now. Jayde Ashton just didn't have a clue about this feeling. Period.

"Sahar?" The thick rasp of passion in his voice kicked her heart into a light stutter. His hand pressed down on her shoulder. "Sahar, I'm sorry, for my behavior, for Tariq—"

More than anything in this world she wanted to turn around, to bury herself in his arms. She wanted to *be* Sahar.

Right now, right at this very instant, it was all she wanted from life—to be Sahar. With no past to worry about. No handlers waiting in Khartoum for her to hand over the man she had come to care for. No worrying about whether or not David Rashid was helping a corrupt government secretly build nuclear weapons of mass destruction...

"Sahar, talk to me."

She drew in a shuddering breath. She still wouldn't look at him. She continued to stare out over the black water as she spoke. "You have nothing to apologize for, David." She tried to hide the tremor in her voice. "You have every right to doubt me. Don't you think *I* didn't wonder why no one came looking for me? And now you tell me there is no physical evidence of my amnesia, that my subconscious cooked it up all by itself. You're right. Tariq is right. It all sounds bizarre. How could I expect you to even begin to understand?"

"Look at me, Sahar." He grasped her shoulders, turned her body to face him.

She looked slowly, warily, up into his eyes. They were dark with a mad and feral kind of hunger. A thick visceral energy emanated from him in slow, heavy waves. He reminded her of a wild jaguar, one that crouched in the night shadow of a jungle, watching his prey, restraining every muscle, controlling every sinew in his body as he waited for precisely the right time to leap, make his kill.

It excited a reciprocal primal appetite deep within her and it wiped her mind clean of rational thought.

"I want you to know something, Sahar." His voice had lowered in tone and it curled through her body like dark-blue mist through a morning ravine.

"No matter what happens, I will be there for you. Do you understand that?" He traced his fingers slowly along her collarbone, awakening sleeping nerves, leaving them raw and tingling in the salt air. Her breath caught in her throat at the sensation. He cupped his hand firmly around the back of her neck, drew her closer to him. "When your memory comes back, you won't be alone. Watson said it could be tough, that it could all come back at once. But I'll be there for you. I want you to know that."

She choked back a lump of tears. "Why, David? Why would you want to be there for me? You don't have a clue who I am…who I might be."

He moved the rough pad of his thumb firmly along her jawbone, tilting her face up to his. She felt the latent power, the absolute control in his hand. He could snap her neck in an instant if he wanted to.

What would he do when he found out who she really was?

"I don't need to know your name to know *you,* Sahar." He scored her bottom lip with his thumb. She shuddered under his touch.

"I don't need a government identity document to reach in and touch the person inside." Her body responded to the dark meaning wrapped in his words by sending a surge of molten warmth down to her belly. With it came an instinctive desire to open up to him, fully, to allow him to touch her inside, to feel the full, hot, maleness of him deep within in her core.

His mouth moved closer to hers. So close. She felt her knees go weak, felt her whole body go boneless at the anticipation of his lips taking hers. But he didn't. He just whispered hotly against them. "I want you, Sahar. I want you so badly I ache."

Her vision narrowed. She opened her mouth to speak, couldn't. His lips almost touched hers. She could almost taste him, his warmth, his maleness, his heat…his tongue.

He pulled back. "No. I can't do this, Sahar." His voice came out thick as molasses. "I can't do this to you."

Yes, you can! Every molecule in her body screamed. She

needed him. It was as if he embodied the power of life itself. She needed to tap into that force, that hot energy, with a desperation that defied all logic.

She leaned into him, pressing the curves of her body against the hard length of his. And her world shrank to just this instant. Just this sensation of his solid strength, his maleness hard up against the silk of her dress. Absolutely nothing else mattered now. Nothing could. She pressed her pelvis against the thick muscle of his thigh, lifted a leg, driven by an aching and potent primal force, a mad hunger to feel him against her.

He caught her knee with one hand, held it against his hip and moaned as she moved against him, the sound guttural, animal. His other hand cupped her buttocks, yanked her hard up against himself. She gasped at the heat that seared through her.

"Sahar." His *R*s rolled in his throat, his Arabic accent swallowing the refined British as his smooth veneer fell away to reveal the rough warrior underneath. "You could regret this. There…there may be someone else your life…."

"No," she whispered, reaching up, brushing her lips along the exquisitely firm and sculpted line of his. "There…there is no one."

He stilled suddenly, grasped her jaw in a vicelike grip and pulled back. He held her face steady, forcing her to look up at him as his eyes bored down into hers, dangerously dark. "Are you *sure?*"

"I'm sure." She was dead sure. She'd never been consumed by this kind of fire before. She'd never felt this kind of emotional longing for a man. Jayde Ashton had never allowed herself to feel deeply for anyone…not since she was eight years old.

"How would you know?"

"I…I just know. I can feel it in my heart." She whispered. There *could* be no one else.

It was an answer that satisfied him. A slash of white teeth glinted in the moonlight as he smiled. A devilish glitter lit his eyes. And her adrenaline spiked at the wicked intent she saw there.

Then he kissed her. Hard. Fast. His tongue probing, stroking, his teeth scoring. She felt his hand move down her thigh. She felt him bunching up her silk gown.

Then she felt his fingers. Rough. Warm. Callused. She felt those beautifully tapered fingers searching, tearing her panties aside.

She lifted her knee higher, widening access. And his finger plunged roughly into her slickness.

A low moan escaped her throat. Her knees gave in and she sank down, melting onto the length of his finger, his hand.

He deepened his kiss, moving his tongue, his finger, inserting another, twisting them inside her. He moved his hand deeper and she felt his palm rub against the sensitive nub between her legs. She could hardly breathe. She moved against the palm of his hand, desperate, hungry, wild. Blind to anything but the instant.

"My yacht," he whispered thickly into her hair.

"It's…it's in the middle of the lagoon," she countered, her voice breathy, her heart hammering as though it would split free from her chest.

"We'll take the Zodiac." He scooped her up, carried her effortlessly in his arms to the small rigid-hull inflatable tethered to the pier. David reached the craft, set her down, leaped onto the boat and held his hand out to her over the water, beckoning her like the desert prince he was.

She reached for his grasp, but as she did a soft lagoon swell surged suddenly with the incoming tide, rolling the boat sharply away from her as she stepped forward.

It happened so fast. David felt her hand slipping from his grasp. He heard her sharp intake of breath. Then the splash. He sucked in his breath. "Sahar!"

There was silence. Darkness. He could see nothing but flecks of gold moonlight glinting on black ripples of water and white foam where she went under.

Oh God, Sahar.

And in that instant David Rashid knew he never, ever wanted to lose this woman. He would do what it took to make her his, no matter who she was. No matter who waited for her. He was going to keep her. On his island. For himself and Kamilah.

"Sahar!" he barked, frantically stripping off his dinner shirt, kicking off his shoes, ready to dive in. Then he heard her laugh.

Dizzying relief ripped through him. He spun around. *Where was she?*

And she laughed again, the sound of a clear brook running through his senses, floating over the swells.

A crazy bubble of happiness erupted low in his stomach and pushed up to his throat. But anxiety kept it locked down. *Where the hell was she?*

Then he heard her again. He spun to his left. And there she was. On the other side of the inflatable, sculling out into the black bay.

The moonlight glinted off the waves, off the slickness of her wet hair and off voluminous silk billows as her gown lifted and flowed around her with the swells. His initial alarm was replaced with a sense of bemused wonder.

She looked like a mermaid! *His* mermaid. She must have dived under the Zodiac and swum up to the other side—just to scare him.

"Sahar!" He said half in anger, half in relief, bewilderment muddling his brain.

She giggled at his shock. It shot a spurt of fuel into the strange cocktail of hot energy and warring emotions within him. She was challenging him. Toying with him. Playing. The way he'd seen her play in the waves. The way he'd seen her play with his child.

That odd, painful ball of happiness and delight spiced with shock exploded through the tension in his throat, erupting into mad laughter. Laughter that boiled from the base of his belly, reverberated up through his torso and out through his chest in glorious release. He threw back his head and just laughed into the night sky like he hadn't since he was a kid. And by Allah it felt fine.

She was laughing, too, sculling farther out into the shallow lagoon, toward the depths where his yacht was moored.

He stilled suddenly, heat stirring his loins once more as he watched her, floating, tantalizing, beckoning. Billows of wet silk fanning out about her.

She was luring him, a man of hot sun and dry sand, into her element. Water. Into depths he'd been trying for years to avoid. He'd known the instant he'd first looked into her emerald eyes that he would succumb and drown in their depths.

"You coming?" she called darkly out over the swells.

And he couldn't resist her siren call. Like an adventurer of old, he left the security of his craft and plunged into the sea, powerless to defy the song of her seduction.

But as he swam toward her, she kept moving just out of his reach, her rippling laughter taunting him, pulling him along like threads of moonlight.

She lured him over a sandbank. The water was now chest high. His feet found the sea bed, and he began to wade aggressively toward her. But still she kept infuriatingly just beyond reach, floating in her sea of silk, toying with him, tempting him until he thought he would burst with his desire for her.

In sheer desperation he lunged at her. But she ducked under, leaving only a ring of empty ripples and glittering phosphorescence in her wake.

He looked to his left, to his right. Nothing. Then he gasped as she grabbed hold of his legs underwater and pulled herself up along the length of his body to the surface. Surprise swirled with a titillating pleasure as she surfaced against him. The thick wet silk of her gown enveloped him as the ocean surged and fell, the folds of it tangling erotically about his legs.

Her hair was slick as a seal's, and water ran creamy over skin made luminescent by moonlight. Her eyes were dark and mysterious. Magic eyes. *Mermaid's eyes.* The eyes of a mythical creature with no name, no place, no memory. He stared into those eyes as the water lifted them slightly. Up, then down. A basic rhythm of the earth. The ocean responding to the moon. Gravity. Essential. Natural. Undeniable.

The water was cool against his skin, but heat boiled inside him. He kept a firm hold of her with one hand lest she bolt again. With the other he traced his fingers up the elegant column of her throat, the throat he'd admired when she lay unconscious in his bed. She responded by hooking one long and naked leg around his clothed one. She placed her palm flat against his bare wet chest, splayed her fingers, moved it slowly along his skin, down his belly. Lower. He swelled hard and hot against the wet fabric of his pants.

He slid his hand along her shoulder, slipped the thin strap of her gown down, exposing her breast. It was milky white, glistening with the sea under the lunar light. He caught his breath, touched her nipple with his fingertips. It reacted instantly, tightening to a hard nub.

He bent his head, sought out the hard tip of her aroused nipple with his lips. He flicked his tongue around it and then sucked, drawing it tighter, to a slick and salty point. He'd ached to do this since he'd watched her on the beach, since he'd watched the rise and fall of her breasts under the white Egyptian-cotton sheet as she'd lain unconscious in his bed, since he'd felt the soft weight of those breasts against his bare chest as he'd hunkered over her on his horse, riding ahead of the storm.

But the pleasure was more than he could even have begun to imagine. It drove his hungering ache to a feverish pitch. He scored her nipple with his teeth, bit.

She moaned, arching her back, pressing herself against him, offering all of herself to him. Her reaction drew a shaft of liquid fire that seared clean through to his groin. A low and hungry growl emanated from deep in his throat. He moved his mouth slowly up the column of her neck, tasting the salt, licking her skin, making her writhe under him with need.

Then he grasped the back of her neck firmly, lifting her face to his, and he forced his mouth down onto hers. He felt her open instantly under the pressure of his lips. Her warmth was salty. Elemental. Soft and deeply feminine.

With a groan he sank his tongue down into her. She responded, her tongue slipping, entwining around his. It cracked his world open into a dizzying rainbow of light. Colors spun riotously inside his head. Music seemed to swell though his core. He was feeding on her brightness, filling a void he hadn't even known existed within him.

He pulled back, stunned, breathless. "Are you for real?" he whispered. "Or are you really something conjured up from the sea?" In his wild sensual delirium, he almost believed she might be.

She murmured in his ear sending hot and cold shivers over his skin. "I can be whatever you want me to be, David."

"Be mine," he growled, lips against hers. *Be my Sahar.*

Jayde didn't want to begin to think about what was happening, what she was doing. What he was doing to her. Her walls had been breached and right now she was utterly defenceless against the raw power that was streaming through them. She was quite simply imprisoned in the present, by her desire, by her desperate passion for this powerful man.

All she could do was lift her face to his. Right now she would be his Sahar. Because deep, deep down, the forgotten part of herself had actually become Sahar. A woman with feeling, emotion, and aching love in her heart. A woman who had been locked away, many years ago, by an eight-year-old child who had been burned by life. Until now.

And now she was desperate. Now she wanted everything she had missed. She looked up into his face. Desire etched his features into dangerous feral planes, his eyes flashed. A quiver ran through her stomach. "Take me, David," she whispered. "Take me."

He crushed his mouth down hard onto hers. She met his urgency, her tongue seeking his, her hands tearing at the buckle of his pants under the surface. She felt him swell free in her hands, his need blatant, hot and hard against the cool velvet of the water. There was no stopping now. It was fast. Furious. Desperate. He shoved the wet, floating silk up high about her waist, grasped at her lace panties, ripped them off her. She wrapped both her legs around him using the swells of the ocean for buoyancy. He pushed his mouth hard onto hers, invaded with his tongue, roughly. Demanding. She was overwhelmed with her own aching need. She arched her back, opened her legs wider around him, aching for him from the very center of her being.

He gripped her buttocks and thrust his full length into her as he pulled her down onto himself. He was hot, hard against her softness. She could feel her own heat pooling between her thighs, around him. He groaned and he thrust deeper. The movement drew cool water into her molten fire. She gasped.

The contrast in temperatures inside her heightened every sensation, awakened every nerve. Her body screamed in delirious and silent delight.

She could hardly breathe. Each movement, each stroke sent her higher, made waves of watery resistance surge between them, their coupling creating a turbulence that fanned out in concentric phosphorescent ripples over the black waters of the lagoon.

Jayde felt as if she would burst. A desperate need to scream into the night air rose in her throat as he drove her higher and higher. She could feel the thick length of him inside her grow hotter. She could feel it quiver and she knew he was near.

That knowledge itself pushed her over the tip. Her vision blurred and she was blinded as scarlet waves slammed into her head and colored her mind. She swallowed her cry as the blinding sensation took hold of her. Her body rippled around him in wave after wave of hard contractions. And then he came, bucking, releasing into her with a final violent shudder.

They held each other, spent, bobbing gently in the water, silently in the swells, breaths coming light and fast.

He brushed his lips over her forehead. "Mmm…that was sublime," he murmured against her skin. "A fantasy."

Jayde began to feel the chill of the water against her skin as her body cooled. Cognizance crept back with the cold. With it came the sharp bite of reality. He was right. It was a fantasy. Only, he didn't know the half of it. And she felt suddenly sick. She was deceiving him. She couldn't do this.

But before she could begin to pull away, David reached up and ran his rough palm over her breast. "Shall we try to make it to the yacht this time?" His voice was dark with fresh promise.

Jayde was shocked by the bolt of new heat that shot to her belly. A pang of guilt touched her heart, but her desire pushed it away. "Yes," she whispered in his ear.

Tomorrow could wait.

Tonight she was stealing time. Tonight she was stealing lost years.

They made love through the night. And as dawn glowed peach on the horizon, Jayde wished in her heart she never had to leave Shendi Island. Or David. They were made for each other.

No, she corrected herself. *Sahar* and David were made for each other.

Jayde Ashton had been trained to be something very, very different. Only, it didn't seem to fit anymore. A part of her had actually become someone else, a woman with emotion and lightness and love in her soul.

She'd been rent in two. And she knew she could never become whole again. Not in the way she truly wanted. Not with David Rashid. Because when he found out who she was, he would never forgive her. He'd said it himself at dinner. There was nothing he abhorred more in life than a liar. And she believed he'd truly meant it.

Surely a man who abhorred lies could not be covertly shipping uranium to Libya and Korea? On the surface, Libya was dismantling its nuclear weapons program, but at the same time the Libyan leader was secretly backing the Falal, a radical extremist group charged with taking the country's weapons program underground—and using Rashid uranium to do it. Jayde was one of the few people in the world who knew about it.

She lay on her back on the large double bed in the cabin of David's luxurious yacht, staring up at the ceiling, listening to the slap of water against the hull, the chink of metal against the mast, the comforting sounds of David making coffee in the galley. And she drank in the heavenly scents of a domestic morning.

No. She could *not* believe he was involved. And she could

not continue lying to him. She would not. She had to find a
way to get hold of Lancaster.

She closed her eyes. God, she wished she didn't have to
do this.

"Morning, gorgeous."

Her eyes flared open. He stood, dark and totally naked, a
Zeus, holding two mugs of steaming coffee, a sinful grin
across his ruggedly handsome face.

She smiled in spite of herself, allowing her gaze to roam
brazenly, appreciatively over his exquisite body, taking in the
broad, dark-skinned chest, the whorl of dark hair that ran
down the center of his washboard stomach and flared out to
cover his godlike maleness.

"Uh-uh." He shook his head. "You look at me like that and
you're gonna have trouble."

She laughed. "I can see trouble stirring already."

He pulled a face, set the coffee mugs down and grabbed a
kikoi. He wound the brightly colored strip of African cotton
around his waist, hiding his swelling interest.

Jayde made a mock moue. "What a shame."

He wiggled a brow. "We could fix that."

Heat spurted to her groin. He sat down on the bed, leaned
over her. She pulled his kikoi free…

But the sound of an engine coming at full throttle over the
bay made them both pull back.

Someone was speeding toward the yacht.

David jerked to his feet, grabbed his *kikoi*, wrapped it
around his waist. But before he'd even made it up on deck
Jayde felt the bump of a small craft pulling up alongside the
yacht. Then she heard Tariq's voice barking over the sputter
of the motor. "I must talk to you, David. Now."

"What is it?" Undisguised irritation laced David's voice as
he clambered up to the deck.

"Not here. In private. There is something you must see. It cannot wait."

Jayde heard David coming back down to the cabin.

"What does Tariq want?" she asked, nerves skittering through her chest. *Had Tariq found something out about her?*

He took her face in both his hands, kissed her full on the mouth. "Business. Wait for me. There's food in the galley. Help yourself."

"David—" she called after him in desperation.

He blew her a kiss. "I'll be right back."

Jayde's heart sank like a stone. She listened to the roar of the engine as Tariq took David away from her. A heavy sense of doom descended on her as the splutter of the engine faded into the distant sound of waves.

She just knew David would not be back.

Not in the way she wanted him back.

It was over.

David stared at the item Tariq had placed on his desk as if it were a poisonous snake from the pit of hell. "Where did you find *that*?"

"On one of the small outer islands. We did a search early this morning, found some boat wreckage, clothing, life jackets, diving gear—" Tariq jutted his chin in the direction of the package "—and that."

"Why did you search?" he snapped.

"I'm trying to help you, David. No one has claimed the woman. I was looking for some clues to her identity."

David picked up the waterproof document pouch and yanked open the ziplock closure. He tipped it upside down. The contents spilled out over his desk. Two diving passes. Airline tickets from London. Two British passports. A boat rental agreement...

And a gold wedding band.

His heart drummed in his chest. His throat went dry. He reached out, picked up the passports, flipped one open. The photo was Sahar.

Except it wasn't Sahar.

It was *Melanie Wilson.* He flipped the other document open. It belonged to Simon Wilson.

A lump swelled hard in his throat. He reached for the diving passes. Simon and Melanie Wilson. He grabbed the rental contract. It was made out to Mr. and Mrs. Wilson.

His heart shriveled in on itself. He struggled to breathe. Slowly he reached for the wedding band. It was cold in his hand. Smooth. A woman's size. He turned it over in his fingers, read the engraving.

"Simon and Melanie forever."

David sank bonelessly into his office chair, the gold ring clutched tightly in his fist.

Mrs. Melanie Wilson. He felt as if every bit of life had been sucked from his marrow. She was *married.* And, inside, a part of him died.

Tariq was watching him silently. David looked up at him, forced himself to ask. "Was there any sign of…of her husband?"

"No."

"Any sign of *anyone* else?"

"Nothing."

David closed his eyes, rested his head against the back of his chair. He tried to steady his breathing. He hated himself with a passion for even beginning to think what he was thinking— that if her husband had drowned there was still a chance for him.

His eyes flared open. He slammed the ring onto his desk, glared at Tariq. "Why has *Mr.* Wilson not come looking for his wife, then?" he demanded. "What man doesn't look for his wife!"

"David—"

"No." He held his palm up. "Don't talk to me. Just phone that damn diving operation and find out why no one is looking for *Mrs.* Wilson. Find out why no one is looking for that boat! Find out what in hell has happened to *Mr.* Wilson! And find out why the goddamn British Embassy doesn't know these British subjects are missing!"

He jerked to his feet. Nothing added up. But he had to go to Sahar. He had to tell her they had an ID on her.

No, he corrected himself, not Sahar. She wasn't Sahar. Not anymore. That fantasy was over. She was Mrs. Melanie Wilson.

And as David made his way back down to the bay, he caught sight of his yacht gleaming white on the water. He stopped and stared at it. She was on that yacht. Waiting for him.

His whole body began to vibrate against the tension in his muscles. Because now he couldn't have her. She belonged to another man. And that meant he had to keep his hands off her. Just the idea of not touching her again made him feel like a bomb ready to blow its casing. He knew it would take every ounce of control to hold himself in check. Both emotionally and physically.

He didn't know if he could do it.

Chapter 11

She had to think fast. There was a chance Tariq had simply wanted David for some other urgent business. And if Tariq had nothing on her, she had two choices. Continue to deceive David. Or come clean and tell him who she was.

She could do neither. Deceiving him now was out of the question. She was just not capable of consciously hurting him and Kamilah in that way.

And telling him? That would jeopardize an international sting operation. And it could endanger lives. It was not feasible.

There was one other option. She could abort the mission.

That's what she would do. She had to find a way to reach Lancaster, tell him she'd been compromised, that she needed to be brought in. ASAP.

Jayde glanced at the antique clock on the cabin wall. David still wasn't back. He'd been gone for over an hour.

It was nothing, she told herself. He was a busy man. He and

Tariq had business. And she could get herself back to shore with the inflatable if she really wanted, or she could swim.

But in spite of her reasoning, she had a sinking sensation something had gone horribly wrong.

She anxiously fingered her ring finger. Then it hit her. *It was missing.* The engraved wedding band she'd been handed as part of her cover with all the other "pocket litter" was gone.

She'd taken the ring off on the boat because wearing jewelry on her hands irritated her. She'd slipped it into the document pouch with the other papers she and Gibbs had been given.

Some people routinely took their rings off to wash their hands and do other things. So technically, it wasn't a mistake, she told herself. She'd been behaving as a normal married woman might have. But in this case, it had turned out to be a critical error. On a deeply personal level. Because maybe if she'd kept the ring on, maybe if she'd been able to read the inscription on the wedding band, she just might have remembered sooner who she was…and why she was anywhere near Shendi Island. Maybe she'd never have found herself this far down the road with David Rashid.

Jayde sat on the bed and sank her fingers into her mass of hair. How could this have happened to her? Why had she lost time again so many years later?

She closed her eyes.

It was the storm. The boating accident. It had to be. It must have shocked her right back to that terrible ordeal off the coast of Cornwall when she was only six…Kamilah's age. That's why she'd felt such a visceral connection to the child.

Jayde got up, made her way toward the bathroom. She leaned over the basin and stared into the mirror. She touched the clear amber stone that hung at the hollow of her throat.

Amber. The name of her twin sister. She covered the stone with her hand and closed her eyes. For a second last night she'd thought David had been on to her. But he'd only been talking about the stone. Not about the sister she'd watched drown with her father in that awful boating accident when she was six.

Jayde and Amber. Her parents had given the twins the names of precious stones. She and Amber had been inseparable. She choked down the balloon of pain in her throat, stumbled back to the stateroom and sank down onto the bed. Her body began to shake. Her breathing became labored. She began to relive the horrific memories her mind had tried once again to blot out.

They'd been on holiday, visiting her grandfather in Cornwall. She and Amber had gone out on a boat with her dad. A terrible storm had risen out of nowhere blacking out the sun and sky. They'd tried to outrun it, but it was impossible. Monstrous waves had swamped the boat. They'd ended up in the viciously churning and frigid sea. Her father had saved her first, shoving her into the heaving lifeboat as he choked and coughed out the salt water in his lungs

Hold tight baby, I'll be right back. Her father's words echoed in her skull. She clutched her arms tight about her waist and swayed.

He never came back.

He went after Amber. But he was tired, too tired to fight the raging sea. He was injured, bleeding. The waves were too big. The water too cold.

She never saw her father or sister again.

For two days she'd lain curled up in the bobbing lifeboat, adrift in the sea, shrouded in thick gray mist. When they'd finally rescued her she was unconscious. The newspapers had said it was a miracle she'd survived at all.

Her mother hadn't been on the boat that day—she'd gone to see a movie with an old school friend. The guilt at not hav-

ing been there to help had eaten at her like a cancer. And it
had eventually killed her like a cancer, when she swallowed
a bottle of pills and bottle of whiskey to hide from the pain.
She never came back.

Jayde was eight years old when that had happened. She'd
found her mother when she'd woken up in the morning. Her
mother's skin had been ice-cold, a photograph clutched in her
stiff fingers, the one where they were all together and smiling under the Christmas tree.

Jayde had called for help on the phone. Then she had
waited by her mother's body until the police arrived. But it
was no use. No one had been able to wake her mother up.

And when the police took Jayde away, she lost herself for
the first time. She went into a dissociative fugue, as the doctors had called it. She simply forgot her name and how she
fitted into the pain of her world. And it had taken her a full
two years to come out it. Two lost years. Two years of hiding
from the agony of her own memories.

Doctors had told her later in her life that the chances of re-
experiencing a similar amnesiac state were much higher after
it had happened once before.

Jayde scrubbed her hands brutally over her face trying to
make it all go away again. That's what must have happened.
When the storm hit off Shendi Island, when the boat she and
Agent Gibbs were on started to go under, she must have regressed, started to relive those terrible memories as she was
once again sucked under the waves. And her old coping mechanism had snapped in. She'd simply shut it all out again.

And now it was back. Every lurid detail. Just like that.

She scrunched her eyes tight. They burned, but tears
wouldn't come. Because she was Jayde Ashton, agent for the
British secret service. And everyone in the business knew
Jayde Ashton never cried. They knew nothing touched her.

Ever. Because she would never let anything get close enough, and that had made her one of the best in the business.

But now? Now she'd been compromised. Now she would have to tell MI-6 about the mental weakness she'd kept hidden from them. She had never dreamed it could one day damage her or her colleagues. She had to assume that Lancaster and O'Reilly knew she was here, on Shendi. Did they know she had amnesia? Or did they think she might be role-playing? Whatever they thought, they were probably waiting for her to make contact. She had to find a way to reach them. But before she could figure out how to do it, she heard the roar of an engine cutting across the lagoon.

David was coming back!

Her heart twisted into an excruciating knot. Panic skittered through her blood. She took a deep, shuddering breath, tried to quell the shaking in her limbs.

She felt the Zodiac knock up against the yacht, heard him thud onto the deck. She held her breath.

David loomed into the doorway, strangling the light in the cabin. Under his coffee-brown skin his face was ashen. A muscle pulsed at his jaw. His neck was corded with tension, his mouth a flat, hard line.

And in his piercing blue eyes Jayde saw a look she'd seen only once before in her life—in the eyes of soldiers faced with an impossible mission, one they knew they would not return from. It was a look of emotional distance combined with fierce determination. A look of the haunted and damned. And seeing that look in him terrified her in a way she didn't think possible.

What had happened? What had Tariq shown him? Had he found out she was a traitor?

A hatchet of fear hacked into her heart. "David?" her voice came out hoarse.

He said nothing. He took something out of his pocket and held it out to her. She stared at it. She knew exactly what it was. A passport. A British passport.

Then he took something else out of his pocket. The wedding band. Her eyes flashed up to his in horror.

"You're married," he said, his voice hollow, his mouth twisting in an effort to hide his pain. "Your name is *Mrs. Melanie Wilson. You belong to another man.*"

He didn't know she was MI-6! Of course he didn't. He'd found only her cover information. Relief plunged through her. Then it flipped straight over and reared up into a horrible black realization. David was devastated not by the fact she was a spy, but by the fact she was *married.* And the agony that echoed through the hollowness of his voice ripped the very soul from her body.

David, the potent desert warrior, was destroyed by the fact she belonged to another man, another world. That she wasn't his.

She choked on the emotion that boiled up into her throat. *It's not true! I'm not married! I don't belong to anyone!* She wanted to scream the words, wipe away his pain. Her pain. She wanted him. Like she'd never before wanted a man in her life.

But she couldn't. She couldn't have him. She couldn't tell him the wedding ring in his hand was a lie. A lie devised to snare him.

More than anything she wanted to tell him the truth. But the truth could cost lives. And the truth was worse. Because then he'd know she was a liar. And in his own words, he was a man who abhorred liars. What would he do when he discovered the extent of her lie, her deception?

Her face dropped into her hands. And agent Jayde Ashton cried. Her whole body shook. For the first time in her life since she was eight years old, Jayde Ashton *felt.* And it was overwhelming her.

* * *

David wanted desperately to go to her, to hold her tight in his arms. He ached with the need. But he couldn't move. His limbs were numb, his brain thick. It was all he could do to clear his throat and say, "Tariq is making some more calls now that we have your details."

Her big green eyes lifted slowly to meet his. And in them he saw an echo of his own devastating pain. He watched as she fingered the amber stone around her neck.

They stared at each other in silence. There were no words that could possibly ease the tension or the hurt. There were simply no platitudes that could fill the void of space and time that yawned between them.

A few minutes ago they'd been so close. Now it seemed as though an ocean separated them. He'd known a moment like this would come. But he'd underestimated the raw power of it. He was an absolute fool for having entertained the notion that things might somehow work out. He deserved this pain. But *she* didn't. She was innocent in this. He should have protected her, not taken advantage of her. This was his fault.

She broke the silence, swiping the tears from her face. "David, I'm so sorry. I…I don't know what to say." She stood up, took a hesitant step toward him, reached out her hand as if to touch him.

He tensed, moved away from her. A small part of him took satisfaction in the fact she didn't seem happy with the discovery of her identity. And that meant she cared for him deeply enough to be sorry to lose him…and Kamilah. But if he allowed her to touch him now, he knew he'd be powerless to stop himself from grabbing her into his arms, holding on to her forever. "I'll take you back to shore," he said, his voice rough, thick. "Hopefully we'll get more details soon."

"Yes. Thank you."

He hesitated. "Now that you know…now that you know your name, does it help you remember anything else?"

Uncertainty flickered through her eyes. Then she nodded. "Yes. I…I think it's coming back, bit by bit. I…I believe I was on a diving holiday."

He felt his fists clench, but he had to say it. "With your husband, Simon?"

She looked away from him. "Yes," she said softly.

His stomach bottomed out so fast he felt ill. "I see," he said. "I hope he's all right."

She nodded, but she was shaking like a leaf.

"Do you remember if there was anyone else on the boat?"

"N-no, there wasn't. It was just us, the two of us."

He nodded. "Come, I'll take you back to my office. We'll see if Tariq is making any headway. Do you remember now where you and your husband launched your trip from? The boat rental papers say Port Sudan. Is that right?" His voice strained against the effort to sound normal. All he wanted was to smash his fists into the wall.

"Yes. We launched from Port Sudan," she said, refusing to look him in the eye.

He frowned. "Why do you think no one reported the boat— or you—missing?

"I…I have no idea."

"Did you register with the embassy in Khartoum when you arrived in Sudan?"

She shook her head. "I know it's recommended but we didn't bother. We wanted to get out on the water as soon as possible."

"And you remember *all* this now?" A strange cold shadow of doubt crossed his heart. This didn't seem right.

She was still shaking, clutching her arms into her waist as if she was going to throw up. "I…I guess I blocked everything out…because of the accident. Do you…do you mind if I make the calls myself? I need to do it…to find out if my…my husband is missing."

"Of course." And with that, David knew it really was final. She was looking for her husband.

There could be nothing more between them.

David showed her into his office. There was no sign of Tariq, and that relieved Jayde immensely. She couldn't face the man's accusing eyes right now. And she needed to do this in private. She needed to contact Lancaster and tell him to bring her in. She looked up into David's eyes. "Do you…do you mind if I do this alone?"

He hesitated. "You sure you don't need me?"

"Yes," she said.

Hurt rippled through his features. "Of course," he said and left the room.

Jayde swallowed her remorse, picked up the receiver on David's desk…and paused. Calling her handler from this phone was a risk. But she had to take it. It was the only way to make contact. She quickly punched in his number.

"Yes?" Lancaster's voice was gruff on the other end.

"It's Jayde," she said.

She heard a sharp intake of breath. "Are you all right?"

"I'm fine. Is…is Gibbs okay?"

"The lucky bugger is in excellent health. He was picked up by a fishing vessel. Good ploy with the amnesia, Ashton. We've been waiting for you to check in."

"It…it wasn't a ploy," she said. "It was for real."

Silence stretched over the distance. "But you're fine now, right? You remember everything now?"

"Yes. But I've been compromised. I need to be brought in, ASAP."

"*They know who you are?*"

"No. It's…I'm not able to…the amnesia compromised me."

"Ashton." Her handler's tone was gruff. "We *need* you there right now. You're right inside his home. We couldn't have orchestrated this better if we had tried. You have to hold steady."

She scrunched her eyes up in frustration. *What did the man want? Did she have to beg?* "Lancaster, I can't stress this enough, I've been irrevocably compromised. Besides, I believe Rashid is innocent." *And I trust him. And he's made me feel things I never thought possible. And I've made love to him. I…I love him.* She choked on a ball of tears that lurched into her throat.

Again silence stretched. "You have any proof of his innocence?"

"No."

"And Rashid has no idea who you are?"

"No."

Silence again. "We have new intel, Ashton. It came in late last night. Hear me out, *then* make your decision. If you still need out, we'll mobilize ASAP."

"I'm listening."

"You just may be right. There is a chance David Rashid could be innocent."

Her heart blipped, kicked into a light staccato beat. She *knew* it! In her gut she just knew it.

"The CIA operative undercover in Libya has made a breakthrough. He saw Tariq Rashid leaving the Falal base in Libya near the Azar border two days ago. He's one of them."

"Tariq is *Falal?*" she whispered.

"Yes. And according to the operative, Tariq is the one organizing Rashid uranium and oil shipments for the Falal. His brother may not even know about the deals, since it is Tariq

Rashid who is now in control of those mines. We have also just learned that the Falal is funding the dissidents in Azar. The Falal is using the Azar rebels to disguise a renewed attempt to seize the Rashid oil fields and uranium mines. Once they have those under their full control, they'll be in a position to mount a coup and take the whole country."

"But the Falal is really just an underground arm of the Libyan government…" Her brain reeled as it hit her. "Lancaster, that means Libya is trying to annex Azar using the Falal. It means David and the Force du Sable are not just fighting against rebels, they're fighting a whole damn country."

"That would be the assumption from the recent intel, yes."

"But Tariq…it just doesn't make sense. Why would Tariq belong to a group fighting his own brother, a group fighting to take over the Rashid mines, his own mines, his own country?" Then with a sinking realization she knew. Once a fundamentalist, always a fundamentalist. Tariq had never forgiven his half brother. David Rashid had been deceived by his own flesh and blood. He was being destroyed from the inside out. And Tariq was running the show.

"There's still the chance that David Rashid could be behind this, Ashton. He could be orchestrating this."

"No, I don't believe it."

"One way or another the Rashids are central to whatever is going down in Libya and Azar. And whatever it is, it's going to end up compromising global stability. If David Rashid is innocent, we need proof."

"I'll get you proof." And by God she would. She'd stake her life on the fact that Tariq was deceiving his brother. The bastard. "I'm staying on Shendi."

"Ah, there's the Ashton we know."

Fire burned bitter in Jayde's gut as she replaced the receiver. She knew just how the revelation of Tariq's betrayal would cut David to the core. He would feel that he had failed to keep his promise to his father. This was the stuff that went to the very heart of what motivated the man. But...she couldn't tell him without blowing her cover.

Jayde's heart sank like a stone. Keeping her cover, staying on Shendi, meant she would now knowingly be deceiving the man she had come to love.

She couldn't do it.

But she had to. In order to prove his innocence, to protect him from a traitor, an enemy within the walls of his own home. His own brother. She stared at the phone. What had she just done?

She felt as if her very soul had been ripped in two by divided loyalties. She pushed her hair back from her brow with a shaky hand. God, David was going to hate her when he found out what she'd done. In trying to help him she was killing any hopes of a future with him. Who was she kidding? There *was* no hope for a future. David would never believe her amnesia was real once he learned who she was. He'd think she'd deceived him and Kamilah from the start. So what difference would it make to see the mission through now? None. Apart from the fact she might save him from the evil of his half brother.

Jayde sucked in a breath, filling her lungs until they felt they would burst. But as she did, she sensed a presence. Someone was watching her from behind. A cold dread seeped through her. Very, very slowly she turned around.

He stood rigid in the doorway, blue eyes crackling with sparks of fury, the muscles of his neck corded and tight.

"David!" she gasped. "How long have you been standing there?"

"Who were you talking to?" His voice was flat, dangerous.

Jayde's eyes shot to the phone, then back to him.

How much had he heard?

"I said, who were you talking to?" he demanded.

"I...I called the embassy."

"Bull!" He stepped into the room, slammed the door shut behind him, locked it, pocketed the key. "Who the hell *are* you?"

She forced panic away. She told herself she was trained for this sort of thing. But she couldn't kid herself. Nothing in this world had prepared her for the situation in which she found herself now.

He grabbed her wrist, tightening his fingers around her like a metal cuff. He yanked her toward him. His eyes lanced hers, stabbing clean through to her soul. "Who was on that phone?" he growled. "What's this about my brother? What about the Falal?"

She stared up into his ferocious eyes. Beyond the crackling anger, she could still read deep pain. A pain she had put there. And she couldn't lie to him. Just couldn't. She knew in her gut that he was innocent. And if his brother was working against him, he deserved to know it.

Jayde drew in a shuddering breath. Telling him would be one hell of a gamble. One that could cost lives if her gut was wrong. And it would most certainly cost her her job, right or wrong. But at this instant she didn't care about her career. Before she'd met David, her job had been her life, her colleagues had been her family, and a sense of duty to her country had been her sole driving force.

But this man had sneaked in when her guard was down, and he'd changed her in some profound way. He'd put the missing part of her soul back into her heart. And life was no longer simple.

Deceit or truth? The choice hung over her head like a sword of Damocles. Her mouth went bone dry. She tried to swallow.

His fingers tightened painfully around her wrist. He was waiting for her response…for the thread to break and the sword to fall.

Tariq waited until he was absolutely certain she'd hung up. Then he clicked the receiver carefully back into place. His hand trembled. Perspiration pricked along his top lip. He swiped it away. He'd been exposed. This was far worse than he could have contemplated. He had to think fast. He had to move fast.

David's fingers squeezed her wrist, and rage circled his heart like the winds of a terrible storm. He'd been betrayed by a woman he desperately wanted to believe in. A woman who'd made him dream once again of a future.

He was an idiot. He should have listened to Tariq. Instead he'd fallen into a trap as old as time. He had little doubt after hearing her on the phone that she was some kind of spy.

The question now was simply, who was she spying for?

She stared up at him with her huge innocent green eyes. But this time he knew they were a lie. "Who was on that phone?" he snarled.

"David, I…I'm…I'm not the person in that passport. I…I'm not married."

A crazy wave of relief swooped through David's stomach so fast he almost threw up. *She wasn't married.* But the sensation bottomed out instantly. He tightened his grip, yanked her closer. And as he did, his nostrils flared in reflex at the scent of her. In spite of himself, his loins stirred involuntarily. Her body was so close to his he could feel her quick nervous breaths against his lips. His blood began to heat.

A dangerous cocktail of adrenaline, rage and furious desire began to spurt through his veins. A dark and primal voice whispered through him that she was fair game now. She didn't belong to another man. And she sure as hell wasn't the vulnerable amnesiac. He need feel no guilt, no shame in taking her now. Right here, on his desk. Hard and fast. His breathing quickened. His blood boiled with rage and lust. His eyes bored into hers.

But instead of challenge, instead of the latent confidence he was used to seeing in those bewitching eyes, a look of uncertainty…and of fear stared back up at him.

It totally threw him.

"Who the hell *are* you then?" he demanded, his voice hard and strange to his own ears.

She sucked in a shaky breath. "David, you have to understand, the *only* reason I'm going to tell you this is because I believe in you. You *have* to understand that."

The desperation in her tone, the insecurity in her eyes set him on edge. "What are you talking about?"

"What I'm going to tell you cannot go beyond these walls. Can you promise me that? Can I trust you, David?"

He could feel her pulse racing wildly under the pressure of his fingers.

"Trust?" He snorted. "Who are you to talk of trust?"

"My name is Jayde Ashton. I'm an agent for the British government."

Anger and an unexpected jolt of sharp pain pierced his chest. He grabbed her jaw with his free hand, jerked her face up to his. She winced in pain.

"What in hell do you want from me, *Jayde Ashton?* Did you get what you came for? Was I a nice, easy lay? Will it please the British government?"

"Don't do this David—"

"Don't do what? Pretend I didn't fall for a professional? Pretend I wasn't taken by your lying sinful eyes?" He shoved her brutally away from himself. "You're a spy!" He spat the words out in disgust. He raised a finger, aimed it at her face. "Tell me what you came for, then get the hell off my island!"

Shock, hurt, ghosted her features then was gone. She steeled her jaw, took a deep breath. "I'm going to give it to you straight, David. I owe you that much."

"You sure as hell do."

"If you are guilty, you will kill me for this." She straightened her spine, squared her shoulders. "*That* is the measure of my trust in you, David. I am prepared to tell you the truth. I am prepared to tell you what I am doing here because… because I just believe—" her voice caught "—I believe in you. With my heart. And if I'm wrong, I don't care. I don't care if I die." Her eyes glistened with hot emotion. "Because…I have nothing I want to go back for. Not anymore."

A spasm of shock quirked through him. *Him, kill her? Was she crazy?* His anger shifted. Confusion swirled through him. Then he clenched his teeth. This was probably just another game, another ploy.

"If I am guilty of what?" he demanded.

"I work for MI-6, the British secret service—"

"I know what MI-6 is," he snapped.

She swallowed. "My partner and I were sent to set up a perimeter surveillance system of your island—"

"Why?" he interrupted. "Why me?"

"You're a person of interest to the British Government."

"And *that's* why?"

"No." She cleared her throat. "Two months ago the U.S. National Security Agency picked up intelligence that led to the U.S. interception of a yellowcake uranium shipment from Libya to Korea. It was a rare kind of uranium, David. The kind that made headlines two years ago, the kind being used in cutting-edge nuclear technology."

His chest tightened. He knew exactly what kind of uranium she was talking about. It came from only a few mines in the world. He owned two of them.

"It came from *your* mines, David. It was being shipped to Korea by the Falal in return for sophisticated centrifuges and other nuclear-weapons hardware and technology. What the U.S. discovered is only a small portion of what is coming from your mines. The rest is going straight to the Falal and the Falal is enriching your uranium and using the Korean hardware to manufacture nuclear weapons for Libya. Falal, David, is a covert arm of the Libyan Government."

David's heart kicked against his rib cage. He said nothing. He felt sick. This couldn't be true.

"The U.S. also learned that illegal oil shipments from Rashid mines were making their way onto the black market and that the funds generated from them were going to finance the Falal. Because it's your company and because you are a British citizen, U.S. intelligence alerted MI-6. The agencies are cooperating. On the surface Libya had abandoned its nuclear-weapons program. But now we have proof the Falal has simply taken it underground. It still exists, and your mines are fueling it."

David felt the blood drain from his head. "It cannot be true."

"It *is* true."

"It can't be. I'd know about it. Or…or Tariq would. It couldn't be done without at least one of us being aware."

"Yes," she said, watching him intently.

He reeled at the implication. "You're trying to tell me my own brother knows about this!"

"Yes."

"No!" He slammed his fist onto the desk. "It's a lie!"

"David, Tariq was seen at the Falal base in southern Libya two days ago." She hesitated. "The U.S. has an undercover operative at that base. He has evidence that Tariq belongs to the Falal. He also has proof that the Falal is funding the rebels in Azar…the rebels you have been fighting."

His vision narrowed and his world spun. "You're telling me that my brother is a traitor not only to his family, but a traitor to his whole country. And that I'm not fighting a small group of Azarian dissidents but I am fighting Libya itself?" He paced the room angrily, raked his hands through his hair, halted, glared at her. "Why should I believe you? You are a liar!"

"Because I care about what happens to you and Kamilah."

"Bull!"

"David, you *have* to trust me."

He felt himself beginning to shake with bottled rage. "You faked an accident to get into my home, you faked amnesia, you insinuated yourself into my daughter's life to get to me. You…you *slept* with me. You are the worst kind of liar…and now you accuse my brother and you want *my* trust?"

She took a step toward him, her eyes burning with desperate urgency. "The accident, David, the amnesia, that was all real."

He stormed over to the door, unlocked it, swung it open. "Get out! Get out of my life! Get off my island!"

Jayde had pushed him too far. But she stood her ground. She had to see this through. She had to ensure the information she'd divulged stayed with him and him alone. "I can help you, David."

His eyes literally sparked with rage. Fury came off him in hot waves. He seemed to swell in size with the power of his anger. He was an awesome and frightening sight, and there was no doubt in her mind David Rashid was a man who could be driven to kill with his bare hands.

"Leave!" He pointed to the door, his voice quavering with rage.

Jayde made her way slowly toward the door, her mind racing for a way out. But as she reached the archway, a terrible scream echoed through the palace corridors. Then another. And another. Coming toward them. Both she and David froze at the awful sound.

They could hear footsteps. Someone running, stumbling. Gasping for breath.

Fayha' lurched around the corner and collapsed against the wall. She was pale as a ghost, her eyes as big as black saucers. Her scarf had been yanked back, leaving her hair uncovered. Her dress was torn and stained with dirt. She opened her mouth. But the only sound that came out was a coarse rasp. Her knees buckled under her and she began to slip down the wall.

David lunged forward, caught her. "Fayha', what is it?"

"Allah forgive me…forgive me."

The first thing David did was pull the scarf back up over his housekeeper's hair. The gesture moved Jayde deeply. David knew how important it was to a Muslim woman to keep her hair covered. The gesture also showed a respect for his housekeeper, respect he no longer had for her and would never have again.

He spoke gently. "Take it easy, Fayha'. Tell me what's wrong."

"Sh…she…she's gone."

"*Who*, Fayha'? *Who* has gone?"

"Kamilah."

David's body went rock still. "What?"

"He…he took her."

"Who?" he barked.

"Mr. Tariq…he…he took her in the helicopter."

David didn't move. Time stretched thick. Then his head turned, very slowly, and his eyes lifted to meet Jayde's. In them Jayde could see the harsh truth of his brother's betrayal beginning to sink in. His whole face began to change as she watched. She saw darkness bleed into the sharp blue of his eyes. His brows lowered, his mouth flattened, his features sharpened. The muscle in his jaw pumped wildly. And she was held prisoner by the intensity of the transformation.

Fayha' thrust a crumpled wad of paper at David. "He…he gave me a note."

David jerked his attention back to Fayha', grabbed the paper, stood up, read it.

And his face went white.

Chapter 12

David read the note a second time. The words had no less impact. It was written in Arabic, in Tariq's unmistakable scrawl. His daughter had been kidnapped.

By his own brother.

He couldn't get his brain around the fact. It didn't make sense. He read the note a third time.

"If you want to get Kamilah back alive you will do everything I say. Expect my call by midnight. Follow orders to the last detail."

This was not possible! How could his brother do this to Kamilah? Even if what Jayde Ashton had said about Tariq was true, surely he would not harm Kamilah, his own niece, Aisha's child? Tariq knew just how vulnerable Kamilah was, how she'd suffered since the death of her mother. This would utterly destroy her. How could he use her like this? Why? What could he possibly want?

David tried to swallow the orb of anguish ballooning in his throat. His fists balled, his jaw clenched, his vision blurred. He hadn't been there for her. He'd been distracted by a woman.

Once again he had failed his daughter.

Rage began to boil deep inside him, surging violently up through his body, his blood. He could feel himself begin to vibrate against the sheer steaming power of it. And he knew he was veering dangerously close to the outer limits of his control.

But he couldn't afford to lose it. He brutally clubbed his emotions back into submission. He sucked in a deep breath, willed the fire of his fury to flatten out into a deadly cold and laser-sharp focus. He had to think fast. Clearly. He needed to be both restrained and ruthless. And he had to move with lightning swiftness.

First he had to contact his insurance company in London. He had kidnap and ransom cover with Sudderby's. They would immediately dispatch Gio Moriati, a trained negotiator, the world's best. And he had to summon Jacques Sauvage to his island immediately. Sauvage would put together a tactical team and the tracing equipment needed to track Tariq's call. If he moved fast enough, they could all be in place and ready for that call by midnight. If the negotiating failed, Sauvage's team would be ready to go in and retrieve his daughter. And David would go with them.

He sucked in another slow, deep breath, filling his chest to capacity, filling his body with control. He exhaled slowly. He ignored the MI-6 agent watching him. He took Fayha''s arm, led her to a chair in his office and sat her down. "Tell me exactly what happened, step by step."

Fayha' was still shaking violently. "Mr. Ta-Tariq was on the phone in the great room. I…I came in to see what dusting needed to be done and I…I saw him there."

"Did you hear him talk on the phone?"

Fayha' shook her head. "No. He was just listening. Then he put the receiver down and…and then…he saw me. His eyes were strange. He asked where Kamilah was. I…I told him she was in the kitchen helping with the dinner." Fayha' began to choke on her own sobs. "She likes to do that, you know… she's such a good child. I…I told him where to find her. I…"

David took her hand. "Fayha', it's not your fault. I need you to think clearly now, we all need to. What happened next?"

She sniffed, smudged the tears from her face. "I followed him. I wasn't sure why he wanted to see Kamilah." Another sob shuddered through her body. "He…he took her to the helicopter. I…I couldn't stop him in time. I tried. He…he was too strong. He threw me to the ground. I…I didn't have time to get help."

"Thank you, Fayha'. You did what you could. Go clean up," he said. "I'll have Dr. Watson brought in. He'll give you something to help calm you down when he arrives."

David turned to the woman at his side, the stranger he thought he'd known so intimately. Her eyes were wide and her skin was white with shock at the news of Kamilah's kidnapping.

But *her* feelings didn't touch him. They would never touch him again. He never wanted to see her again. But right at this instant he needed her on his side. He needed every ally he could possibly think of. Working with the woman who betrayed him might help save his baby. He wasn't going to miss a single possible play. He'd do anything in this world to bring his Kamilah home safe.

He glared at her. "Tariq must have heard you on the phone."

She swallowed. "I know. I have to call in. If Tariq heard me it means the American agent in Libya has been compromised." Her voice was small. "He will be killed if they find him."

He stared at her beautiful face, at the raw pain and regret

in her eyes. And his heart sent a ripple through him. He quashed it instantly. This woman had done more than betray him. Because of her actions, the most precious jewel in his life had been taken from him. He could never forgive her that. He had to hold on to anger, channel the energy of his emotion into hate, revulsion. It was the only way he would be able to keep functioning.

"I want all the information your people have gathered on Tariq," he told her, his voice cold. "And I want whatever intelligence you have on the Libyan Falal, their southern base, the black market exchanges, details of the Falal connection with the Azar rebels. You will deliver this to the Force du Sable tactical team in the great dining hall as soon as you have assembled it. We need the information by midnight. Use my phone."

She said nothing. She'd lost her fight. She was no longer challenging him. It was as if a part of her had died. It made something sink inside David. Again he shoved it brutally away. He watched her move woodenly over to his desk and pick up the phone.

Guilt weighed heavily on Jayde's shoulders. In allowing herself to open emotionally to David, in falling for him, she had allowed him to become her one weakness, the chink in her armor. And in trying to help David, in being honest with him, in being true to herself in the only way she possibly could, she'd ended up putting his daughter in jeopardy, and now possibly a colleague.

She'd done what she had for all the right reasons. She could not have behaved otherwise. And everything had gone wrong. There was no reward for being true. There was no justice in this world. This was life. Not a fairy tale. And life was cruel.

She swallowed against the dryness in her throat. She loved

that child. She understood her. And now she knew why. It was because she had been there. She knew what it was like to lose someone you loved to the sea, what it could do to your soul, how it could kill a part of who you were, and how it could destroy a family. She'd promised Kamilah a happy ending. A fairy-tale ending…

Jayde gritted her teeth suddenly. *By God she was going to do it!* She was going to do whatever it took to deliver that happy ending to little Kamilah, or she would die trying. She grabbed the phone and punched in Lancaster's number for the second time that day.

She knew that when she'd finished telling Lancaster what she'd done, she would be without a job.

She'd lost everything. First her memory, then her heart, then the man who'd stolen her heart. Now she'd lost his child and it would cost her career.

But she was not going down without a fight. She would not let Kamilah and her father down again. This was her fault. And she was prepared to do whatever it took to make it right.

By the time Jayde made her way to the dining hall it was eleven o'clock and dark, with a waning crescent moon low in the sky. She'd gathered her wits and was now sharply focused on the task that lay ahead.

Lancaster had seen the need to keep her on the job—for now. He made no bones about the fact he would deal with her later. He and O'Reilly had delivered the bag of gear and information she'd requested from them earlier in the afternoon. They'd flown it in by chopper and they were now on standby in Khartoum in case she needed additional manpower. Lancaster had also told her the American undercover agent was safe in Azar. He'd left Libya with a group of dissidents under the guise of picking up another uranium shipment. His cover was still tight. But most of all, he was still alive.

But it did little to ease Jayde's conscience. She would rest only when Kamilah was safe and back in the arms of her father.

She strode down the palace corridor dressed in light cargo pants, an olive-green T-shirt and army boots. Her hair was tied in a neat braid that hung down the center of her back. She'd pulled herself together and she meant business. She knew this was her last mission with MI-6, the organization that had been family to her for most of her adult life. And she was going to make it count.

She pushed open the double doors, entered the dining hall and did a double take. The grand hall had been turned into a war room in the space of hours. There were maps tacked onto the wall and spread over the table. Electronic equipment, computer monitors and wires covered another table. The telephone was connected to a microphone, to speakers, and linked into the computer equipment. Lights blazed brightly over the whole affair.

It was a far cry from the candlelit atmosphere she'd shared only hours ago with Tariq and David at this very table. She had to hand it to David, when he went into warrior mode, he sure as hell moved fast.

David was in deep conversation with three men gathered around the far end of the long table. One of them was the most powerful-looking black man she'd ever laid eyes on: bald head, gleaming ebony skin and bone structure worthy of an ancient gladiator. The other two were Caucasian, and equally potent in build. Both were deeply tanned. One had dark hair, another was sandy blond.

They looked up in unison as she approached. Each wore an expression of business. David's mouth flattened at the sight of her. He didn't bother to introduce her.

She nodded at the men, dumped her pack on the table. "I'm agent Jayde Ashton," she said. "MI-6."

The dark-haired man at the head of the table stood to a towering height. His icy silver eyes appraised her with cool and calculated concentration.

Jayde knew his face instantly. It was unmistakable. All hard angles with a scar that sliced from the corner of his left eye to the base of his sharp jaw. It was a ruthless and rugged face, one that had graced many a paramilitary magazine. It was the face of a man who had piqued the attention of the world's governments with the way he'd single-handedly challenged the international community's perception of mercenaries and armies for hire. He was the legendary Jacques Sauvage, the formidable head of the notorious Force du Sable. The founder of the first private military operation to lobby for United Nations sanction. The man giving soldiers of fortune respectability.

In spite of herself she felt a prickle of awe run over her skin.

"Jacques Sauvage," he said, holding out a large, roughened hand. She held out her own. His grip was as powerful as he looked.

"And this is December." He motioned to the large black man at his side. December tipped his head and lowered his eyes in sullen greeting.

"And this is Gio Moriati, K&R point man for Sudderby's of London."

Jayde nodded to each. She knew K&R stood for kidnap and ransom and that Moriati would thus be handling the negotiations with Tariq. But she suspected he would have little success. Tariq was not after money. He was after his brother's soul. And a country.

She sensed David's eyes on her. She turned to look at him and she felt color rise to her cheeks under his intense scrutiny. She held his gaze, but his features remained implacable, his eyes cold and hard. Like the men he'd assembled around him, David Rashid was in combat mode. These were the men he'd chosen to guide him into battle. These were the men he was relying on to help save his daughter from his own brother. They made a formidable team. And she was going to show them she was every bit as good as each one of them.

Jayde pulled out a chair and joined the men. She had less than an hour to table everything she had on Tariq, Falal, the Azar dissidents and the black market trades.

She methodically laid out her case, her eyes continually trying to read David's as she did. But he'd make one hell of a poker player. Nothing she said about his brother seemed to touch him. She felt as if she'd never known him, never even glimpsed the man she knew lived under that shell.

By the time the clock ticked down the final minutes to midnight, they had a preliminary battle plan drawn up. They assumed Tariq would hold Kamilah at a Falal base just over the Libyan border. It was an old French fortress in the Sahara desert with a sheer ridge of rock to the north. They would trace Tariq's call with state-of-the-art satellite technology. They needed to keep him talking for only thirty seconds to confirm his location.

They would hear out his demands, and Gio would try to get proof of life and keep negotiating as if in good faith. They would stretch the negotiations out as long as they could in order to buy time for Sauvage and a small team of crack paratroopers to mount an offensive from the north.

"He will not expect us to hit from within Libya's borders," said Sauvage. "They will be looking for us to the south, to Azar. We'll launch from here, in the Egyptian desert near the Libyan border." He jabbed his finger at the map. "We'll fly in at night, low, under Libyan radar. We will drop off here, behind this ridge just north of the fortress." He moved his finger over the map. "We will approach the fortress from this direction using the ridge as cover."

Jayde tried to place his accent as she listened to Sauvage speak. It was a rich and eclectic blend of French and South African with the hint of American drawl. She could not pinpoint his origin. No one could. He'd come out of the French Foreign Legion, a man with no past.

"Once we have our package," he said, "we will radio for pickup at this point just south of the fortress. We will make it over the Azar border and fly in to Al Abèche, this small settlement here." He poked his finger at a spot in the desert.

Jayde studied the map. Al Abèche was nothing but a name in the middle of miles and miles of Sahara sand.

Sauvage glanced up at David. "You will wait for us at Al Abèche."

"I'm going in with you."

"No," said Sauvage with the ease of one practiced at command. "I understand your need, David, but you must let me do my job. Kamilah will need you when we get to Al Abèche. But she will need me and my men to get her to that point. While you are in Al Abèche, you will remain in constant contact with Gio, who will stay here on Shendi. Tariq must at all times believe you are still here. *Ça va?*"

Jayde watched David's Adam's apple move as he tried to swallow. His eyes, however, remained emotionless. When he spoke, his voice was flat. "Understood," he said. And Jayde knew just how torn this man must be in spite of his stolid exterior. It made her heart ache.

"Bien," said Sauvage. "At the moment this is a bit of a mug's game until we know exactly what Tariq's demands are and where he is. We will adjust as needed."

David glanced at his watch. Jayde checked hers. One

minute to go until midnight. The air seemed suddenly thick. Time stretched, and silence hung ominously over them as they all waited for the phone to ring.

The door behind her swung open. Jayde almost leaped out of her skin at the sudden interruption. But it was only Farouk with tea. She let out a shaky breath as he set the tray on the far end of the table. She hadn't realized just how tense she was.

The phone rang.

For a nanosecond everyone froze. Then December moved instantly over to the tracing equipment, seated himself in front of a computer screen. He held up three fingers.

David nodded, waited until the third ring, picked the phone up. It clicked over to the speakers.

"Rashid," he said, the strength and power in his voice belying the angst that most certainly had to be chewing him up from the inside out.

"I have Kamilah."

David's body tensed visibly. His knuckles whitened as his hand tightened into fists. Jayde's heart squeezed. She held her breath. Sauvage watched. December tapped quietly at the computer keys.

"Do what I say if you want to see her alive." Tariq's rough voice echoed dissonantly through the speakers, bounced off the mosaic walls and drifted up to the glass dome above them. Jayde could see the sliver of the sickle moon shining down through the reds and oranges of the stained glass high above their heads.

Sauvage made a fast rolling motion with his finger, indicating to David that he must keep talking. David nodded. "Let me speak to her, Tariq."

"No. You will do as I say. Until then, you will have no contact."

The muscle in David's jaw jumped wildly. Jayde could see the veins in his forearms, his neck, popping out. He was visibly straining against violent impulse. But they all knew the plan was to stay steady, to stay in control, to calmly sound Tariq out, to hear his demands without antagonizing him and driving him to make an irrational move. This would set the stage for Gio to take over negotiations. David had to make it clear to Tariq that he would have to deal with Gio and Gio alone.

"What do you want, Tariq? Why are you doing this?"

He laughed, the sound harsh. "You know what I want. My views have never changed. We want what is ours. The oil fields, the mines, Azar, the desert."

"We?"

"Those of *pure* blood."

David flinched. Fire began to crackle in his eyes.

Sauvage rolled his finger.

David nodded. He cleared his throat. "You mean the Falal?"

"The people to whom the desert belongs. The people you and my father sold out to the Imperialist West."

David's fists clenched. Sauvage made another motion with his hand, telling him to go slow, take it easy, stay calm.

Jayde knew it had to be killing David.

"I have sold out to no one." His voice leashed his fury. But barely. "You speak the propaganda of Falal, Tariq. You are a fool. A puppet. Nothing but a means for Libya to take control of Azar's wealth, a wealth that belongs to *my* people."

Tariq cursed in coarse and guttural Arabic.

Sauvage held up his hand, motioning to David not to inflame Tariq further.

David sucked air deep into his lungs. Jayde could see him straining for control.

"Why take Kamilah? She is innocent. She is harmless. She cannot withstand this. It will destroy her. You know that."

He laughed. "It will destroy *you*."

And in that instant Jayde knew Tariq had no intention of ever returning Kamilah alive. They had to move in. And they had to make every second count. She caught Sauvage's eyes, then Gio's. And she could see they, too, had reached the same conclusion.

"You would not harm Kamilah! I cannot believe it. Not after what she went through with the death of her mother."

Tariq snorted, the sound ugly and harsh. It bounced around the cavernous hall mocking them from all angles. "*I* took Aisha's life. You and Kamilah were meant to die with her."

Jayde gasped. The blood drained instantly from David's face. He grabbed the back of a chair, steadied himself. All eyes were on him. The tension in the room was suddenly as thick as pea soup. But David didn't speak. He didn't blow his control. He simply waited for Tariq to continue. Jayde's heart bled for him. She got up, moved around the table and touched his arm. He pulled back.

"It was meant to look like an accident. And in the event of the death of your entire family, I was ready to mount a legal challenge to take control of Rashid International, to take back what my father denied me. Except you didn't die. And you restructured your company, changed your will to put in place a trust to ensure your plans in Azar would go ahead in the event of your death. Killing you was no longer an option, brother. So I found a new way."

David's grip on the chair tightened as the sheer scope of his brother's betrayal set in. Tariq had never stopped hating him. Not for an instant. He had killed Aisha. He had caused Kamilah untold pain. And he was prepared to do it again.

When David spoke, his voice was rough like gravel rolling through a metal pipe. "What must I do to get my daughter back?"

"You have exactly one week to withdraw *all* Force du Sable troops from Azar. If one soldier is left in the country, Kamilah will be executed."

Everyone looked up, exchanged glances. Withdrawing Force du Sable troops at this point would amount to a coup. The rebels would move in, and Azar would fall into the hands of the Falal. It would in effect be annexed by Libya, and the international community would be powerless to stop it. Everyone at the table knew that. And everyone knew that the ripple effects of the takeover would shift the balance of power not only in the Middle East but the world.

December shot his fist into the air in victory. He'd pinpointed Tariq's location. Sauvage jabbed a pin into the map marking the spot. They were right. He was at the old fortress.

"I want the country, David. Or I will take the life of your daughter. Your choice."

"There is no choice. I will have my daughter back!"

"Then show me you negotiate in good faith. I want the troops in Li'shal gone by nightfall tomorrow. The next day you will remove troops from Benghusi."

Fury glittered in David's eyes. "Give your demands to Gio Moriati," he snapped. "He is my negotiator. From here on, his voice is mine. And may God save your soul, brother. Because I plan to send you to hell!"

David stormed from the room.

Jayde found David down at the cove, where he'd ordered a bonfire lit to keep vigil for Kamilah. It was the same beach Jayde had washed up on. It was where Kamilah herself had kept a vigil for her mother, waiting for a mermaid to come from the sea.

David stood in his daughter's place now, staring out over the black swells, straining to reach out to his child in every desperate way he could.

Jayde could almost feel the man's mind calling out over the waters. Calling over the ocean, across the desert sands, to where his Kamilah waited for him. And Jayde knew that the most difficult thing for David to face right now had to be the waiting. He was a man of action. And this must be killing him.

He didn't hear her approach. The roar and spit of the bonfire drowned even the sound of small waves on the shore. And his mind was focused outward, on his daughter.

"David?"

He jolted, spun around. His eyes shot to hers, then he turned abruptly away from her to face the sea.

But in that brief instant, highlighted by the orange light of the flames, she'd seen the rawness in his eyes. It grabbed her by the throat, tore at her insides.

"I'm going with you to Al Abèche," she said.

He didn't move a muscle, didn't look at her. "No."

"I have to."

"I don't want you there."

"I can help you."

"No."

"David, look at me, listen to me, I can help Kamilah when they bring her out. I know as well as you do how fragile she is. And you know as well as I do how she opened up to me, how she needed *me* to be able to talk. Who knows how she will have regressed, what this trauma will have done to her. She will need me there, David." Jayde hesitated. "She will need *both* of us there. *Together*. It will make her strong to see us as a unit. After that I swear I will get out of your life. You'll never have to look at me again."

His eyes flashed to hers, held. Jayde swallowed. The intensity she saw in his features put her on edge. But she could also see she'd found a chink in his armor.

"Why would she need to see us together?" His voice was cracked. He was a caged and wounded tiger that could strike a lethal blow in an instant. She had to tread carefully.

"It's part of her fantasy to see us together," Jayde said softly. "I know how her mind works."

"How in hell would *you* know how her mind works?" he snapped.

"Because I've been there, David. I've been through what Kamilah went through. I was the same age when it happened."

Something shifted in his eyes. But he said nothing.

"I lost my sister and my father to the sea, David. I know what that can do to a child, a family."

He stared at her, the shadows of flame and night dancing across the angles of his face. She knew she'd snagged something in him. But he was too angry to ask about what it was she'd been through.

So she pressed further. "Kamilah's fantasy is to see the mermaid and the prince find a happy ending, David. Not the ending she's read over and over again in Andersen's tale where the mermaid sacrifices herself. She has a dream of seeing us together."

"That's preposterous. It'll never happen."

"I don't doubt it. But seeing the two us together will give her a measure of faith that could end up pulling her through the initial days after her capture. She needs stability, David."

He glared at her. "Damn you! You're the one who filled her head with this fantasy nonsense. I should've put a stop to it right away."

She held his eyes. "No. It wasn't me who put the fantasy in her mind. It was there already. I'm just the one she opened up to."

"You fueled it! You gave it form. You were a bloody curse brought in with that wretched storm. This is all your fault."

Her frustration piqued. Her fists clenched at her side and her nails bit into her palms. "This is *not* my fault. This is Tariq's fault. I refuse to shoulder the blame for his actions. Yes, at first I felt responsible. But not now. Yes, my actions have resulted in disastrous consequences. But I picked up that phone and called in because I couldn't lie to you, David. I picked it up because I cared, dammit."

Shock jolted through his body. His eyes widened. She could see the stark question in them.

"That's right. *I care.* For you. For Kamilah. For everything that is good and true and honest in this world. I lost my mind and I fell for you, David. And by God I'm sorry I did. Because look where it got us. But the reason we're here is precisely because I could never knowingly lie to you. And I swear on my life my amnesia was real. I swear I never meant to hurt you or Kamilah. When my memory returned, when I realized what was happening, I picked up that damn phone in your office to tell my handler I wouldn't, *couldn't* finish the job."

His features shifted. She was getting through to him. "Whether you like it or not, I'm going with you to Al Abèche. I'm going to do everything in my mortal power to make this right."

"Jayde—"

"I have nothing else to live for, David." Her voice wavered. "I've lost everything since washing up on your bloody island. Don't take this away from me, too."

Chapter 13

He clenched his jaw, biting in emotion. Hot orange sparks exploded into the black night and leaped above the flames of the bonfire. His heart hammered in his chest. He stared at her. What did she mean she had nothing left to live for? Was this all just another lie?

Not by the naked anguish in her eyes. But then, she was a trained agent, wasn't she? It was her job to wear fake emotions, to insinuate herself into peoples lives…into their very souls.

She took a step closer to him. His body braced. His fists clenched. He didn't trust himself this close to her. He didn't trust what was raging through his blood.

"You've *got* to believe me, David. The amnesia was real."

Could it be the truth? It sure as hell had looked real to him. Watson had said she could be faking. But he'd also said she may have dissociated from her identity to protect herself from some trauma, and that when her memories did come back she might go through great pain reliving them. Was she feeling that pain now? Was that what he could see shimmering in her eyes?

Guilt stabbed sharply. Deep down he ached to reach out, to touch her, to comfort. But he couldn't bring himself to crack out of the armor he'd barricaded himself behind. He could not bring himself to ask about her past, to ask about the sister and father she lost to the sea. He didn't want to know any more, to feel any more. He wanted to shut her out. He wanted to hate her.

So he turned away from her.

"David," she said softly. "Please don't hate me for this. The only mistake I made was to fall for you. I regret it deeply. It's the biggest mistake I've made in my entire adult life. But you have to understand, everything that has happened over the last hours relates directly back to that one fatal error. And if you look at it that way, you too must shoulder your share of the blame." She sucked in a shaky breath. "This is also your fault, David. You made it impossible for me not to…to love you."

His breath caught sharply in his throat. He clenched his teeth. His head pounded wildly. But he refused to look at her. *Love?* His heart twisted. He tried to breathe.

She was right. It *had* all been a terrible mistake. One that belonged to him as much as to her. The mistake had been not resisting the impossibly powerful force of attraction that simmered between them.

He turned, very slowly. And swallowed. Because it was still there. That force still simmered. It burned fiercer than ever. He only had to look into those emerald eyes to feel the heat of it smouldering deep down in his core. And right at this moment he couldn't hold on to the hatred he was so desperately trying to direct toward her. In its place was an overpowering urge to grab her and to squeeze her so tight she could barely breathe. He wanted to hold her so close she'd feel his pain

right through her skin. He wanted to share the feelings that
boiled inside him, the anger and anguish of a betrayed brother,
of a man who still was being rendered incapable of resisting
the force of the enigmatic woman in front of him, of a father
who'd lost his child.

He'd been through a meat grinder. But, hell, so had she.
And she was right. Kamilah would need her. No matter what
he thought about it, his child had formed a deep bond with
this woman.

"I'm coming to Al Abèche, David, whether you like it or
not," she insisted. "I'll be ready by first light."

He brushed her statement aside. "What happened…to your
family?" He wanted to know. Needed to know.

Her lip twitched. But her eyes held his.

"Tell me…Jayde." He used her name for the first time, and
it stuck in his throat on the way out. "What happened?"

She shivered slightly, in spite of the warm night air. "When
I was six…I was in a boating accident off the coast of Cornwall. I…I watched my sister…my twin…"

"Twin?"

"Yes. Identical twin. Her name was Amber. I…I watched
the sea swallow them. Amber and my father." Her eyes were
bright with emotion but her voice was flat. "My dad saved me
first. He went back for Amber but he…they never made it. My
mother wasn't with us that day, but it destroyed her anyway.
She killed herself two years later. That's…that's when I had
my first amnesia episode. When I was eight. After I found my
mother. I lost two whole years, just blanked out, forgot who
I was."

An odd ball of pain expanded in his chest. He knew just
what it was like to watch someone you loved being sucked
down by the waves. "Is that why you think you connected with
Kamilah like you did?"

"Even with my amnesia, a part of me deep down inside must have sensed the similarity of our pasts. I…I didn't want to see the two of you destroyed by this, David. I…" She looked away quickly, trying to hide the glimmering tear that escaped her eye. "I think that by trying to help you and Kamilah I must have subconsciously been trying to fix my own wretched past. I…I just wanted to put it all right."

She sniffed and angrily smudged the trail of tears shining on her cheeks, then gave a soft, derisive laugh. "I…I never cry, you know."

He ached to hold her.

She sniffed again, rubbed her nose and took in a deep, shuddering breath. Then she pulled her shoulders back, lifted her chin. "That's why I'm going to Al Abèche, David. I have to make it right."

He studied her in silence, the fire crackling. In spite of what she had done, he could only admire her strength, her determination, her desire to set things right. "It will not be easy," he said finally.

"I can handle it."

"The Sahara respects no man…or woman," he warned.

"I said I can handle it."

"We will fly into Tabara, the capital. But from there we will have to travel three days and nights by camel in order not to arouse suspicion. Any air or vehicle traffic into Al Abèche will alert Falal or rebel informants."

"I know."

"You ever ridden a camel?"

"I can ride camels. I can speak Arabic. I've worked in Algiers and in Egypt—"

"Right," he snapped. "How could I forget? You're a trained agent."

"Exactly," she retorted. "That's why you need me."

She spun on the heels of her army boots and stomped over the sand and up to the path that led back to his castle. "I'll be ready at dawn," she called out of the dark.

David blew out the pent-up air in his chest and turned to stare back out over the ocean. He felt as if he'd been shoved right up to the very edge of his existence. And beyond was wilderness. Uncharted territory. Tomorrow he would be over the ocean, in that wilderness, in the blistering heat of the desert under a wild, open sky. Alone with Jayde. With no place to hide from each other. He knew they would both be stripped naked by the blistering winds and harsh environment they would have to traverse to reach his child.

Summer in the Sahara held no mercy.

Jayde packed her backpack with grim determination. It was nearly three in the morning, but sleep eluded her. She needed to keep moving. She carefully checked through the supplies Lancaster had shipped to her. Among them she had a military issue compass, knife, binoculars, night-vision gear, pencil flares, sat-phone and cash. She'd also asked for some more serious hardware, and Lancaster had obliged by sending her some small but highly effective weaponry that included thin bricks of malleable plastic explosives along with strips of chemical reactant. He'd also thrown in chemical darts that would render a victim paralytic for several hours, and a small grenade launcher that could be fitted to her rifle. The launcher could be used to deliver an array of both lethal and less-than-lethal munitions including teargas rounds, smoke, signal flares and revolutionary electromagnetic pulse grenades.

Jayde studied the e-grenades. They'd only just come through highly secretive British military trials. They were hand-held versions of the bigger electromagnetic bombs the army now had in its arsenal.

Jayde knew the big electromagnetic pulse bombs could overwhelm the electrical circuitry of an entire city with an intense electromagnetic blast. Instead of simply cutting off power, an e-bomb literally overloaded and fried everything that used electricity. A big enough e-bomb could thrust an entire city back two hundred years or cripple a military unit. These mini versions in her hand would delivery enough power to knock out the communications and security capability of the Falal fortress. Not that she'd need them. That was going to be Sauvage's job. But she was now prepared for any eventuality. And that's the way she liked things.

"Thank you, Lancaster," Jayde whispered as she packed them carefully with the rest of her gear. She checked her watch. In a few hours they'd be on their way.

She prayed Tariq hadn't harmed Kamilah yet. She wasn't going to even entertain the negative. They were going to get her out. Safe. And to prove it, she was going to pack a bag for Kamilah. She would need some fresh clothes once they'd extracted her. And maybe something familiar and comforting from home.

Jayde made her way down the corridors to Kamilah's room. The palace was ablaze with lights even at this hour. David had lit up his castle like a beacon. He was letting nothing rest.

Jayde opened the door to Kamilah's room, and the instant she saw the unruffled covers on the little girl's bed, agony clawed at her heart. Where was Kamilah sleeping tonight? How had she reacted to the monstrous change in her uncle? Was there anyone with her to comfort her when she cried?

Jayde set the small bag she'd brought from her own room onto the bed and began going through the closets and drawers sorting out some clothes for Kamilah. She folded them neatly and packed them into the bag with military precision.

Some training died hard, she thought ruefully. Well, she might need that training to help get this child back.

Then she caught sight of the small teddy bear lying on Kamilah's pillow. Jayde hesitated, picked it up and buried her nose in the soft fur. It smelled so innocent. Like sunshine. Like a kitten or puppy…like Kamilah's hair. Emotion stabbed behind her eyes and ballooned in her throat. She swallowed it down. She tucked the teddy into the bag and began to zip it up, but something peeking out from under the white ruffles of the pillow sham caught her eye. Jayde reached for it. She pulled out a leather-bound book. *The Little Mermaid.*

She fingered the embossed gold lettering. This time she couldn't swallow the emotion away. It spilled hot and furious down her cheeks, and her chest jerked with a powerful sob. "Hold strong, baby," she whispered clutching the book to her heart. "We're coming…we're coming to get you. We're not going to let you down."

Jayde Ashton swiped away her tears. This crying business was the pits. She had a sneaking suspicion that this new part of herself wasn't going to squeeze back into any bottle now that it was out. She turned to search for a scarf or piece of fabric in which to wrap the book…and froze.

He stood in the doorway. Watching her. A dark and silent specter, a strange and unreadable look in his dark features.

"David?"

He stared at the book in her hands, then he looked up into her eyes. He held her gaze, and a current of connection surged between them. In that instant they were bound. She knew it. He knew it. They were in this together. They were joined by a fierce drive to save this child. And the very thing that united them was what also tore them apart.

Jayde swallowed against the sheer oscillating power of it. "I…I was just gathering a few things for Kamilah."

His eyes shifted to the small bag on the bed. Jayde saw his throat work, the muscle pulse rapidly at the base of his jaw. He nodded. Then he spun on his heels, and she heard the clack of his boots on stone as he marched down the corridor.

She let out a shaky breath. Through the window, dawn was already a peach hint on the distant horizon.

They had to get going.

Heat lay thick like treacle over the dusty desert capital of Tabara, and the air shimmered like a mirage above the ancient buildings. The sand was everywhere. Constantly moving, propelled by the kinetics of wind and gravity. The Sahara literally drifted along the streets, blowing into lobbies of crumbling hotels, frosting traffic lights and piling in drifts in alley corners and ancient doorways. It was so fine in texture it made table salt look coarse by comparison.

After being here only a few hours Jayde had simply given up trying to resist it. It was in her clothes, her hair, her eyelashes, under her fingernails, in her mouth. And the heat slowed her every movement, making her feel sluggish.

David had left her in a small earth-brick hut on the crumbling outskirts of the city where thin goats roamed and children played in ragged clothes. He'd gone to the bustling market in the city center to buy camels and grain.

Her job was to pack the food supplies they'd bought as soon as they'd arrived and to have the bags ready to load onto the camels.

Jayde secured the rice, tins of sardines and dates in the final bag and then she lugged everything outside to wait for David. He wanted to have their camels watered by the evening and he wanted to be gone by nightfall when the oppressive air cooled a little. They would travel through the night. The next day would be tougher because they would continue their trek through the blistering midday heat of the Saharan summer, stopping only briefly to feed and water the camels before pressing on again.

Their goal was to stay low-key and under the radar so as not to alert rebel spies. Jayde was dressed in the manner of an Azarian camel herder, with a loose-fitting muslin shirt that hung to her calves and covered her arms. Under it she wore light muslin pants. On her feet she wore battered old flip-flops and a head cloth hid her hair.

She shaded her eyes and squinted into the haze. The sun was already beginning to dip down toward the distant desert horizon but there was still no sign of David. Jayde felt her jaw beginning to tense. From this last ring of small earth houses that fringed the northern outskirts of Tabara, the Sahara stretched like an undulating ocean in tones of yellow, ochre, cream and amber as far as her eye could see. She felt as if she was standing on the very edge of civilization.

As they trekked into that sea of sand, moving north to Al Abèche, toward Libya, she and David would enter the most arid and hostile region of the Sahara, where moisture was virtually nonexistent and dunes reached four hundred feet and more in height. Al Abèche was a town that hung onto a thread of life in that desiccated wasteland, and they would travel an old Bedouin route to get there.

It was tough for Jayde to get her head around the fact that it would take three days to reach their destination while the urgency of the situation was so acute. But as Sauvage had said, Tariq's demands had afforded them the luxury of time to get it right. *"We have only one shot and we must make it a clean one,"* he'd said. And traveling into Al Abèche any other way would most certainly alert any informants or rebels in the area. They had to try and blend in as best they could. It was that or stay on Shendi and wait. And neither she nor David were the waiting sort.

And while she and David traversed the desert, Sauvage would gather his team in Egypt and Gio would keep the lines of negotiation open with Tariq.

Jayde heard a sound to her right. She swung around. It was David. She sucked in a breath of relief. He was striding toward her, camel stick in hand, three camels in tow. Two were a creamy white, the other one red. He'd already saddled them. Two goatskin water bags, or *guerbas,* were strapped to one. The others were loaded with grain. From one dangled a blackened cooking pot and an old kettle.

"What took you so long?" she called out to him.

"Camel shortage at the market," he called back. "They had mostly calves or untrained bulls that turn into frothing demonic man killers if the mating urge hits." He jerked his head toward the three beasts in tow. "Found these three geldings at the butcher's yard. I reckon they have some life in them yet."

David grinned as he neared, his teeth a slash of stark white against his skin, which was already darkening from the fierce desert sun. It sent a crazy spurt of desire through her. She hadn't seen him smile since they'd made love on his yacht.

He was dressed in similar garb to hers, but he had his *jambiya* thrust through a tie at his waist. But even in peasant dress he was regal. He looked like the sheik, the true leader that he was. And like this crumbling and once-majestic desert city of Tabara, he had one foot in an ancient world, another in a new one. If anyone was to build a bridge between the two ways of life, this was the man. Seeing him like this, she could suddenly understand him in a profound way. She could almost feel the spirit that drove him. And it only deepened what she felt for him already.

She brushed the sensation aside. She couldn't afford to feel anything. Because once they rescued Kamilah, he and his daughter would walk away from her. It would be over. She knew that. He hated her for her betrayal. He blamed her for this tragedy. And the only reason he'd brought her with him now was for the sake of his child.

But she couldn't take her eyes from him. She was entranced by his enigmatic presence, the way he moved in this environment with the elegance and ease of a man born to the sands of the Sahara. Right now there wasn't a trace of Anglo-Saxon about him, apart from the unsettling blue of his eyes against his dark skin. The color was made even more striking as it picked up the indigo blue of the cotton head cloth he wore.

"What are you staring at?"

"You."

He grunted and handed her the head rope of the red camel. "You sure you can handle these creatures?"

"I am." She took the rope from his hand.

David watched, ready to leap to Jayde's aid.

She allowed the beast to sniff her, then she tugged on the head rope and expertly couched the animal. He raised a brow in surprise. This woman was something else. She acted like a desert native.

His admiration flattened almost immediately. That's exactly what she was trained to do. To insinuate herself into situations and blend in like a native. She'd been trained to deceive, and because of this very skill he was admiring now, she'd been chosen by a government agency to betray him.

He felt his jaw clench. He watched Jayde proceed to lug her big bag over to the couched animal. She hefted it up and began to meticulously secure it to the saddle horn. It looked heavy, cumbersome. "What's in there?" David asked, watching carefully as she tied the knots, making sure he wouldn't have to recheck them once she was done.

"Nothing much."

"Put it on the other camel, the one for the supplies."

"No." she simply. "I need to keep this one with me."

"Why?"

She shot him an odd look. "It's my personal bag."

He frowned, watching as she secured a second bag to the camel. A much smaller one. His chest constricted. It was the little bag with Kamilah's things. His hand shot out in reflex. "I'll take that one."

Her eyes flashed to his. She hesitated. "Sure." She handed it to him. Their fingers brushed as he took the bag from her. The electricity of the touch stilled them both. Their eyes locked. And neither needed words to share what was going on their minds. This little bag was a symbol of why they were both here in the desert. And the magnitude of what still lay ahead hung heavy between them.

They worked in silence to load the rest of the bags. Then David watched again to make certain Jayde knew how to mount these notorious desert beasts.

She slipped into the saddle with ease, pressing her heels into the camel's neck. She tugged on the rope, made a clicking sound with her tongue, and the beast rose like a wobbly leviathan.

And in spite of himself, a grudging admiration arose in David. The woman knew what she was doing all right. He wasn't going to have to worry about her abilities. He could now focus solely on the task ahead.

With the three camels loaded and strung together, they left the outskirts of Tabara and made their way down the cascading dunes to a small wadi, a riverbed where dark water pooled and a few date palms straggled in sand as white as snow. There they would water their camels and set out as soon as the sun dipped over the horizon.

A handful of children ran behind them on skinny brown legs as they made their way down to the wadi. Their grubby little faces ranged in shades from dark chocolate to pale coffee. The colors of Africa. And in their eyes, David saw Kamilah's. And in their laughter, he heard hers.

His stomach clenched violently. His hand fisted around the head rope. He lifted his chin to the distant horizon. And in his heart he said a silent prayer. He prayed the gods of the desert would spare his child from the crazed wrath of his half brother.

By the time the sky turned to purple velvet and only a faint violet streak lingered where the sun had slipped behind distant dunes, they had their camels watered and supplies once again secured.

They set out at a rhythmic pace. David let Jayde take the lead. He followed up the rear, behind the camel that carried supplies and grain. Keeping distance between the two of them had been automatic since the moment their hands had brushed over Kamilah's belongings.

The air was still viscous with heat, but the wind was now smooth and soft against his face. They settled into the undulating and mesmerizing rhythm of their camels, traveling in absolute mind-numbing silence for hour after hour after hour.

The sky above them was vast. Stars moved across the heavens in a transcendent display as the hours ticked down toward dawn. Every now and then the movement of a falling star caught David's eye and he began to feel that familiar sensation descend on him as he traveled into the sandy void.

It was a feeling he didn't really have words for. It was spiritual, one of the reasons the Sahara had kept pulling him back throughout his life. Out here David was acutely aware of the fragility of his humanity. He got a sense of perspective he could only imagine was akin to the feeling space travelers got when they looked back at the brilliant blue marble of a planet they called home.

Quite simply the desert helped him put life in perspective. It was where time warped and everything seemed possible.

Even getting his daughter back.

As he rode he watched the hypnotic and sensual sway of the woman on the camel ahead of him and he found himself wondering if it was the same for her. What was she thinking as they headed into this void of sand? In so many ways she was a woman after his own heart. She challenged him in more ways than he could imagine. And she did things to his body he hadn't dreamed possible. As he let his mind go, he found himself wishing it had been different. That there had been a possibility of a future for them. That she could have been his *Sahar,* a gift to him and Kamilah from the sea.

He shook his head.

He was beginning to feel the effects of fatigue. They'd been going all night without a stop. He looked to his right and saw that a copper tinge was already beginning to bleed into the sky, heralding the arrival of the sun.

He settled back into the hypnotic sway of the camel. And almost instantly his mind took off again. He found himself wondering if perhaps there could still be a future for them.

No.

He jerked his mind back. He was being a fool. She was a government agent doing a job. And once this mission was over she'd simply move on to the next. She would slip as effortlessly into some other world as she had into his. And perhaps as easily into another man's heart. There was no room for him and Kamilah in a future like that.

Then her words echoed like a ghostly taunt in his head. *You made it impossible for me not to…to love you.*

His throat constricted. Yeah, so maybe she'd fallen for him. But it had been the biggest mistake of her life. She'd said so herself.

He swallowed the bitterness in his mouth. That was then. That was Sahar. This was now. This woman was Jayde.

But something still ate at him, something he just couldn't let go. The need to know began to, once again, burn in his gut as the copper on the horizon fired into a livid orange and the Sahara sands began to glow.

He clucked his tongue, urged his camel to move faster until he'd caught up and was riding alongside her.

"Jayde?"

She swung her head around and her eyes caught his. David's heart stalled. She'd never looked more beautiful to him as she did right now in her peasant gear with a piece of cloth tied like a turban over her head. In the golden dawn light her eyes were a liquid and lambent green made only more beautiful by the deepening bronze tan of her skin. In spite of her obvious fatigue, she looked proud. Regal. A princess of the desert.

"What is it?" she asked.

He'd lost his train of thought the second he'd looked into her eyes. "I…ah…back on Shendi, you…you told me your amnesia was real."

"It's the truth, David."

"When, Jayde, when *exactly* did your memory return?"

She halted her camel, shifted around in the saddle to face him. "Why?"

The sun exploded over the horizon, and the sands around them caught fire. He squinted as his eyes adjusted to the flare. "I need to know. Did you remember before…before we were together, on the yacht?" *Before we made love.*

The look that shifted into her eyes made his heart sink. "David, you told me once you abhorred a liar. I'm not going to lie. Everything I tell you from now is the whole truth." She studied his face.

But he said nothing, just waited.

"I began to remember first in little bits and pieces. I didn't now what was happening and I thought I might be imagining things. It scared me. Then…then when you showed me to your office and I saw the map of Azar with all those little pins, I got a big chunk of the picture. And then, at dinner…when I saw Tariq's face, that's when it all really started amming home. It all just came down on me and I was totally confused. I needed to sort it out…in my mind."

He glared at her. So she *had* known. He clenched his jaw. he had known before he went to her on the pier. He kicked is camel forward.

"David—"

He ignored her. She'd known who she was when she'd ade love to him. And that burned like all hell.

"David!" she demanded. "David, stop! Listen to me!"

He stopped, turned slowly back to face her.

"What I felt for you was true, dammit. *That* was not a lie. Vhat we shared was *not* a lie!" Her eyes flamed like the rowing globe of heat rising fast in the sky. "You put life back to me, David." Her voice caught. "Don't you see? I had *othing* before I met you. Dead to emotion from the day my other killed herself. You made me live again! And I didn't sk you to do it. I didn't ask you to make me feel again." Ferocious emotion brought angry spots of color to her cheeks. e could feel heat beginning to rise from the sand.

"And now—" her voice quavered "—and now that I've felt hat it's like to…to love…I've lost it all. Everything. Every amn thing that means anything to me. I've lost you. Kamih. My job." Her voice broke. Tears shone in her eyes. "Don't or one minute think I'm enjoying any part of this. I didn't sk for this. I didn't ask you to sneak in under my guard."

His chest cramped. "Jayde—"

She held up a palm. "Forget it. Just forget it. Don't say thing. We've got a job to do and that's the only reason I'r here. You know it. I know it. So let's get on with it."

"Jayde, I…I'm sorry." And he truly was. For her. For him self. For his child. For what had happened to his brother. Fo the unfulfilled promise to his dead father. For his mother wh could never love the desert. "I'm sorry," he said again.

Her mouth opened.

"Yes. I'm sorry. For everything. I…I wish it could hav been different."

She stared at him. Then something shuttered in her eye: She pressed her mouth into a tight line and kicked her came forward in a spurt of dust.

He let his camel drop back. He felt shaken. Shut out. Unsure And in love.

Yes. He couldn't hide from it. He was in love with thi incredible woman. And there was a desert of distance be tween them.

Chapter 14

The sun shrank to a scorching white-hot ball as it climbed into its zenith. It bleached color from the world and set the sand blazing with blinding light. The dunes swelled in size like monstrous waves, torrid and desolate as far the eye could see. And beyond the heaving sands, the horizons simply vaporized into a blur of white heat.

Jayde felt her breathing become labored, and she could see her camel was suffering. They had dismounted and were walking to give the beasts a break. Her feet burned, and sand rubbed blisters into bleeding patches of raw skin. The *guerbas* were almost empty and Jayde knew no man or woman could last longer than one day in this heat without hydration.

"How far to the next water?" She called out to David, her voice hoarse, her lips thick, cracked.

"Should be a wadi over the next ridge," he called back. "We can water there if it hasn't dried up already."

Great, she thought as they pressed laboriously on up one dune and down the next, the distant ridge never appearing to get any closer. Her calf muscles felt as if they were tearing apart. Her back ached and her tongue felt swollen to twice its size. The sides of her throat literally stuck together. She was seeing bright pinprick spots and swarms of black dots in her peripheral vision. She was beginning to feel dizzy and slightly crazy as desert madness and the sheer size of the place tried to grip her mind.

She stumbled in the shifting sand, fell to her hands. It was blistering hot against her palms. David moved instantly to her side. "Here." He reached for the *guerba,* held it out to her. "Take some."

She shook her head. "What if the wadi is *not* over the next ridge?"

"It will be. Here, drink."

She let a small sip of water moisten her lips, but she knew how dangerous it would be to finish every last drop. Nothing was a given in this desiccated environment. There may *not* be water over the next ridge. She knew David was only saying that to ease her mind. "Thanks." She handed the goatskin back to him. "I think I'm going crazy. I'm getting mad visions in my head."

"The jinns," he said. He helped her to her feet. "Wait here with the camels. I'll head to the top of that dune and see if I can see the wadi."

She watched him move up the monstrous mountain of sand until his image wavered in the glistening heat and she thought he might be a ghost, a trick of her mind. She blinked against the glare trying to track his movement to the top. What if he got lost? She'd be dead on her own. She didn't have a clue where they were. Panic struck her heart. It boiled through her blood. She began to scramble wildly up the dune after him, leaving the camels.

"David!" She yelled as she stumbled up the mountain of sand, slipping back down as fast as she moved forward. "David!" Everything turned to fire around her. The whole world was burning. *She was going to die!*

"David!" she screamed. She fell to the sand, and a world of fiery flames spiraled around her.

"Hey, hey, it's okay." She felt his arms supporting her, lifting her up. Her focus began to return.

"It's all right, Jayde, take it easy."

She looked up into his eyes. His skin was even darker and his eyes more blue. Right now he looked like a god. Her savior. She gripped his shirt with her fists. "Don't leave me, David."

Something shifted in his eyes. He smoothed her cheek. "It's okay, Jayde, it's just the jinns talking."

"Don't leave me. Ever."

"Don't worry, I won't. We're in this together, all the way. The wadi is just over the ridge. Come. Before we lose the camels and our gear." He helped her slowly down the dune. And she realized just how vulnerable she was without him. And what a terrible fate could have befallen them if the camels had wondered off because of her mad carelessness.

The water in the dry riverbed was almost nonexistent. It was dark and smelled bitter. But it was water. And right now that meant life. David used it to make *zrig,* a blend of water, powdered milk and sugar. They sat under a small rock overhang alongside the wadi and drank copious quantities of it.

Jayde could feel her body and her mind slowly begin to return to normal as the moisture and sugar seeped through her system. She took the last sip of her share and returned the bowl to David. She watched as he cupped the enamel basin in his deeply tanned hands and lifted it to his lips. There was something so basic and so beautiful and powerful about this man, she thought. Something so honest.

Maybe it *was* the jinns. Maybe it was the effect of the desert. Because she felt as though there was nothing to hide behind out here, nothing to veil emotions. And she'd surprised the hell out of herself by begging like a fool for him to never leave her. It was as if something deep and primal had ripped loose and erupted out of her very soul.

Now she felt embarrassed. "I'm sorry, David. I think I lost it back there," she said. "And I could have lost the camels. I was totally irresponsible."

His eyes caught hers, held. Then he grinned suddenly, his teeth impossibly white, fine wrinkles fanning out from his cool blue eyes. "Like I said, the jinns got you."

She nodded. "I guess they did. And they don't get you?"

"All the time." He sipped the dregs of the *zrig*. "We'll rest here a few minutes," he said. "Why don't you lie down, try and close your eyes."

The notion was overwhelmingly appealing. She desperately needed rest but she hadn't wanted to hold up their progress by telling him so. She tried to inch farther into the thin line of shadow under the rock. She lay back on a faded blanket and covered her head with the fabric of her head cloth. Trying to hide from the heat and blinding glare of the sun proved futile. She nevertheless drifted into a dazed and delirious state somewhere between dream and sleep.

And in her dream she was drowning in the sea. The waves sucking at her. But she could see the shore, the beach, his palace up high on the ridge. She could see Sheik David bin Omar bin Zafir Rashid, an untamed warrior galloping over ancient dunes on his white stallion, the platinum-hot glare of sun at his back throwing his profile into stark and menacing shadow. He had his arm raised high above his head, brandishing his *jambiya,* as a blood-curdling battle cry emanated from his throat. He charged over the dunes, over the sand toward the sea, toward her.

Fear clutched her heart. She began to go under, salt tearing at her throat, burning her nasal passages. But the thundering hooves bore down. David reined his stallion and rode over the beach sand and into the white froth of the waves. He swung low over the side of his horse and scooped her naked into his arms.

She clutched onto his shirt, stared up into cool indigo eyes under his turban. He grinned at her, a piratical slash of white against the deep brown of his face.

Then she was riding behind him on his stallion. Naked. Wild. Free. Laughing. She'd survived. She hadn't died.

And she felt the delicious ache of desire pump blood through her body. And for the first time she could remember, she realized she was truly alive.

Her eyes flashed open. Her heart was racing. Through the cloth covering her face she could see that the sun had moved across the sky. Panic kicked at her. He'd let her sleep too long. They would lose too much time. She jerked up. Her brain was thick. David was no longer beside her.

Her panic mounted as she squinted into the sun trying to find focus, to scan the surroundings.

Then she saw him. Relief swooped through her. He hadn't left. He'd moved into the meager shade of a rock. His back was to her and his head was bent low over something in his lap.

She got up and went over to him, the muscles of her legs aching with each step.

He looked up as she approached. And in his eyes was something unreadable. Then she saw what he held in his hands. A leather-bound book, *The Little Mermaid.*

She sat quietly beside him.

He closed the book and ran his strong brown hands over the cover. His eyes were liquid ink. "I'd never read it, you know."

She nodded. She didn't know what to say.

"All this time and I never read her favorite story. How could I have let that happen?"

"David," she softly, "don't be so hard on yourself."

His eyes lifted to hers. "Thank you, Jayde." His voice was low and full of gravel. "Thank you for being there for Kamilah...in...in a way I never was. I just didn't see it. I didn't know how. *This* is what I should I have been doing all along. Reading to her. Fairy tales. Indulging her in her childish fantasies. I should have been playing with her, allowing her to be a child. I should have let her know it was okay to have fun...that it wasn't a slight to her mother's memory."

She placed her hand on his arm. "You needed to let *yourself* know it was okay to live again, David. And that comes only with time. Don't blame yourself."

He sucked in a deep breath, closed his eyes and held his face up to the sky as if to stop the kinetics of gravity drawing the tears down from his eyes. "And time we've had. It's now time to move forward. We'll get her, Jayde." He whispered up to the heavens as if convincing himself as well as the universe. "We'll get her. And we'll let her be a kid. I won't let her down again. *Ever.*"

Jayde's stomach tightened into a ball. He was saying "we." But she knew she would not be a part of the equation. Not once they'd freed Kamilah. There wouldn't be a place for her. He'd made that clear enough. "You have never let her down, David."

"I did. By not saving her mother. She blames me. She holds me responsible for her mother's death."

"No, she does not blame you, David," she said softly. "She has never blamed you."

His eyes flashed to hers. "How would you know?"

"Because she told me. She told me what happened that day, what she saw through her own eyes. And she told me how hard you tried to save her mother and she told me how very proud she is of you."

His mouth pulled sideways as he tried to contain his emotion. "She *told* you that?" His voice was thick.

"Yes, David," she said softly. "Yes, she did."

He opened his mouth and let out a whoosh of air. Then he turned to look at her. "Thank you," he whispered, his eyes tunneling deep into hers. "Thank you, Jayde."

Then he clenched his jaw. His eyes turned cold and determined. He jerked to his feet. "Come," he said, holding his hand out to her. "Let's go and give my baby that happy ending. The one you promised her."

Jayde reached out, grasped his hand. And she felt a new connection between them. A solidness that hadn't been there before.

He strode over to the camels he'd hobbled near the fetid water, showing no sign of the fatigue that gripped her. "If we keep moving through the night," he called out as he untied the camels, "and throughout tomorrow, we could be in Al Abèche before next nightfall."

They stopped once more in the late evening and then pressed on into a night that was as stinking hot as the day that had preceded it. The moon was an almost nonexistent sliver, and the only light that guided them came from stars splattered over the huge black dome of sky.

The farther north they went, the drier the desert, the more hostile the terrain, the blacker the night. In places, sand dunes gave way to sharp rock ridges, and flint in the stone glinted at them like sharp teeth in the dying light of the waning moon.

Jayde knew that once they reached Al Abèche they would be only twenty miles from the Libyan border. The Falal fortress was only another ten miles into Libya. There they would contact Gio Moriati and they would wait for Sauvage and his team to bring Kamilah to them. They would then fly out by helicopter. Dr. Watson would be waiting to treat Kamilah on Shendi if all went according to plan.

She ran over the timeline again and again in her head, trying to stay awake on her camel as dawn once again seeped up from the horizon.

As the sun burst into the sky and rippled the sand with orange color, a wave of heat descended on them that was so oppressive Jayde thought it might just end up killing them by midday.

Even the wind had stopped, making the air thick and gelatinous. It sapped her energy and it slowed the camels. Jayde began to feel tense, edgy, delirious as they waded through the heat and sand. She tried to shake it off. But in each distant ridge of rock she saw monsters lurk. She couldn't tell north from south anymore. She felt alarmed at the hostile vastness of landscape. She tried to tell herself it was the jinns playing tricks with her mind again.

But this time she could see David was edgy, too. He kept peering at the horizon to the right of their little caravan, as if expecting something.

Then she saw what he was looking for, what he must have been sensing all along. A clot of angry red cumulous clouds began to boil up high over the distant horizon. She caught her breath as it changed before her eyes into a terrifying monstrous black claw of sand and wind. She watched in horror as it roared toward them, covering miles in seconds. She glanced around in panic. There was nowhere to hide.

David moved fast.

He yanked her down from her camel, thrust the animal's head rope into her hand. He yelled above the screaming sound as the wall of sand advanced. "Hang on to this no matter what! Pull that cloth over your face! Lean into wind!"

She couldn't move. She was held prisoner, awed by the sheer scope the advancing, twisting, spiraling whorl of blackness.

David worked quickly to secure the camels. "There should be a deep wadi up ahead," he yelled. "If we can find it in the storm, we'll have shelter."

The sound slammed into her head the same instant light was blotted from the sky. It was a sound so awful it seemed to emanate from the very bowels of the earth itself, screaming up from the core into the sky, sparking a primal terror deep within her.

Then the sand hit, instantly choking her nose, her throat, her lungs. She reeled back, then forced herself forward into the teeth of it.

It cut into her skin like a billion needles. She couldn't see a thing. She staggered blindly forward, clutching onto the head rope knowing her life depended on it.

David steered them into the raging blackness. As they inched forward, the wind and sand filled her head with whispering voices, senseless moaning, screaming, in a thousand unidentifiable tongues.

She had no idea how long they battled against the storm. She moved like a dulled automaton, foot before foot. She no longer felt the pain. Then she felt his hands on her, pulling her, guiding her, forcing her down into a crevice of rock. She felt his solid body tuck in next to her. He pulled a blanket over their heads, held her into him, shielding her from the worst of the storm.

They huddled like that, breathing in each other's hot air as the sound and sand tore at their senses for what seemed like hours.

Then as suddenly as it had come upon them, it was gone. An eerie silence filled the desert. David threw back the blanket, shaking out layers of fine sand. Jayde coughed and spluttered as she tried to wipe the grit of sand from her eyes and mouth.

She looked up at David. He stared at her. They'd made it. *They were alive.* Behind him Jayde could count all three camels present. And beyond the camels, she could see water, life-giving water gleaming in a depression in the dry riverbed.

Her body shuddered with a crazy sob. She felt as if she'd been stripped of everything in that sand, like she'd stared into the black maw of death. But they'd survived. And she was staring at a pool of water in a depression of snow-white sand fringed by a handful of straggling date palms.

She began to cry. And laugh. Crazily. Hysterically.

David grabbed her by the shoulders, pulled her into him, held tight. And she could feel the force of fierce life flowing through his hands, his arms, his entire body. The same force seared wildly through her.

She laughed and sobbed into his neck until tears ran in muddied rivers down her cheeks, until every last bit of tension had been drained from her body.

She pulled back, stared up at him, and began to laugh all over again. "Oh, my God, don't tell me I look anything like you do."

He grinned, and his eyes twinkled fierce blue through the sand that caked his face.

He studied her. And he began to laugh, too, a sound that came from deep in his belly and burbled up through his chest. He laughed so hard it brought moisture to his eyes and it ran in streaky trickles down the sides of his face.

He took her hand and they ran down to the water like abandoned spirits under the dome of empty blue sky. They furiously shed their clothes, tossed them onto the white sand of the riverbed and plunged into water that embraced their hot and burned and raw bodies like cool silk.

Jayde sank under the water and rinsed the sand from her hair. She surfaced. "This is heaven. This has *got* to be heaven. I have died and gone to heaven."

A strange look filled David's eyes.

She went silent at the darkness she saw in them.

Then he grabbed her, yanked her into him and kissed her brutally on the mouth. She kissed him back, hard. Tongues slipping, fighting, mating, teeth clashing. Breathless, Jayde pulled back. And in his eyes she saw the pure rawness of primal male hunger. It was as if the winds of sand had unleashed something savage in both of them. It scared her. "We…we should move on," she whispered.

"Yes." The muscle in his jaw pulsed hard. "We must water the camels," he said, his voice thick.

"Yes."

They stared at each other in silence.

He broke it. "Come," he said, his voice rough. "If we don't feed the poor beasts they'll never get us to Al Abèche."

The chores of living were paramount out in a place like this. Jayde could see that now. Wrapped in a *kikoi,* her hair drying in the sun, she worked alongside David to water the beasts that had brought them this far. Then she sat on a blanket spread under the shade of the straggling palms and watched as he spread a tarp on the sand. His *kikoi* was wound around his waist, and his chest was bare and strong and dark with hair that ran in a thick black whorl to his waist. She couldn't take her eyes from the way his muscles moved under his slick skin as he poured piles of grain on top of the tarp.

Then he stood back as the camels began to splutter and hiss and bite at each other, serpentine necks fighting for the food so that it scattered and spilled off the tarp and onto the sand.

David chuckled. "That'll teach 'em not to share." He came and sat beside her, his body touching hers. The electricity was inescapable, and what happened next was as unavoidable as the passage of the sun over these heavens.

He reached over and tugged her kikoi loose from her chest so that it spilled off her. She sat as naked as the day she was born. His eyes ran over her, sending a spurt of liquid heat through her body. He reached up and grazed his rough palm over her breast. Her nipples hardened instantly. "You have the most beautiful breasts," he whispered, looking into her eyes.

The warm, dulcet tones of his voice seeped into her blood and pooled in the base of her belly.

He ran his roughened hand down the length of her leg and slowly, very slowly, up along the inside of her thigh. Her breath caught in her throat and she instinctively relaxed her thighs, letting her legs fall open to him. Heat spilled to her groin as his hand moved up to the apex of her thighs, his roughened fingers searching her wet folds. He leaned over her, his lips finding hers as he slid a finger up into her heat. She groaned, opened wider, moved against his finger. He plunged it deeper into her, stroking her as he deepened the thrust of his tongue in her mouth. The movement of his hand brought her to an almost unbearable pitch of pleasure.

He straddled his leg over hers, used his knee to force her thighs even farther apart, and as he did, his *kikoi* fell loose. He was solid with need. She moaned, arched toward him.

David couldn't hold off a second longer. He leaned her back onto the blanket, mounted her and thrust himself deep into her slick heat. She moaned, bucked under him, and it drove him nearly wild. Naked under the skies with camels crunching grain quietly over to the side, they joined their bodies in a fierce obsession that knew no shame. They tangled their limbs in feral abandon. And for David there was no past and no future. Just the present. And the woman under him was not Jayde. Not Sahar. Nor a mysterious mermaid. He didn't know her by a tag. But he knew her nevertheless. In a most intimate way. He'd come to know her when she didn't have a sense of self. And he'd discovered the pure, giving soul that existed at her very core.

He'd come to know this woman in a way he'd never dreamed he could know any woman. And at this moment, he was not David Rashid, British aristocrat. He was not Sheik David bin Omar bin Zafir Rashid, descended from a line of fierce and noble nomad warriors. He simply existed. An Adam in the desert united with his Eve under the sky, only a raw and primal honesty between them.

He cried out in wild release as she shuddered under him.

And in this instant he knew in his heart that this was the only woman for him. Spent, he sank back and lay on the blanket beside her. In silence they stared at the sky through the dried fronds of the palm as the heavens turned livid orange and violet. He laced his fingers through hers, squeezed her hand. She squeezed back in response. He wanted to keep her by his side forever. But he couldn't allow himself to think of forever until he'd saved his child. He could offer nothing to the world or to any person in it until he rescued his daughter.

Jayde sat up, traced her fingers along the side of his jaw and over his lips. She smiled at him, a smile that reached right into her eyes and made them dance with pale-green life.

She opened her mouth to say something but a sound jerked them both back to reality.

It was the sat-phone. Ringing in the saddle bag. They exchanged a stunned glance. It could only mean one thing.

David grabbed his *kikoi,* wound it around him as he strode over to their pile of supplies and pulled out the phone.

"Rashid."

"It's Moriati, David, we've got bad news."

The muscles across his chest snapped tight like a steel band. "What news?" he barked. He was vaguely aware at how Jayde jumped at his tone, grabbed her *kikoi,* came over to his side.

"Sauvage and his team have been captured in Egypt."

His brain spun. "How?"

"Egyptian authorities were tipped off. It was Farouk, David. He's been working on the inside for Tariq. I've dealt with him."

"He confessed?"

"Yeah. He got word to Tariq and Falal about our plans to attack the fortress from the north using Egypt as a launch. The Falal then fed a line to the Egyptian authorities telling them Sauvage and his team were planning trouble in Egypt. It's tied them up in bureaucratic tape, David. They've got them behind bars. It will take weeks for Sauvage and his men to get out of this."

"We'll get another team together."

Moriati was quiet on the other end of the line.

"Moriati, what is it? What are you not telling me?" he barked.

"Tariq has lost patience. He demands to have all Force du Sable troops out of Azar by midnight tomorrow or he will harm Kamilah."

"Talk him out of it."

"David...there is no negotiating with this man."

"Buy time, dammit!"

"Can't. He's cut off all communication. This is his endgame, David. We have no choice but to give him what he wants. And—" Moriati paused "—I have to be brutally honest with you, even if we do deliver, I'm not sure he'll uphold his end of the bargain and give us Kamilah."

David's throat constricted, shutting off his air passages. His heart jackhammered in his chest. Adrenaline balled every muscle in his body. "Give him what he wants! Give the order, Moriati. Pull the troops out of Azar. And in the meantime, I'm going in myself. I'm going to get my daughter."

"They'll kill you."

"So be it. If my daughter dies, I die, too." He clicked the phone off. His limbs shook.

"What was that, David?" Jayde asked. But she could already guess.

"Sauvage and his team have been captured in Egypt. Farouk tipped Tariq off, and the Falal in turn tipped the Egyptians off. Now Tariq has brought his deadline forward to tomorrow midnight. I've given the order to move the troops out but I'm going in get my daughter."

Jayde studied his face, his eyes. He was serious. Deadly so. "They will kill you, David."

"They will kill Kamilah if I don't."

She knew he was right. She'd believed it all along. Only an extraction would save the little girl. Not negotiation.

"I'm going with you."

"No. No way in hell."

"Yes way. I'm in this all the way, David." Her eyes flashed to her bag. "I can help. You need me. I've been trained in covert operations. You haven't."

"I can't let you do this, Jayde. I can't ask you to endanger your life this way."

"No, you can't. But *I* can. And I'm not letting you do this alone."

"You said it yourself they will kill."

She reached up, grabbed his shoulders, her eyes lanced his. "Then we will fight, David. Then we will fight back."

Moisture filled his eyes as he stared down into hers. "Do

you realize what you are doing, Jayde? Do you realize what you are saying?"

"I do."

Emotion spilled out from his eyes. He grabbed her face in his hands, kissed her hard on her mouth, held her tight in his arms. "I can't...I can't let you do this."

She pulled away. Her eyes bored into his. "I've never been more determined about anything in my life. Give me that phone," she demanded. "What's Moriati's number?"

He handed it to her and watched her punch in the number.

"Gio," she said with crisp efficiency as she crouched down into the sand and picked up a small sharp piece of rock. "I need the satellite specs of the Falal compound. I need to know the layout of the fort. I want to know where you figure they're holding her, how many guards." She began to draw in the sand with her rock as she listened. David watched as the shape of the fort emerged in the sand. She marked *X*s for guards and soldiers. This was her job. This is what she did for a living. This was what he had hated her for. And now he saw what good she could do with it. And respect for her swelled inside him.

She clicked off the phone, slanted her eyes up to him.

"See," she said pointing her finger at her map in the sand. "This is where Gio reckons they're holding Kamilah. Satellite heat-imaging shows a small and fairly stationary figure here in this room on the ground level. This—" she pointed her finger at an *X* in the sand "—is probably a guard. There's only one outside the door. And there are surprisingly few people in the fortress. Moriati reckons they might feel safe with Sauvage's rescue attempt thwarted and they might be mobilizing for the anticipated coup attempt once the Force du Sable troops are out by midnight tomorrow."

"We stand a chance, then," he said, hope blossoming in his heart.

"Maybe," she grinned up at him. "But only if you follow *my* orders."

He pulled a face. "I've never taken orders from a woman."

She stood up, bussed him on the mouth. "First time's the hardest, Rashid. Get used to it. Because I plan on being around for a while."

Incredulous, he watched her march over to the camels and start loading their gear. She'd sown the seed of a promise in his heart. *I plan on being around for a while.* He let her words sink in, feed the promise.

She spun around "Hey, you gonna help or not? If we move now we can be in Al Abèche by nightfall. We can dump our stuff, regroup and be at the fort sometime after midnight. That will give us a few hours of new-moon darkness before dawn," she yelled as she hefted a bag onto her red camel.

In spite of the gravity of the situation he felt a delinquent smile tug at his mouth. "Yeah," he whispered. He was going to make damn sure she stayed around. He wasn't going to let this woman go. Not now. Not after she'd been through all this with him. Not after what they'd shared in the desert.

And suddenly saving his daughter became something even bigger in his mind. It became a need to kill the cancers of the past to ensure a future. It became a driving need to make all three of them whole…him, Kamilah and Jayde. A family.

Because all of sudden he could see with incredible clarity that the very thing that had been driving them apart is what ultimately bound them together—love.

With new fire searing through his blood, he set about loading the camels. And he began to plot. He knew people in Al Abèche. Loyal villagers. Men who would stand by them to fight the Falal. But they had to hurry.

The clock was ticking.

Chapter 15

A moonless night brought them invisibility. With fresh camels, eleven additional men from the village of Al Abèche, and a small cache of black-market weapons, including the stash Jayde had brought, they'd crossed into the Libyan desert undetected just after midnight.

They were all dressed in black. Jayde and David had extra clothes in their saddle bags for their return journey. Jayde had borrowed a chador from a Muslim woman in Al Abèche. The plan was to hide Kamilah under it and for her and David to pose as a simple Bedouin man and wife if they encountered any rebels as they fled. She and David would go one way. The villagers, who were to create a distraction to the north of the fort, would flee in another direction. They would all meet up in Al Abèche…*if* all went according to plan.

It was almost three in the morning. They didn't have much time until first light. Jayde and David lay flat on their stomachs against the warm sand of a dune that provided them cover. The village volunteers, all experienced guerrilla fighters who'd fought Azarian rebels for Sauvage and his team, had stolen around the west end of the fort and made their way into the rocks of the northern ridge armed with grenades, explosives, AK-47s, *jambiyas* and scimitars.

David scanned the fort with night-vision binoculars while Jayde rolled onto her side, carefully attached the grenade launcher to her rifle and inserted a small e-bomb canister, making sure she had another ready to go as soon as she'd fired this one. She checked her watch. "Two minutes," she whispered.

The seconds ticked by interminably as they waited for their men to detonate explosives along the cliff face to the north. That was where Sauvage's men were supposed to have been, according to the plan Farouk had given to Tariq.

Tariq would think David had found a replacement team, and the attention of the few Falal members left at the fort, the ones who had not yet mobilized for the Azar coup, would be diverted northward while Jayde and David crept in from the south.

The plan was for Jayde to fire her e-grenades over the compound as soon as the distraction to the north commenced. The e-grenades would knock out all electrical communications and surveillance equipment in the fort. She and David would then creep in using night-vision gear and neutralize the two guards at the southern entrance.

They would move quickly into the fort and find the room where they assumed Kamilah was being held. They would have to deal with one guard there, according to Moriati's satellite specs.

The first explosion went off on cue, cracking the silence of the desert night. Then the next, and the next. They heard yelling, gunshots, general confusion as the few Falal fighters still in the fort scrambled to cover the northern side of the compound and began firing into the dark.

"Now!" she whispered, firing the launcher. Equipment began to explode and cook under the massive electrical surge. Even from their vantage point a hundred yards away in the dunes, the acrid smell burned their nostrils. Jayde reloaded, fired again. The fort was plunged into blackness.

They raced like silent black ghosts over the sand, using night-vision gear. Through it they could make out the green-gray shapes of the two guards at the entrance. The two men were focused on the ruckus north of the fort.

They caught them unawares from behind, jabbing them in their necks with Jayde's chemical darts. The guards slumped with soft thuds to the ground.

Guns fired to the north. Another explosion rocked the ground. The Falal fighters were fully engaged by their men. David and Jayde ran down the right-hand corridor. They came to a sharp corner in the passage of the old stone fort. David pressed his back against the stone wall, peered carefully around the corner. Ahead, left unguarded, was a thick wooden door with metal hinges. His heart clenched. This was where satellite imaging showed a small and fairly stationary figure they presumed was Kamilah.

He motioned to Jayde that all was clear. They ran to the door, still using night-vision gear in the blackened fort. The door was locked. David fought with the bolt. Jayde touched his shoulder, gestured he move aside.

He watched as she deftly wound two different shades of malleable substance together. "One thread's explosive," she whispered. "The other contains a chemical that will detonate it in seconds. Be ready to get back." She moulded the plastique against the door lock. They both ducked back around the corner in the passageway.

A muffled thud sent shockwaves down the passage. They raced toward the door. David shoved it open. And in the corner, on a pile of old blankets, her eyes big and black in the darkness, was the gray-green silhouette of his baby girl. His heart clean stopped, then kicked sharp up against his ribs. She couldn't see them. She was clearly terrified. "Kamilah!" he whispered. "It's me."

Jayde stood guard at the door.

He rushed toward his child in the dark corner.

"Daddy?" said a tiny voice. Emotion exploded violently in him. She was alive. Speaking. His hands began to shake. "Oh, God, Kamilah, are you all right? Did they hurt you?"

"I'm scared, Daddy. I can't see you. It's dark."

He scooped her up, hugged her tight to his chest. "I've got you, baby, we're going to get you home."

"I knew you'd come, Daddy. I knew."

"Of course, baby. Of course—" He halted as he heard a muffled cry behind him and the sickening sound of a body slumping to the ground. He swung around, Kamilah still clutched tight in his arms.

David's heart stalled. Jayde was curled in a limp pile on the floor, a black stain spreading under her. *Blood.* Tariq stood over her, a bayonet in one hand. *He'd stabbed her!*

Then light from a flashlight cut the darkness. David winced against the pain that screamed through his eyes and into his brain. He whipped off his night-vision gear and, blinking into the glare of the light, slowly set Kamilah down. "Get behind me," he whispered to his child. "Get in the corner, cover yourself with the blankets." His fingers curled around the hilt of his *jambiya* as he spoke. Rage was boiling through him. A sick fear curled through it. *What had Tariq done to Jayde?*

With one hand, Tariq aimed his bayoneted rifle at David's heart. With the other, he pointed the flashlight at David's eyes.

David blinked again, a little more accustomed to the glare of the light. He stared at the blade mounted on the end of Tariq's gun, the blade stained with Jayde's blood. "Tariq," he said hoarsely, "let Kamilah go. Let Kamilah and Jayde go."

Tariq nudged Jayde's limp form with his boot. "She's not going anywhere. Neither are you." He stepped close to David.

Every muscle in David's body strapped iron tight. He slipped his *jambiya* slowly from its sheath as he spoke. "Let us talk, Tariq. Let us work this out. For our father's sake."

Tariq snarled. "My *father?* The man who took an English bride and made a bastard sheik?" He moved even closer.

David's teeth clenched. He angled the curved blade of his *jambiya* slowly up in front of him, poised should his brother take one more step in his direction. "Let my daughter go, Tariq." He waved his *jambiya* menacingly in front of him, feeling the familiarity of the hilt against his palm. "I'm warning you."

Out of the corner of his eye David could see Jayde move ever so slightly. *She was alive.* His heart kicked his ribs. Then he saw her hand move slowly up to her head. She lifted the night-vision scope still attached to her eye. *She was more than alive. She was preparing to make a move.* She caught David's eye, signaled to him to draw Tariq away from Kamilah.

New fire seared through David's blood. He edged slowly to the corner of the stone cell, away from his child, away from Jayde.

Tariq followed David's movement with his flashlight, his finger curling around the trigger of his weapon.

Jayde's hand inched across the crumbling stone floor, groping for a loose chunk of stone. David saw her fingers close around one. She hefted herself up on one elbow and flung the rock at Tariq's head.

Her aim was dead-on. The rock cracked against his skull.

A grunt escaped Tariq. He spun around, aimed at Jayde, and David hit him abruptly from behind. Tariq's shot went wild as he stumbled forward under the impact, the rifle and the flashlight skittering across the floor.

He spun instantly back to face David, his hands empty. Thick black blood was oozing down the side of his face from the gash in his head. He drew out the dagger at his waist, swinging it threateningly.

The light in the cell was dim, the flashlight lying on the stone floor pointing a halo at the far wall.

Out of the corner of his eye, David saw Jayde crawling over to the pile of blankets, to Kamilah. He had to hold Tariq's attention, give them a chance to escape.

Tariq's eyes were wild with anger. He inched closer to David, crouched, his knife swaying.

David raised the point of his dagger. "Don't move, Tariq. Don't force me to do this. Just let us go. We can put all this behind us."

"Never," Tariq snarled, inching even closer. "Even if you get past me, you'll never make it over the border. I have already alerted Libyan troops. There is a column moving in from the east as we speak."

David's heart clenched.

Tariq came closer. Then in the blink of an eye, he lunged at David.

David jerked back, just missing the thrust of the blade. His heart pounded like a drum. He could see Jayde gathering Kamilah into her arms and hunkering down over her as she shuffled out of the cell.

Tariq lunged again, taking advantage of David's distraction. David moved quickly, once again narrowly missing the swing of the blade.

Then Tariq came at him again. David jumped. But not fast

enough. This time Tariq's blade sliced his forearm. David felt the searing burn, the warmth of his own blood. But he could not bring himself to lunge forward, to plunge his *jambiya*, his father's *jambiya*, into his brother's body.

Tariq now had him backed up into the corner. He came at David with a final thrust. David swung to the side. Tariq stumbled forward with his own momentum. Before he regained his balance he lurched sideways after David. David tripped backward over the loose stone floor, and Tariq came down hard on top of him, right on top his David's dagger, impaling himself on the blade. A soft grunt escaped his body as the blade sank deep into his chest.

David's heart stopped. Tariq's eyes were huge with silent shock. David could feel the wet, hot blood of his brother seeping thick over his hands. He rolled quickly over to his side, pushing his brother onto his back. The *jambiya* was buried in his chest to the hilt. His brother gaped up at him. Blood started to dribble from the corner of his mouth.

David got to his knees. "Tariq!"

His brother groaned.

"By God, Tariq, what have you done?"

A sound bubbled up from Tariq's throat with the blood and spittle. He choked as he tried to speak. "I…I die for my people. I…go in peace. You…you will not escape…" He coughed, choked. And his head lolled to the side, his eyes wide and suddenly empty.

David stared at his father's *jambiya*. The symbol of his unfulfilled promise. And tears spilled hot and furious down his cheeks. His whole body began to shake. "Why, Tariq? Why?" The pain in his own heart grew unbearable. He bent his head low over his brother, kissed his face and said a silent prayer for the salvation of his brother's soul. And for his own soul. He closed his brother's eyes.

Then he remembered the Libyan army. He could not afford to waste time. David left the *jambiya* stuck in his brother's heart. He would not be able to bear ever touching it again. He covered Tariq with a blanket from the corner in which he'd found Kamilah. And then he fled down the passageway after his woman and his child.

He found them in the dunes with the camels. Jayde had already donned her chador and was mounted on her beast with the folds of her garment wrapped around his daughter.

"How is Kamilah?"

"She's doing okay…considering."

"And you, Jayde…your wound?"

"Surface. He struck in the dark, missed his mark, missed the vitals. I was lucky. I'll be fine." She stared at his arm. "You're bleeding, David."

"It's nothing." David couched his camel, mounted. "The Libyan army is on our tail," he said quietly. "We must flee. We'll take the southeast route and circle back into Al Abèche. They'll be looking for us to the southwest, the direct route. Have our men gone?"

Jayde nodded. She clucked her tongue and kicked her camel into action. The southeast route would take them into the worst desert, and they had little water. But no choice.

They raced through what was left of the night. They slowed as dawn leaked blood-orange into the sky. "We must be over the border now," David said. "Are you all right, Kamilah?"

His daughter was burrowed into Jayde's chador. From under the folds she nodded her head, eyes still wide. She was in shock. They needed to get her treatment as soon as possible.

"Do you think they'll cross the border?" Jayde asked.

"I don't doubt it. We must keep moving." He dug into the saddlebag and pulled out the sat-phone. Moriati picked up on the second ring. "We've got Kamilah. We're in Azar, heading into Al Abèche from the east."

Gio was silent. Then he spoke. "I don't know how you pulled it off. Congratulations."

"Halt the withdrawal of Force du Sable troops, Moriati. Ready them for a coup attempt."

"Done."

"And we need a chopper in Al Abèche ASAP. And have Watson on standby in Shendi. We have to move. The Libyan army is on our tail."

"Jesus, have they come over the border?"

"We're not sure but not risking it, either. We hope to make Al Abèche before nightfall."

The sun was high in the sky. Jayde's mouth was bone dry. She could see David was suffering, too. They'd given Kamilah what was left of their water. Their camels were under strain. They rode in limp and undulating silence as the desert sand blazed relentlessly and the sun beat down on their heads. They had only a few miles left to go by David's calculation. They'd made record time. And were paying for it.

Then something caught David's attention. He halted his camel, squinted at the northern horizon. A faint plume of orange dust rose in the air and feathered into the blue sky.

Jayde's heart clenched. "What is it?"

"Trucks! Move!" He whacked Jayde's exhausted camel on the rump, kicked his own into a gallop. They began to race across the dunes.

But the dust plume across the ridge grew at an alarming rate and began to close in on them, circling around to the west cutting off their access to Al Abèche.

And for the first time, Jayde felt defeated. She was exhausted. She'd lost blood. She was in pain. Her thirst was excruciating. Then she looked down at the little child that clung to the saddle in front of her. She couldn't let her down. She had to make good on her promise. A happy ending. She gritted her teeth, tightened her grip on Kamilah and focused on speed.

But their pursuers were closing in. They could see the black line of vehicles clearly now like huge ants crawling across the sand ridge. Jeeps and a truck.

They could never outrun them. They were being cut off from their only hope of survival. If they were forced back into the desert, they would be dead by tomorrow.

The caravan of vehicles crossed around the ridge and started coming at them from the south.

They were done for.

David halted his camel. Jayde halted hers. They were both breathless. David stared at Jayde. And she knew what he was thinking. They had both known it could come to this.

But as she opened her mouth to speak she heard a chopping sound in the shimmering white-hot sky, growing louder and louder. Helicopters. She squinted into the sky.

Two black choppers materialized like prehistoric beasts over the shimmering heat of the desert. Goose bumps ran over Jayde's skin. The three of them stared in stunned silence as the copters bore down over their heads...and straight onto the convoy ahead of them.

Flashes of light and sound streaked from the machines, and instantly the jeep convoy erupted in explosion. Flames and waves of sound roared over the dunes. Black smoke spiraled into the sky. Fire crackled from the burning out hulls of vehicles in the distance.

Jayde stared at David, dumbfounded. "What was that?"

David smiled wryly. "Force du Sable. Sauvage's men. The best damn private army in the world." He blew out a huge breath and grinned. His eyes were alive with light. "Ladies, I think we made it."

"I think we did," she whispered.

"Yaaah!" he cried, whacking her camel on the rump. And they galloped over the last stretch of sand into Al Abèche.

A week later Dr. Watson gave Kamilah a clean bill of health. According to him, she'd fared exceptionally well. He credited this to the fact Jayde and David had arrived as a team to rescue her, restoring her faith in the world.

David stroked his daughter's silken hair. Her eyes smiled up at him. Warmth spurted through his chest. "You sure you don't want another bedtime story."

"Daddy," she said. "You've read nearly *all* my stories. I have to get new ones now."

He kissed her on the forehead. "I'm making up for lost time, sweetness." He tickled her in the ribs. "Just one more? Huh? Huh?"

She squealed and giggled as he tickled her.

"*The Little Mermaid,* maybe? How 'bout I read you that one."

She stilled, her eyes suddenly dark and serious. "Nope. I don't need that one anymore."

He sat up in surprise. "You don't?"

"Uh-uh. I don't like the ending of it anymore." She grinned. "I can make my own happy endings now."

Emotion pricked hot behind his eyes. "Yes, sweetness, that you can." He kissed her and closed the shutters. "Good night, baby."

"'Night, Daddy." And again his heart squeezed at the sound of his child's happy little voice. He made his way out of her room.

"Daddy?" she said as he was about to close the door.

"What is it, sweetheart?"

"Will she stay?"

He was silent for a while. "I sure hope so. I'll let you know in the morning."

David made his way out onto the terrace. The moon was rising and the swells were slow and languid out over the ocean. Jayde stood at the end of the terrace, the hem of her white dress ruffling in the breeze around her calves, the tendrils of her hair blowing with the warm wind. He slipped his arm around her waist, and together they stared out over a horizon as clear and vast as the future that lay before them.

"Jayde," he said. And inside he quaked. Because he was terrified of what she might say when he asked her.

"What is it, David?" Her eyes were so big and so green. He wanted to wake up to those eyes every morning for the rest of his life. He wanted to drown in them forever. "Jayde, if I asked you to stay, would you?"

Her eyes searched his in silence.

His heart balled into a knot. He wanted this above anything else in the world. He wanted her at his side forever. He wanted them to be a family.

She sucked in her breath.

He braced, waiting for her words.

"David," she said, "out in the desert, I said some things. And you said it was the jinns talking…"

His stomach bottomed out.

She lifted her face to his. "It wasn't. It was *me*. It was me talking from my heart, me stripped of every damn defence I'd ever built up around myself. In those dunes I pleaded with you to never leave me. I also told you I intended to stick around." She smiled. Her eyes shimmered. "I meant it, David. All of it…if you'll have me, that is."

Tears filled his eyes. He grasped her face with both hands and kissed her hard. Then he stopped, backed off. "What about MI-6?"

A wicked twinkle lit her eyes. Her hair billowed softly out behind her in the jasmine-scented breeze. "I have a new job."

"What?"

"I work for Sauvage now,"

"I don't understand."

"He wants me for the North African intelligence and research team he's putting together. It's part of a new service he will be offering his clients. The mercenary business is shifting more and more into this field. He says I can do the bulk of my work out here, as long as I make myself available for client briefings and meetings in London and at the Force du Sable base on Sao Diogo."

His face was priceless. She'd rendered him speechless. She loved him right now more than anything in this world. This powerful man who'd become her one weakness was the very person who had made her whole again. He'd put the feeling back into her soul. He'd given her life. Real life. In all its messy guts and glory.

"How long have you and Sauvage been in cahoots?"

She chuckled. "A lady has to have some secrets, no?"

He took her face in his hands. "Damn, I love you, woman. You truly *were* a gift from the sea," he said. "Marry me, Jayde. *Be* my happy-ever-after."

Her heart clenched. "You mean Kamilah gets her fairy-tale ending?"

"We all do. She gets her voice back…I get the mermaid."

"And I get the prince." Tears pooled in her eyes. She kissed him. "Yes, David. Yes, I will marry you."

And for the first time in Jayde Ashton's life, she believed fairy tales really could come true.

* * * * *

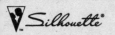